Blind Date With God

Blind Date With God

CHETAN CHANDAK

NU VOICE PRESS

First published by NU VOICE PRESS 2024
An imprint of Hubhawks Pvt. Ltd
www.nuvoicepress.com

This edition published by NU VOICE PRESS 2024

ISBN: 978-81-966888-0-6

Typeset by Saanvi Graphics, Noida
Printed at Thomson Press
Published by Nu Voice Press

Contents

Author's Note

It took a heart shattered into a million pieces to embark on an intriguing journey. My destination? To confront God himself. Determined, or perhaps just stubborn, armed with nothing but a relentless thirst for understanding and a head full of questions, I embarked on a journey to know the very essence of my existence.

I left no stones unturned. From the dusty shelves of abandoned libraries to the dimly lit and mysterious *Ashrams*. In the pursuit of divine truth, I met scholars and priests, engaged in spirited discourse, and navigated the labyrinthine corridors of faith. And let me tell you, dear reader, each step propelled me closer to the elusive presence I sought.

A soul-stirring odyssey that transcended blind beliefs, social boundaries, mind illusions, and thoughts. Truth was peeking from the far end of the tunnel. With each discovery, I found myself shedding the shackles of conditioning and preconceptions. With my heart laid bare, I embraced the boundless expanse of the unknown.

Now, humbled and awestruck by the magnitude of my journey, standing on the threshold of revelation, I am compelled to share its echoes with you. Blurring the lines between reality and fiction, this narrative is woven from the threads of personal experience and the fabric of collective wisdom.

So, dear reader, journey with me beyond the boundaries of familiarity. Where the only thing more bewildering than the mysteries of the universe is the absurdity of our own existence. For in the exploration of the divine, we may just discover the most profound truth of all—the light at the end of the tunnel is not an illusion, the tunnel is.

Chapter 1
The Voice

"I know how hard this is for you, but please have faith, my son. God will help us weather any storm. Look at me, I have always been blessed. In times of…"

My father's voice got abruptly cut off on the phone.

BANG!

I rushed to the hospital. There he was—my father, unconscious, with his chest and left arm plastered. His face had an ugly contouring of bruises and cuts, and his head was swathed in white bandages, with splotches of blood permeating through. The doctor's arrival shook me out of my tense stance.

"Look, it was a serious accident, the sort that can potentially cause instant death. But, by some miracle of God, he is alive. Your father is not out of danger though. He has been unconscious for some time, but we're working on bringing him back."

The so-called God's blessings hit me hard, and I felt his fury.

We waited anxiously and fearfully at the hospital. Sorrowful wails of a large group reverberated around the floor. As I slouched on the bench outside, I could not help but overhear this uncalled-for sermon from one of them: *"Death starts its journey towards you the day you are born. If it didn't arrive today, it is sure to arrive tomorrow."*

The following day, at eleven o'clock, the doctor ushered us into his office.

"Your father has suffered serious brain damage and memory loss. He may not recall anything, so please be patient. Go easy on him and treat him like a baby."

The days that followed were bizarre and intriguing. For the first two or three days, dad gazed around with bewilderment and curiosity, with no sense of being. Mom wasn't spared of this callousness either. Our relentless efforts to feed his cognizance proved futile. I combed through him deep enough but could not find my father—his achievements, his status, his power, his ego—in those childlike eyes.

The truth of the fabricated mind lay exposed. My father worked hard and endured many hardships to secure his stature, his fortune, and his family. But with his memory gone, all of that was lost forever. I wondered, are we just one medical condition away from losing it all? Scary.

My mother had ornamented the small Lord Ganesha statue made of green jade, which she brought from our *Pooja* room and placed it at his bedside. My father found this extremely uncomfortable. In a fit of rage, he would throw it on the ground. My mother would immediately pick it up, and overcame with guilt, ask for forgiveness from it while cursing my father for doing such a horrific thing. I was flabbergasted.

Seconds before the accident, my father was giving me a sermon about the magnanimity of this green, shiny idol, heaping praises of the power of Ganesha's blessings that he always felt upon himself. He swore by it, always remembering to pick up fresh jasmine flowers for this jade idol on his way home from the office. One hour of his day was dedicated to beautifying and engaging with this idol. If he failed to pray in the morning, he spent time with Ganesha in the evening asking for his forgiveness. He often preached about how Ganesha watches everything we do and that we should act accordingly.

The worst beating I had ever received was because of this idol, and I still resent it for that. I was in the third grade. The jade idol was always locked in the tiny and dark, air-conditioned Pooja room; it wasn't allowed to come out. One day I picked it and brought it out in the rain to play. Ganesha enjoyed his much-needed freedom, dancing, jumping in the puddles with us. He was drenched; the ornaments fell off, the red mark on his forehead spread all over his body. Discovering this, my father was horrified and slapped me twice in rapid succession. "How dare you dishonor God?" he had said.

He quickly returned the idol to the confines of the Pooja room to pay back the respect it deserved. While I was locked up in my room for two days, I harbored pity for Ganesha, who had been imprisoned for years in that small room. For four hours straight that day, my father apologised in front of his prisoner.

I wondered how my father's unconditional love, devotion, and faith for the glossy green Ganesha had turned into such anger? Was Ganesha just a conditioned imagination, a trained thought in my father's brain, which has evaporated now with memory loss?

It was seventeen insufferably long days at the hospital before my father's memory was rehabilitated. That Friday, we welcomed him back home. Ganesha was imprisoned again. Exhausted, I decided to take a two-day break.

Something strange was stirring within me. I found myself

reflecting on how fragile the mind can be. How swiftly it can vanish our beliefs, accomplishments, progress, and even our pride. A new feeble voice, never heard before, seemed to emerge from deep within me, outside the purview of my mind, urging me to pay attention. It was questioning my mind, trying to expose it and uncover something. I started to identify this voice each time it came up. It sounded like a wake-up call, compelling me to introspect.

Deep asleep, my mind withdrawn into itself, engulfed in nothingness, I could not resist a strong nudge by this voice, trying to awaken me. It finally convinced me for a morning jog and accompanied me.

It was still dark outside. The gentle breeze of December was stroking my face and rousing my sleeping hair follicles. The silence was broken by the wind rustling the leaves, orchestrating them to jiggle. I reached the forest area in my city—Sanjay Gandhi National Park.

The darkness was giving birth to the golden boy. Orange rays illuminated the forest floor, dispersing the greys instantly. Nature embellished my surroundings like a mother dressing her daughter. A moment later, my eyes shyly fixated on this woman jogging towards me. Her warm gaze, through her blue-framed glasses, penetrated my heart and melted it. Her morning face was kissed bright rose by the chilly breeze. My surroundings got blurred as my eyes dilated, and she seemed to jog in slow motion. Her hair danced to the morning *ragas*. As she drew closer, she smiled, and I was smitten, almost intoxicated. The divine aroma of this goddess faded away as she crossed me. I hesitantly looked back a couple of times, but nothing. The *voice* impelled me to wonder, what just happened? What are these mighty emotions, beyond the scope of mind? A mere smile took me to the seventh heaven.

The place was now relatively crowded. I decided to rest along the trunk of a distant tree. As I was resting, my attention was driven to the ants on the ground, laboring hard. They were disassembling a dead bug to take home. Each ant transported twice its weight towards their home under this trunk. While the ants were still trying to dismantle the insect, out of nowhere, a crow flew in, picked up the dead insect with the ants surrounding it, and flew off. The hardworking ants, some sucked up by the crow and others squished by the crow's claws. Everything they'd worked for and everything they'd stored to eat so far, was all gone in a jiffy.

All of life's efforts and struggles, but nothing to show at the end. The voice questioned within me, is life and its labour so worthless? Should I not divert my attention to something more valuable—wisdom?

Just then, seeing me sitting far away from the crowd, an old man carrying an infant approached me. He was bent as much with his rags as with years. His body was heavily wrinkled, but in his arms, the baby's body was fresh from the oven, brown and cushioned.

The old man begged, "*Maalik*, please give us some money

or food. My granddaughter's parents were crushed by a truck; we have not eaten for two days."

I asked the old man to rest beside the tree while I got some milk and food for them. A few vendors were assembled on the street corners catering to the early morning enthusiasts. While waiting for the vendor to return my balance, I saw a mother teaching her unwilling son how to offer milk to Lord Shiva, a matte black oval stone plugged on a raised platform of a tree. I don't know about the black stone, but the old man would have surely given blessings, if that milk was poured on him.

The old man plucked a leaf, folded it from one side to make a spoon and fed the baby. I asked him to let me hold the baby so he could have some bread. He looked confused, but then agreed to my insistence.

In the relatively cold December weather, the baby was shivering painfully. She was wrapped in a cloth which was damp from the night's dew and possibly her pee, which gave off an intolerable odor. I unwrapped her, making sure she got some of the early morning sun on her. Once my gaze met the eyes of this marvelous creation, the odour vanished. Her sparkling curious eyes, deep like an ocean, were gazing at me in judgement. It was as if her expectation of a parent was renewed.

After having the leftover milk and some bread, the old man tried to lift himself up, to take the baby and carry on. I was worried about this beautiful baby, how will she survive in these conditions and who will take care of her, in a few years or months from now, when the old man's clock would stop ticking?

"Obviously, you can't take care of this baby," I said to the old man. "Why don't you just give her up for adoption?"

The old man replied with pride, "Maalik, God takes care of the baby. He gives food and shelter to everyone who needs it. He will provide for her, when I die."

I hoped he knew that his God lets almost three million kids die of malnutrition each year. Also, the fact that his God allowed the baby's parents to be taken away. I asked him to be practical.

"Maalik, I deserve this. I did bad *karmas* in my earlier lives. God is only being just."

Even after all this suffering, why does man reject reality, logic, and just relies on this unmoved psychological deity, always justifying his existence and grace? The beautiful thing about reality is that it always strikes.

The baby started to cry. The old man quickly rescued her from me and tried hard to calm her. But she would not stop crying. She seemed to be in deep pain, and her bawl was starting to alarm the people passing by, but no one came forward to help.

"Maalik, she has gastric ulcers. She wept for twenty hours the last time. She nearly died. No one gives me work and no doctor sees for free. We sleep on the sidewalks. Her crying and hunger keep my aching body awake. The next day comes unwanted, and I drag myself again in pain. I curse the heartless Satan. I don't know why God created Satan and why can't he stop him. Right now, you are God for me, please give me money."

I gave him some money and asked him to hurry to a doctor. While leaving, the last thing he said was, "God loves you, may God bless you."

When this made up God does not bless the needy, why will he bless me? How can he love me, when he is so uncompassionating towards the poor beggar, who believes in him? Why do people live on whims and fancies of someone they fantasise?

Even if the so-called god existed and he created everything, how could he be this cruel? Why has he burdened us with suffering, disease, hunger, poverty, natural calamities, accidents, hatred, wars, and so many other evils? *Was he not capable of creating a perfect world?*

I walked home. In the bustling city streets, a Hindu procession and a Muslim gathering unfolded in parallel, each showcasing their faith with fervor. Drums beat loudly, and announcements from huge speakers were also too loud for comfort. There has been tension between Hindus and Muslims in North India, over the last few weeks. These processions seemed more like displays of power than genuine religious devotion. I put in my air pods to drown out the noise.

Rest of my Sunday, this mysterious questioning voice within me insisted to ponder on this entity named God and his marketing agents—the various religions.

Each of the religions has convinced people that there is an invisible man, who rules us from the sky above. That he has a set of rules and if we do not follow them, he has made a place called Hell, where we shall burn and suffer eternally. But we should not worry, as he loves us.

The existence of any religion is dependent on these ideas. Without these ideas there would be no religions. Without the idea of Hell there would be no fear, without the idea of Heaven there would be no desire. *A fearless and desire-less soul needs no religion, only a fearful and desiring soul needs religion.*

This idea of Heaven and Hell, is the foundation stone, common for all the religions. All religions define fear or "Hell", as the extent to which a human mind can conceive agony and anguish. Then "sin" is synthesised as the acts that lead one to hell. They claim man is born sinful and destined for hell. By now, man is afraid and guilty. Then comes "Heaven", a carefully crafted hope profile that defines pleasure to the extent conceivable. Then they make the path, the rituals, rules, and dogmas, which will help one to get rid of Hell and deliver Heaven. Religions live and survive only on the hope that these ideas exist.

Sitting in the balcony that evening, the voice within compelled me to record some verses, questioning the so-called God. I paraphrased them later.

You, the unknown, unseen, unheard, unproven one,
How did your idea start in the human mind and spun?
How did the mind perceive you, construct & finally yearn?

You have no evidence and have never left any cue,
However, they still justify your existence so true,
And construct an image of you in their mind's view.

You the invisible, believers believe you to be everywhere,
Why do they bother searching if you're already there?
Why don't you just show up and end their despair?

You fear that on being known, you shall become ordinary like us,
Losing your decorated identity, rank, stature, and shining lust,
Is that why you choose to be unknown, to be God the robust?

You worry that we'll lose interest in you, if the truth is unsealed;
You delight in slaves remaining unaware and concealed.
Is that why you hide behind your veil, only perceived?

You, who were you before the title of "God" was bestowed?
Did people's worship create your divine abode?
Where will you reside if humanity or its belief in you erodes?

You, do you have any knowledge of us and our suffering below?
Or are you ignorant, as we are about you, and don't even know?
Are we seeking each other, just out of ignorance's flow?

You the director, why force us puppets, into your grand play?
Why then punish the Devil, and bless the saint, with no say?
Or do you bless the one, justifying his assignment in your grand play?

You create desire, then punish those who crave?
Why make the mind a slave, to lust and greed's embrace?
Why create duality, with good and bad, at odds and in place?

You the mighty, are you not capable or are you not willing,
to create this world with goodness and bliss, sans any suffering?
Would that ruin the fun you were having creating & viewing?

You the merciful, why divide lands and people into so many kinds?
Why some flourish in your love, while others suffer and grind?
Are you unable or unwilling to be equal and merciful, in kind?

You wield your magical powers, to create the mysterious nature,
So why not use them to eradicate, all suffering and war's torture?
Why claim the wonders of creation, but not own up to its cruel ventures?
You claim the soul transcends mortal frames, yet bind it to fleshly cages;
Why do some bask in abundance and others suffer through life's stages?
Why do lies flourish while truths wither away through ages?

You, people have died & killed, in search of you, without any gain,
Why allow such killings in your name, causing so much pain?
Why not stop people fighting, and let peace, love, and harmony reign?

You give different names and addresses, to people of different faiths?
Do you have a real name and address, or is this just a faith-based race?
Why not reveal your true name, address, and end this confusion's case?

You are one and the same, why then religions fight in your name?
Why not reveal the true path, and end this cycle of blame?
What fun do you have in seeing religions manipulating this game?

You are "you" & I am "I", Why? If nothing else exists besides you?
Are you for real, or not, this entity, inside, who is it, is it you?

The voice was overpowering. I decided to sleep early. The creation with all its beauty and suffering began to ebb away from my brain. Now there existed neither me, nor my thoughts, nor my questions.

Chapter 2
Journey Begins

My mind dwelled in this null where nothing existed—time, past memories, future hope, my body, or the world. I marched into my dream, unabashed.

There I found myself dribbling Ramos, a serene nutmeg, parading the ball on the right, shooting from almost thirty-five yards. The ball curled nervously, picked up velocity, ending up in the top left corner of the goal. As I staged my celebratory moonwalk, Barcelona fans chanted my name in harmony, "CHICHO… CHICHO… CHICHO!" My heart poured wine, the mind soaked in it, bliss, a feeling of joy like no other. We celebrated the derby win over Real Madrid all night. Messi and I left in my shimmery white breed, Bugatti La Voiture Noire.

Our next game was against Atletico Madrid. "CHICHO… CHICHO!", the orchestral cheers from the crowd triggered gallons of adrenaline in me. It stimulated my drive right from the half line with ferocious pace and vigor. Approaching the D, I was about to shoot. One leg firmly planted on the ground and the other ready for a savage swing, but a sliding tackle by Ramos and a hammer pounded the knee of my grounded leg.

There was a distinct cracking sound. My whole body was

trembling with excruciating pain. The pain was so bad—it jolted me from the dream.

Such was the life-like feel of the dream, my mind was in a dilemma. Was I this woken self who was dreaming of being Chicho, or was I Chicho, dreaming to be my woken self? This brain which now alleges that I am a nobody, just a while ago assured me that I was the celebrated Chicho. *Does it deserve my trust anymore? I wondered, did my dream snatch away my reality, or did it snatch away, just another dream, called life?*

My father's accident had taught me that reality is shaped by the mind alone. Mind is so prone to being hypnotised, it is so fragile. I have been dreaming almost all nights of my life. Every time I awaken from my dream, I am made to realise that it was not true. But my mind refuses to register this fact. Why isn't it ever aware? In the sleep state, it persists dreams to be real, to only tumble into reality of it not being real, the very next morning. How does it unlearn every single day? Can it not be mindfully aware of the "fakeness" while the dream progresses in the sleep state?

My newly discovered inner voice was trying to expose my mind once again. *If my mind bluffs me while I am dreaming, what stops it from fooling me while I am awake?* If my mind is not capable of being percipient, is my waking up as bogus as my dream? Am I ever aware of my being?

Why do I think dreams are illusions and waking a reality? Wakefulness disproves dreams, so do dreams disprove wakefulness? Both states are just experiences and memories.

Dream state lasts from night to morning, while wakefulness lasts from birth till death. The ultimate leveler death will eventually wipe off memories of both states and reveal their emptiness.

So, who am I? Am I the dreamer or the dream? Am I both the dreamer and the dream? Am I just a projection of myself as a dream-figure? Are both the awakened state and the dreaming state, only creations and illusions of mind? Is there a state beyond these two?

Moving on, I left for my office. The traffic was horrifying. It was so congested that a snail might have made it in better time. If I was late for my nine a.m. meeting, it could seriously affect my performance review. I became irritable and fidgety. My driver seemed unperturbed the entire time, as he hummed a familiar tune and bopped along to the beat.

At around eight o'clock that evening, my wife called. She was tense and asked me to come home immediately as my father's health was not good. My father retired last year, and after recovering from that terrible accident, he had been showing signs of depression. He does not get proper sleep and is disturbed in his thoughts. My mother keeps her patience. But often, she blames him saying depression is his punishment for humiliating Lord Ganesha.

When I reached home, the main door was open. Everyone gathered in my father's room staring at him as he sat at the foot of the bed—sweating profusely with eyes wide open and in shock. After a few minutes, he started screaming, "Please go! Please go!" All this while, he was staring at the opposite wall. I did all I could to console him, and eventually, he felt relaxed and slept.

Next morning, I felt curious about what had happened last night and wanted to know if everything with dad was fine now.

Dad sat up and informed me that he had been having terrifying nightmares for the past week. At midnight, every night, a devilish figure appears in his dream and gives him a countdown until "you become mine". He described the horrifying satanic figure to be about ten feet tall, almost completely black in colour, with bull-like horns, scary red eyes wide open, and carrying a variety of weapons. He kept threatening dad about the number of days he had left, after which eternal suffering awaited him. He had started with 303 days, and as the number of days reduced, he described harsher punishments to dad.

A phase of bad dreams, I thought; but the way he spoke—all petrified, was intimidating. My mother however insisted that everything I was hearing must be genuine because it is written in the holy books. At the conclusion of one's life, the Devil appears to the spirit to impress upon him the value of his time on Earth. My father added, "He also challenges me saying—'go and figure out if someone can save you from me'."

"All my accomplishments, wealth, repute, and pride, which I accumulated in my life so far have no meaning, being

confronted by death now. I want to go out in search of truth. Your mother says that learned saints and religious places have the answer to this question. I want to seek their help and get rid of this treacherous Devil."

I wasn't convinced by the Devil story, but I could identify with my dad's outlook on life. My parents were still discussing as I went to the office.

The mood in the office was dark, and everyone seemed to be in disbelief. The cause for this was an email from our MD, warning of a possible hostile takeover by our main rival. The implication was that the future is cloudy and difficult to predict. Our future performance review, pay, and employment status are all up in the air. My heart sunk and my mind froze. Life was heartlessly uncertain.

I left the office early, when I got home, my parents were having coffee with our family doctor, Dr. Shah. My father stayed adamant about finding answers to the Devil's challenge. Mom had called Dr. Shah to check if dad would be okay to travel so much. The doctor said that he could travel but would not be able to do it alone, he would need someone beside him every minute. For as long as I can remember, my mother has stayed at home to take care of our family. We all understood that she couldn't manage the demands of travel and caregiving at the same time.

As I accompanied the doctor out to his car, he said, "Medicines can do as much as they can. His state does not look good; he may be falling into deep depression. I would recommend this tour. Maybe this search for God can help him."

In all my years, my parents have never once made a request of me. Their lives were on the line, and they had no one else to turn to but me.

All the events in my life seemed to align and propel me on this journey.

* * *

My uncle Sonaram was a pious person. His wife died at the age of thirty-five. Since then, he has been sojourning around religious destinations to explore the meaning of life. He was residing in Banaras at the time, so I decided to call him and discuss this journey. He was excited and asked us to come to Banaras as he knew a lot of people who could probably help us.

Our first stop was Banaras or Varanasi, a city on the banks of the Ganges in North India. It is the holiest of the seven sacred cities in Hinduism. It is believed that dying in Banaras helps one attain nirvana.

On arrival in Banaras, we boarded the taxi which I had pre-booked to reach the hotel. Our driver, Hiralal Yadav, started to impress my father with his talks on religious beliefs and tales from around the city. I turned a deaf ear to their conversation as I was looking at the city and noticing how different it was to the fast life of Mumbai. Everybody in this city was in the business of selling something or the other in the name of religion.

Our hotel was old and lacked the sophistication of modern amenities, but the air smelt heavenly because of the incense sticks floating around. My uncle joined us at the hotel around three at noon. We discussed at length the state of my father, and it made me happy to see my uncle so confident about resolving the issue. We planned to go to the Ganges Aarti in the evening. On our way back, uncle told us about Siddhiram Babaji, whom we would visit tomorrow. He mentioned that Babaji had not eaten since he was fifteen years old. At sixty-three now, he had answers to all the questions.

As darkness started to rule the skies, I could see my father's face turn pale and I knew he feared the Devil. I slept beside him and hoped the night would pass calmly. At fifteen minutes past midnight, I woke up to my father's scream. It was the same scene again. He was so scared that I could hear his heart beating. We spent a restless night together hoping to get a solution tomorrow.

The next morning, feeling hopeful, we started towards Babaji's *ashram* on the outskirts of Banaras. We were greeted by one of the disciples on arrival, and he asked us to wait in the lobby. At the centre of the ashram was a Shiv temple surrounded on one side by a meeting hall, and on the other two sides, by rooms.

Fifteen minutes later, we were summoned in. Babaji, a fleshless structure weighing no more than thirty-five kilos, was sitting on a raised platform in the meeting room facing the temple. He was draped in a thin white cloth and his projected bones decided the flow of the fabric. His hair and beard, covering a major part of his thin face, were grey and black. He was chanting something with closed eyes when we were presented before him. My uncle touched Babaji's feet in respect, my father and I followed suit.

"I know why you have come here," Babaji said.

I looked at my uncle, he nodded—an indication that he had not pre-informed Babaji about anything.

"Babaji please help me! I am petrified of the Devil. He doesn't spare me even one night, every night he…" dad started to say, but Babaji interrupted and said, "He scares you about your death."

We were shocked.

"Yes! Yes, Babaji! You know it all, I am so happy I have come to the right place. Please help me."

"*Jai Mahakaal!* you are already too late. You spent your life all for yourself and never thought about Lord Shiva, the mighty one who lives in you."

"Please Babaji, please! My responsibilities have kept me so busy that I never had the time to think about the mighty one, nor did I have the company of a learned person like you to guide me," my dad pleaded.

"One of your responsibilities was also towards Lord Shiva."

My dad broke into tears now. On seeing this, Babaji agreed to help us. He raised his arm and out of thin air produced an apple. My father was zapped, but I knew this trick.

"Jai Mahakaal! From now till nine in the morning tomorrow, only eat this and sit in meditation from six in the evening to six in the morning."

Babaji then asked my father to come closer and uttered some *mantra* in his ears, which my father was supposed to keep repeating, while in meditation. Even if I did not believe in any of this, we were hopeful. We took blessings from Babaji and were about to leave. The person who greeted us at the entry door earlier accompanied us on the way out and persuaded us to donate twenty-five thousand rupees to the

Shiv temple. I was quite reluctant, but my father was so happy that he did not hesitate once before donating the entire sum.

Back at the hotel, at exactly six, my father sat in meditation. For the first 15-20 minutes, he seemed to be ok, but then he seemed to be in complete discomfort. His body was not accustomed to this, so he kept changing his posture in search of comfort.

Around two at midnight, I woke up to the usual scream and scene of my father petrified. The Devil came as usual and told my father that all this meaningless repetition of borrowed words is worthless. That it's not that easy. My father needs to find God and the purpose of his life. He also told him that God has gifted freewill, which should not go futile. The Devil sounded logical.

My uncle came in the morning and insisted that we should go to Babaji again. He doubted that father would not have stayed up in meditation and might have dozed off. Why do they always doubt us and not the promise? Reluctantly, I approved of meeting Babaji, on the condition that I would lead the conversation this time.

The scene inside was scary. Babaji was roaring his sermon from his raised platform, with baked eyes scanning his audience. The disciples were terror-struck, shrinking further at each word. We sat behind the seven rows of petrified disciples, while Babaji continued,

"Your skin will be burnt and then peeled off. Then they will lay you on the ice, put salt on you. They will break every bone in your body into pieces, make holes in you and then let insects crawl within you. They will put you in hot oil, boiling over the eternal flame. Believe me, they know no mercy. You may cry as hard as you can, but you will not be heard. You will not even be allowed to die; you will have to live in that pain eternally."

HOW DOES HE KNOW THIS DETAILED?
HAS HE BEEN THERE?

For a moment even I was terrified with this description of Hell. The women were wiping their tears and I could hear them sobbing. The men stared at one another in shock. A few kids began to howl. But Babaji did not stop. He went on for another twenty minutes describing even more terrorising stuff.

Then, Babaji paused and threw in the pacifier. "Jai Mahakaal! I have been showing you the way to *Kailasha*. If you obey my commands with absolute sincerity, utter the mantras and remain loyal to your creator Lord Shiva, you will go to the Heaven of Kailasha. Do you still not desire to be in Kailasha? Where you will have rivers of milk, where every wish will get fulfilled instantly, where the most beautiful angels will be at your service all the time and where it rains of gems and pearls."

He followed it up with an emotional sermon, "I remember, I was fourteen when Lord Shiva came in my dreams and showed me his wonderful abode, Kailasha. The next morning, I left everything—my house, family, and clothes, and became an ascetic. For years, I meditated in the jungle before I finally got free from all my desires. I could live happily with my Lord Shiva, but he ordered me to devote all my life to preaching and guiding others, spreading the message of Lord Shiva."

He assured his devotees that they are God's special people and had nothing to fear. They have taken refuge beneath his wings, and he will see to it that they all make it to Kailasha through him. He went so far as to promise that on the route to Kailasha, they would get an outside look at the torment endured by other, less enlightened souls in the fiery depths of hell.

He warned, "Jai Mahakaal! As you travel to Kailasha, ignorant souls will call out to you, but you must ignore them and press on. You will pass by other enticing dwellings, but you should ignore them because they lead to deception and illusion. Do not let them trick you and keep moving until you reach Kailasha."

With each assuring word from Babaji, the mood and actions of his disciples transformed. Overwhelming emotions all around. Some clasped hands and bowed down before Babaji. Some others continued to sob uncontrollably as they swayed their arms wildly and yelled Babaji's praises. Two of them jumped viciously, collapsed at Babaji's feet, and huddled together in sobs. In that moment, anyone could be fooled to believe in Babaji and his promise.

After Babaji's speech, one of his disciples announced, "If anyone has any questions, please come forward and ask." I stood up and was asked to come forward. Throughout the whole discourse, Babaji didn't look at us for even a second, probably intentionally. I was now standing right in front of him, staring at him, not giving him any escape route as I questioned him.

"Your mantra did not work Babaji, the Devil has warned my father that mere repetition of borrowed words won't help."

Babaji smiled; "Son, your father did not meditate as advised. The fault is not in the mantra, but the one who recites it."

What does one say in response to that? These agents of God are all in the business of selling medicine after all, so how can that be wrong? It is undoubtedly the patient who gets it wrong all the time.

My inquisitive inner voice was interested in investigating the medication and the seller of the medication.

"Why should one fear Hell, if he has done nothing wrong in his life?" I asked Babaji.

"Jai Mahakaal! you can't even imagine the atrocities and sufferings of Hell. Everyone should fear it. Firstly, there is not even a single soul which stays righteous his whole life and even if one does, he will still have his past karmas of previous life. He surely cannot escape from them."

"Do you mean to say that every human being is destined for Hell? And only the few people, who fear Hell, follow you, recite your mantra, and have faith in Lord Shiva, will be saved from Hell and go to Kailasha. Is God so cruel? That he has destined all human beings to Hell and only pardons them, if they follow a set of your rules?"

Babaji, controlling his anger somehow said, "Do not speak such words for Lord Shiva. He is merciful. Seeing our plight, he invites us all, mercifully, to his abode. Yes, it's only by obeying him, one shall be saved."

"If you say Lord Shiva is the creator of all, was Hell and all its punishments also created by him?"

Babaji, now clearly in discomfort—"No, No, it's not Lord Shiva, it is *Kaal*, or the one you call Satan, who created Hell.

Lord Shiva is the Mahakaal, who resides over Kaal and saves us from him."

"So, this powerful Kaal, who created him? If Lord Shiva is the ultimate creator, what reason would he have to create such a powerful and cruel entity, who destines everyone to suffer?"

Babaji stayed quite, he somehow escaped my gaze and started looking at his disciples. I also looked around, no one was crying anymore, all were curious. I am sure Babaji, who was scanning around, would have seen the appetite in everyone's eyes for an answer from him. Even if he tried, he could not escape.

"Jai Mahakaal! You would not understand this; your mind isn't capable of it yet. You are still in this materialistic world, running around headless for pleasures and desires. Only when your mind starts to think over and above this materialistic world, will you be capable of understanding the answers to such questions," Babaji mocked.

This was going nowhere, and it was familiar territory. I had such debates with my mom, dad, uncle, grandfather, and a few others, in the past. Invariably all debates ended up, questioning my "unqualified mind". I did not want to end this debate with Babaji, for sure. If not for me, it felt that I was debating on behalf of the silent disciples of his. Conceding to the incapability of my mind.

"Babaji, you say that we should not waste our time in this materialistic world, running in search for our pleasures and desires. Then what is the purpose of life, what should we do?"

Babaji released the wrinkles of his forehead and his tone got calmer. "Son, one should not run after pleasures and desires. One should be content. One should devote his life to his creator, Lord Shiva. Follow his orders, do the rituals, have faith in him."

"What shall I get from doing all this?"

"You shall be saved from Hell. You shall be in Kailasha with him, where there is no suffering, only pleasure. All your desires will be fulfilled; you will be in eternal bliss."

"As I hear you, our purpose of life should be to follow Lord Shiva, recite his mantras, do our rituals, be righteous, all this for our desire to be in Kailasha, to enjoy all the pleasures it has to offer. Isn't it? So basically, the purpose of life should be driven by this desire for Kailasha? But didn't you say that one should free himself from all desires and pleasures?"

Babaji's delusional calm was shaken. His anger snubbing his mind's advice, came out in full vigour. He tore his gaze from me and started addressing his voiceless hypnotised disciples.

"Jai Mahakaal! This young generation has no belief. They dare to question the almighty God. This is why Lord Shiva hides himself and does not end the sufferings. To teach them a lesson, Lord Shiva will surely ensure Hell for them."

I shamelessly interrupted, "If I go to Hell, so will your Lord Shiva, right? You said that Lord Shiva resides in each one of us. So, If I go to Hell, he will accompany me, right?"

Babaji thumped his stick on the ground, harrowing in anger, "You know nothing, you disrespect an ascetic, you shall burn in Hell!" I wanted to yell, but controlled my anger, I replied in a hush tone, "I agree I know nothing. But you seem to know everything about Hell, have you been there?"

He stood up with support from his two disciples and walked away, as fast as his fragile body could. By this, his team, his personal army of disciples got vocal, they wanted to show their support for Babaji. They surrounded us and pushed us towards the exit, as if we were showing any resistance.

I called our taxi driver. We sat on the bench placed just across the road, facing the ashram. Uncle and dad unexpectedly were quiet, looking down, lost in their thoughts. I had no hard feelings for my uncle or Babaji. Babaji has just been following a tradition, an old, stale Indian tradition. It's his stone-blind belief and hope in this story of Kailasha, which makes him act in the manner he has. The moment you try to question this hope, there is no other option left, than to revolt with anger.

In the absence of an actual realisation, they need to shield their belief and suppress the questions somehow. If they let their belief be attacked by logic, what will be left for them? I understand, one's individuality is nothing but his beliefs, his ego, and Babaji was just protecting it.

Had God been a reality, this eternal search for him in the human mind, would have been concluded once and for all. But that's not the case, the search for God, the search for hope, the search for a much better place, the search for a mirage in this conceived desert goes on.

It's these religions, these cults, who benefit from this inappeasable human desire for greener pastures. These religions give the human brain, a belief, a hope in the future but not now, that this thirst will be quenched by the mirage, the secret abode. They try to satiate the human mind, by giving it a crowd for support, and a promise it can hold on to.

A personal god, a personal abode, a personal scripture, something to feel special about—all the things which can boost the ego and prove that he or she is the chosen one, superior to others. They also build a wall around this belief—the fear of hell. If one tries to flee this belief, he would be destined to hell.

After so much thinking, I desired a strong filter coffee once I reached the hotel. I sat there content, knowing that this desire of mine will surely be satisfied, unlike the ascetic's desire of Kailasha. As we were waiting for our taxi to arrive, a foreigner approached us. I recognised him, he was one of Babaji's disciples sitting in the front row. Tall, lean, with a Greek nose, and short curly hair. He had a mole on the right side of his lofty forehead, and approached me with a warm smile. He introduced himself as Mr. Eden Hart, from the UK.

"I appreciate your questions to Babaji. When I came to India, I had similar questions in my mind. Would you fancy a cuppa tomorrow, to discuss it at length?" Mr. Hart said.

Sure! I was more than happy to have someone who thinks like me, steer my exploration. We decided to meet at a coffee shop near our hotel, the next day.

Chapter 3
Science Vs God

"Alright mate, why are you searching for God?" Mr. Hart asked me when we met the next day.

"I am not searching for God. I am searching for a solution to get rid of the Devil," I said with a frustrated look on my face.

"A Devil?!"

Sitting in the sunlit, red-cushioned, corner seat of a roadside modern coffee shop, I told him my story. I don't know what it was, the coffee, or my story, that made Mr. Hart grin. His lips spread in a sly smile as he said, "Wow, another way of god to help us find him, the Devil."

Yet again, God was omnipresent. Mr. Hart had conveniently plugged God and that seemed to have answered every question in his mind. He had appeared to be a rational person when we'd first met, so I asked him, "How can you just as easily accept that your God is behind all this?"

Mr. Hart said, "It seems like you don't believe in God, why?"

"Because he has been created by humans, because his form and his address is different for different people. Truth is the same for all, if god is different for different people, he can only be false. Because he fails to explain the sufferings, because he is just used for filling up the gaps where no other explanation fits, because he can only be explained in faith and belief, no logic or rationality dare touch him."

Mr. Hart leaned over towards me, placing his arms on the table, "Mate, is it God, you don't believe in or is it the gods of the various religions?"

I thought about what he asked for a second, "I guess it is the gods, which have been described to me by the various religions. Even if there is a god, how can he be a Jew, a Muslim, a Christian, and a Hindu at the same time. All religions and their gods are manufactured. All religions describe god in the way that appeals to their demographic. Chinese have a flat nose god, Greeks have a sharp-nosed god, Indians have the wheatish complexion gods. They dramatise him to feed their imagination. They project him to be the biggest superhero and then divert our desire to know and meet this created superhero. Then these religions go to any extent to establish their superiority over other religions, they even murder people in the name of this superhero. The leaders of these religions hide behind this superhero and fulfill their personal imperialistic motives. There seems to be no God, except the ones manufactured by these religions."

Hart placed his left palm on his chin and said, "Indeed, but I have come to realise that these religions like a crystalline stream, which once flowed with untainted clarity, quenching

the thirst of those seeking wisdom. At the pinnacle of their inception, the divine message still glistens like pure water, untouched by the imperfections of the world below.

"As time wove its intricate patterns and human hands intervened, the sacred stream began its descent, meandering through the realms of humanity. The once-pure waters grew murky and polluted, clouded by the weight of the egoistic leaders of religion and their misguided interpretations."

An optimistic smile embraced Hart's face.

"So you see, there exists a choice—a choice to either remain at the banks criticising the polluted river, or keep offering mere tokens of devotion to the adulterated religions, keep polluting them further. Or, you can dive into the river of religion, swim against the currents of complacency, and ascend the mountains of devotion in pursuit of the crystal-clear waters that still glisten at the stream's source. It takes thirst, time, and unwavering courage to reach the sacred summit, where the essence of truth awaits the diligent seeker.

You see, when Jesus was asked by his disciples, why he teaches the common man in parables, he said: "The mysteries of the divine kingdom are reserved for the earnest seekers, while the parables serve as lifeboats for those lost amidst the mysteries, distress, and perplexities of life. A simple moral like doing good and avoiding bad was enough for them to understand. In the heart of every religion lies a timeless reservoir of wisdom, accessible only to those who seek with an adult's discernment and a yearning for enlightenment."

I saw some sense in what he was saying, but could not help being sarcastic in my response.

"If this crystal-clear water exists and has the power to quench the human thirst for God, why has no one brought it down to the common people? That should end all the thirst, all the curiosity about God. That should save the world from all these religious dogmas and fooling around."

Hart ordered one more coffee and continued, "But mate, people don't want the truth, they just want the reassurance that what they believe in, is the only truth. They are not thirsty, they do not want water, they are ok with whatever has been written about water. The urge and determination to know the truth changes everything. The truth has been revealed by a lot of teachers in the past, but the truth is never accepted that easily. Truth must fight against the massive, ever-growing army of false claims.

"The truth about the earth revolving around the sun, had been brought to light by Indian philosopher Yajnavalkya in the ninth century BC, then by the Greek astronomer Aristarchus in the third century BC. But it was never accepted. It was believed that the earth is the fixed centre, and the sun revolves around it—a theory which benefited the religious leaders as it approved the religious texts and proved their superiority.

"Most of these truth revealers, like Jesus, were killed or punished for heresy. Only a few dared to follow Jesus. So, you see, the truth is not for everyone. Just like Jesus taught us, it is only for the ones with the urge to know the truth, the true seeker."

"You seem to know about this crystal-clear water, the truth, the one which quenches curiosity. So please solve the mystery of the Devil," I said, bluntly.

"Mate, I am still exploring the river, finding a way to the top. You see, I am a seeker not a believer. But you are no kid either, so how do you explain the Devil?"

"I believe it is psychological, a mental illness. Some chemistry of neurons in the mind which creates this illusionary Devil in his dreams," I said skeptically.

"Indeed, I knew it, so now you are trying to fill the gap with science."

"Why not! Science does not take the support of faith and belief; it attempts to answer things rationally. It has come a long way to explain most of the things in our universe."

"Like?"

"Like how creation started, how nature works, how our body functions."

"Correct," Hart interrupted. "You see, science has come a long way in discovering the 'How' of things but has deliberately kept itself away from questioning the 'Why' of things. Say the illusion of Devil is created by some neurons in your father's mind, but will science give you the answer as to why is that illusion being created? Scientists can explain how the creation started, the big bang theory, the intelligent design theory, how nature works—rains, earthquakes, volcanos, and even how our body operates or how the reasoning mind functions. But try to replace how with why. Science will never have answers to, why did it all begin? why creation? why us? why are we here? why birth? why death? why nature? why consciousness? why desires? why sufferings? why this questioning mind itself?"

I was stumped by this. But Hart did not stop.

"Mate, I am a physicist and have studied science in detail. Science ultimately explains everything with energy, it is the fundamental factor in all its answers. Energy is the core of all elementary particles, all atoms and therefore all things. Energy manifests into matter, into motion, into heat, into light. Science has nothing except energy.

"This energy cannot be destroyed or enhanced; it remains constant. Scientists have never been able to create or destroy anything, they have just assembled energies or broken them down. Quantum Physics revealed that this energy can be observed as a particle or wave. It depends upon the observer which form he wants to observe. It all stops at this. I wanted to explore more, but science had its boundaries. I was left with no other option but God, who they said was beyond these boundaries and had answers to the 'Why'. Since then, I have debated science and God in my head for years and then arrived at a conclusion."

I was impressed and curious. I realised that I was no different, instead of filling up the gap with god, I was filling it up with science. But I didn't understand either. I have been lazy to seek and explore, blindly choosing science to pacify my questioning mind, like others use religion. I requested my friend Hart to share his mind's debate on Science vs God.

"You see, this study called science originated just to find and know the greatest unknown, termed as 'God'.

Interestingly, scientists' religious beliefs played a significant role in guiding their work. All the great pioneers of science like Galileo, Kepler, Pascal, Boyle, Newton, Faraday, Clerk-Maxwell, CS Lewis, Einstein, all were believers in God."

"Wow, is that so?"

"Indeed, the great theory of 'Gravity' by Newton was also discovered with a reference to God. Gravity is unseen but like God, explains a lot of things. According to Newton, while gravity accounted for planetary motion, the precise positions of orbits and stars, beyond gravitational influence, were attributed to only divine understanding. Galileo and Kepler also said that the pursuit of rational order and laws of nature in the universe are God's imposition, revealed through the language of science and mathematics. They insisted that we all should use the gift of intellect, gifted by God.

"Even Darwin, with some doubts, found the grandeur of the universe and conscious existence too awe-inspiring for mere chance, acknowledging the argument for God's existence. For Maria Mitchell, scientific investigations unveiled new aspects of God's work and brought deeper revelations of the unknown. While CS Lewis insisted that men became scientific only because they believed in the laws in nature, established by god."

"Hmm, I have read one quotation of Einstein: 'science without religion is lame and religion without science is blind'."

A subtle smile graced my friends face. "You see, I consider Albert Einstein to be the greatest scientist and saint of all time. He said that he isn't interested in this or that phenomenon, but wants to know the thoughts of the creator who created this mysterious and marvelous creation. He did not believe in the religious definition of God—a God who rewards and punishes the objects of his creation or a God who thinks and acts like us. For him religion was a humble admiration for the unknown superior spirit who reveals himself in the slight details which we can perceive with our frail and feeble mind. He was convinced that a supreme spirit is manifested in the laws of the universe and that we, with our modest powers must feel humble.

"This enigmatic, mystical, coordinated, and limitless creation has fascinated almost all scientists. But their study has always remained restricted to the limitation of the tools available to examine this endless creation. The telescopic lens and the speed of light will always limit research. Science cannot study anything beyond our senses or brains."

Moved by the moment, I felt compelled to lend my voice. "Yes, I read this in one of the science journals, that our cosmos is continuously expanding. That scientific instruments have been able to calculate the diameter of the cosmos to be ninety-three billion light years until now. But our scientists think the cosmos is one-fifty sextillion times bigger than what has been discovered, making the Earth an invisible dot in the cosmos."

Hart concurred, "Indeed, our earth is insignificant in the observable universe. Two trillion galaxies exist, our galaxy alone has over one billion stars and planets. Our insignificance is inconceivable.

"In this insignificant universe, our science started by finding answers to the questions which rose against the supreme hypothesis, God. The questions never ceased, as God is too complex a hypothesis, so they replaced this hypothesis, God, and substituted it with unseen electrons, energy, gravity, etc. As Thomas Huxley stated, the great tragedy of science is the slaying of a beautiful hypothesis by an ugly fact. Science says all living things including humans, coordinated nature, and creation are scattered, incoherent, chaotic atoms and energy. It's like saying paint made the painting without a painter.

"Science originates from bounded minds and is relative. Our scientific theories are certainly superior to those of the ants. Superhumans or superaliens with minds considerably more evolved than ours may exist in the cosmos. Above every knowledgeable one, there is one who is more knowledgeable, isn't it?"

My friend Hart believed that religion and science are meant to co-exist, support and aid each other. He claimed that science lies within the boundaries of the mind and the universe, which act as a canvas to conceal the hand of God.

I doubt, because if not science, even God has never answered the 'Why' questions. We met regularly. These discussions with Hart, awakened the seeker in me.

Meanwhile, my father and I had sleepless nights. The Devil, he said, is relentless, that he keeps repeating 'find a way out' or 'find God' to get rid of me. I still believe that it is just hallucination, but Hart has dented my belief. He has forced me to think from a different perspective, a spiritual perspective. *The Devil's constant emphasis according to him is a call from God, to come and find him.*

I am in constant touch with my father's doctors back in Mumbai. They emphasise that the medicines should be taken on time and also that I should pray for his health. The medicines aren't yielding any improvement or relief. The more I converse with my friend Hart, my perspective goes through a transformation. I am starting to get convinced that if we can find a way out, find answers and bring my father's mind at peace, we would get rid of these dreams and Devil.

I now want to figure out the truth about the perceived God. Not only to help my father, but to satisfy the newly awakened seeker in me.

We met at the same red upholstered coffee table everyday. I had done some homework to impress my friend this time.

"Last evening, I was surfing the web and your Einstein impressed me as well. He stated that science could only be created by those who are infused with the aspiration for truth and that the source of this feeling only springs from the sphere of religion. What drove me towards him is his take on how science can aid religion. According to him, the goal of religion should be to liberate mankind from the bondage of egocentric cravings, desires, and fears.

"He said that science aids this goal, as it strives to simplify complex connections by breaking them down into the smallest independent elements. Through this process of understanding, scientists free themselves from personal biases and aspirations, adopting a humble mindset towards the profound reasoning embodied in the universe, something beyond human reach."

"I am so happy, mate. You made an effort. According to Einstein, science also helps remove the human tendency to attribute human qualities to divine entities and conceive god in man's image. Science contributes to a spiritual elevation of our understanding of life."

The seeker in me questioned, "You say religion goes beyond the scope of science and have answers to the 'Why' questions, then why do we not have any answers yet?"

"The creation is so elaborate, multifaceted, and bewildering that its creator is inarguably complex. Understanding him would require determination and intensive study. But no one wants to spend time on something which is considered impossible to decode. The catch twenty-two is that we tend to criticise and dismiss ideas we haven't given a fair chance to.

"The material world, needs of our perishable body and our inappeasable desires, have always kept us busy and conveniently led us to choose the easy way out when it came to the 'Why' questions in life. We either assign these questions to the religion we are born into or leave it to science. We are least bothered to see if the questions are answered correctly or not. Just looking at the sea won't help you cross it. Becoming a seeker requires one to put in the necessary energy, time, and study before diving headfirst into the sea of inquiries."

Ahead of schedule, we began our day. As we walked to our reserved booth, we noticed that the café workers were just donning their aprons. Ravi, waiter at the cafe, brought our regular coffee and cookies without us having to ask. I wanted to know more about my friend. What has led him to this path?

Hart became nostalgic while explaining to me how science helped him become an explorer, how he got fascinated with God, and what led him to India.

"You see, I was fascinated with science in my school days. In the ninth grade, we were introduced to Einstein's Theory of Relativity, $E= MC^2$. Till date this has stayed as the most revelatory thought in my mind. It asserts that everything existing in this cosmos is just energy or can be converted to energy. But, what is this energy?

"I was explained energy in terms of mass and if I asked what mass is, it was explained in terms of energy. Both were just defined relatively and not in absolute terms. Strangely our professors never used to encourage us to develop our own approach. We were asked to either adopt an idealistic view or become a critic of other's point of view.

"I was born a Christian. We were asked to be loyal to Jesus and have complete faith in him. I was skeptical and my mind used to explode with questions, is this energy 'God'? Questions were not encouraged; I was asking something out of the syllabus. They told me to keep blind faith. Faith is itself blind and I wondered what blind faith was then. They used to quote me verses from the Bible, which questioned the questioning mind itself.

"They said, sorrow awaits those who argue with their creator. Can a clay pot question its maker or dispute how it's shaped? Who are we to talk back to God? He does as he pleases and no one can question his actions."

"Nothing new; every religion condemns curiosity and questioning God," I interrupted.

"Indeed, so I tried to seek answers in Bible, but realised that it's been made into a history book and not a teacher's guide. I am sure that our Bible is not as Lord Jesus would have liked it to be. The complex and spiritual interpretations were crushed, as it was decided that a religious book should be the one in which the common mass establishes faith and does not question it."

"Faith has to murder questioning to survive, does it not?"

"Indeed my friend. So you see, neither did science or my religion help me know about the omnipresent energy. I clearly remember, I was in my final year of college. I was handed a pamphlet at the Leeds railway station, which had details about a lecture by an Indian mystic sage. At the bottom of the pamphlet was written in bold letters—IT IS ALL MAYA (ENERGY).

"I went to his lecture, which was held in the open ground. I could see a bloated body sitting on an elevated dull cane chair. The mystic asked us what we saw in the water placed in the eight different-sized bowls before him. All of us observed and replied that we can see the moon in all the bowls. Then he asked us to tell him if that moon was different in different bowls or the same. The reflected moon appeared different in each bowl, depending on the size and the ripples in each bowl.

"The mystic then explained that the moon is like the unmoved supreme consciousness. That we are like bowls of water in which the reflections are seen. Though the supreme consciousness is unmoved, the air or energy which makes ripples in the water, makes the reflections of the moon vibrate and active. The bowl filled with water to the brim, ego, will form more agitated ripples relative to the bowl filled with less water. He concluded that one should not be illusioned by the agitated ripples being formed by the energy or *Maya*. One should know that he reflects the supreme unmoved consciousness which is neither the doer, nor the enjoyer, nor the sufferer."

"That's confusing, what did you make of it?"

"It sure was. I even thought, what is this supreme consciousness, the moon? The moon is also just energy. If ripples and moon both are energies or Maya, why is he teaching us to not be fooled by Maya? As everyone was greeting the sage one by one, I also decided to go to him. I put forward this query to him. He asked me to wait, while he was receiving greetings from the last set of attendees. After everyone was gone, he called me and said, 'try emptying the water from the bowl, neither the ripples would exist nor the moon'."

"So if one let's go of his ego, the illusionary world and supreme consciousness both will not exist. Then who will?" I inquired.

"I still don't know. But this analogy changed the way I perceived religions, and I started reading up on the many faiths of the world. You see, that is how I came across Hinduism. In Hinduism, the secret teachings remained apart from the mainstream canon. They have two different sorts of scriptures, one that is designed for intellectuals and one that is meant for the uninformed and the simple-minded.

Christianity had a similar split, but the division meant for the intellectuals was never allowed to percolate down with time."

I resisted to disagree and permitted him to continue.

"You see, the intellect division of Hinduism seems to be a philosophy, rather than a religion. It encourages inquiry and deliberation. What has been discovered by science today, was already discovered and described by this philosophy thousands of years ago. This philosophy provides a comprehensive account of such diverse topics as time, space, cosmology, metaphysics, and creation.

"What we call matter and energy today, was termed as *Brahman*—the primordial matter, and Maya—the primordial energy.

"The scientists know that matter is necessary for everything, but they haven't found it. What is observed is that 99.99% of any subatomic particle is just energy. When the atom was discovered, it was thought that mass is present only in the nucleus of the atom. With the progression of science, scientists discovered quarks and gluons, building blocks of protons and neutrons. But these too are nothing but bundles of energy. Am still not sure if mass exists at all? Or just like any other thing, it is just a bundle of energy."

While talking, my friend has a tendency to embark on a tangent. I interrupted him as his coffee was getting cold. After a few sips, he continued.

"In one of the literatures on mystical philosophy of India, I came across an explanation to this invisible primordial matter. It validated that primordial matter or God can only be known, once we learn how to nullify the primordial energy which creates the illusions. In scientific parlance, I inferred that, till the time energy exists, one may never be able to grasp or know the primordial matter."

"So are you inferring that God cannot be known until illusions exist? And as per your mystic in Leeds, if illusions are negated, nothing would exist, neither God nor us. It's super confusing."

"It indeed is, mate. These questions have pushed me on this seekers quest. There have been a lot of collaborative studies on science and religion. Unfortunately, these studies have mostly been done in the west. It has been forgotten, that the founder of western philosophy, the great Pythagoras in the fifth century BC, who introduced the word 'philosophy' in Europe, had adventured to India in search of wisdom. I wonder about the outcomes of a collaborative study between science and the much-ignored eastern philosophy, today. I came to India for this collaborative study. I feel that my journey has just begun, and I have a long way to go."

As we had our last coffee, Hart looked at me in hope and excitement. "I wanted to talk to you at the ashram, because you seemed to be a logical seeker, your questions reminded me of my past. I would love it if you could join me in this journey."

What option did I have? Science or medicine was doing its bit in curing my father, and I had no say in that matter.

When medicine fails, doctors ask us to turn to the last resort, God. Why wait for that? I decided to seek answers that could convince the Devil or so to say my father's mind. But I persisted with my questioning.

"What's the purpose of this journey, finding answers to the 'Why' questions, believing in it or not believing in it? It all seems the same to me."

With that optimistic smile of his, he explained, "Indeed, a rational thinker's mind will always lead to this question. What is the purpose of exploring religion? So yes, the real debate is not Science vs God, but it is nothing vs something. Science and religion both believe in something, while atheism believes in the nothing theory. So, the base debate is nothing vs something or atheism vs theism.

"The problem is that the atheists of today do not know the meaning of atheism. Atheism describes a true atheist as a person who has explored everything, dived deep into every possible explanation and then arrives at the conclusion of the nothing theory. While the new atheism says—do not waste time in exploring the unknown, because it is unseen and unknowable.

"The Atheist of today fails to understand that radio waves are also unseen. One needs to tune into a frequency to bring them to reality. I once asked a learned person: why can't I see god? He asked me back: have you seen yourself? I replied, yes, surely, every day I see myself in the mirror. He asked me again: do you see yourself, or, do you see your face, your body, and your hair. Yes, I can see only my body, my face and not myself. My soul stays unseen, but I still believe in it."

I knew this was pointed towards me. I nodded, to accept, that's exactly who I am, a modern-day atheist, without any sense of existence or purpose. As I was nodding my purpose arrived. My father was calling my cell, reminding me of my purpose to find a solution to his problem. I informed him that I was on my way back to the hotel.

Hart had plans to meet someone tomorrow. He delightfully asked if I would like to join him. He told me that he was meeting a true atheist-turned-saint tomorrow and that we could take the discussion forward with him.

I was waiting for an auto to arrive, but then decided to walk back to the hotel. My mind was still caught up with the debate and unknowingly involved in the sensations derived from the debate. I walked on the sun-bathed streets, making my way through the crowded religious *bazaars*. The background score, all the while I walked was a mix of chants from the temples and namaz from the mosques, not very different to the sales pitch of vendors in the bazaar. The energy described by Hart was flowing unobstructed on the streets. The air, often distracted with the inauspicious marriage of brown dust and fragrance, liberating itself from religious activities around.

Kids wearing masks of Hindu gods ran on the streets, shouting and chasing each other. The next moment, one of them tugged my pajama, took of his mask and asked for money. Seeing his perseverance, I gave him a ten rupee note. The kid flew off to his gang flaunting the note, and the competition started. I could see the kid with a mask of Ganesha approach a lady in a red saree. She was carrying a decorated tray in her hand, with offerings in it, for her god in her temple. Lord Ganesha, the kid, tried hard to convince the lady to give him the money, which was bouncing in the tray, craving for attention. The lady shooed the kid away. Why did he not get it? The money was meant for the inanimate stone god in the temple and not for the living god.

Everything seemed so dramatic, I was crossing the ghat adjacent to our hotel, there were a few dead bodies being cremated on wooden beds. The fire transforming the body mass into scattered atoms in the air, reminding me of how Hart narrated that everything burns down to energy. A scary thought penetrated my mind—all this to be ultimately burnt down and scattered in ashes.

The band playing nearby, helped me forget this thought. Playing of a band at every funeral, seems to be a thought-out tactic to blind us from the harsh reality of death. The synchroniser ensured synergy and sync among the various instruments, bringing my attention to this focal point. If each instrument chimes randomly without any symphony and order, it would be so chaotic. My mind resurfaced what Hart was mentioning just yesterday, that our universe is so synchronised, that there must be a master musician who is arranging and synchronising all the chords.

My father was watching the National Geographic when I got back to the room. I sat quietly behind him by the window. Looking out, the sun was dipping and dyeing, taking his last few breaths. On the contrary, an elephant calf coming fresh out from the womb, was about to take his first breath, on the television screen. Unable to stand or see, magically the calf approaches the breast and starts sucking milk. It was indeed a site of wonder; who taught him this and who supplies the breast milk?

I wanted to rest my mind. I retired to the bed, but my thoughts wouldn't dose off. The only way was to pour them out. I got up, picked up my brown diary and tried offloading.

Mission Update

I have spent my entire life wearing a mask of nonchalance, doing what I was told to do, running in circles, and refusing to take off my blinders. This was the first time in my life that I was given the chance to really reflect and wonder about the meaning of existence. The newly discovered voice and the Devil in my father's dreams have pushed me to go out and see the world.

The unfathomable stunning creation, the intricate detailing in it, the unfailing laws of nature, the synchronisation of each element, the perfect randomness, the love in the air, the colours and visions beyond imagination, the music, my heartbeat, all drive my interest in God now. Is it him? The grand master, the supreme painter, the unmatched musician, the paramount craftsman, the numero uno coder, the last hope?

I am intimidated to believe in God after all, and am keen to know him as he is.

Chapter 4
Why bother about God?

I got up early the following day, resolved to educate myself about science, atheism and theism before having meaningful conversations with Hart. I took my father along and met him outside our coffee shop as pre-decided. Hart's pale white face was illuminated by the pink colour of cheerfulness, "I am so excited for you to meet this learned person."

Hart directed the cab to pull over next to a dilapidated vintage house. This type of house was common on the street. Ascending the wooden stairway, we found ourselves on the third floor. The door to the large hall was left unlocked, and we were ushered inside without delay. All the walls of the hall were lined with books. Some were neatly arranged in the wooden bookcases, some were strewn about on the floor, and still more were spread out, abstracted, and open on the reading table. A middle-aged man wearing loose *kurta pajama* entered the hall and greeted us. His offbeat spectacles highlighted his grey learned eyes on his thin face. Hart officially introduced me to him while we shook hands.

"Govindji, over the past few days, me and my mate here have been discussing the purpose of life, atheism vs theism, and if one should perplex over these things or just let life follow its own pace with time. I could not think of anyone else but you, who can give some valuable and meaningful insights on these subjects."

Govindji looked at me, in anticipation of my opening statement.

"Yes sir, I am an atheist. Not because I don't believe in the unseen god, but because I cannot conceive the idea of a supreme powerful God being overpowered by the cruel sufferings ruling this creation. My rational mind is in a constant impeachment of this postulate."

"Don't get me wrong, but an atheist is always aware of his ignorance. He knows that he does not know—what will happen after death or the motive behind his creation. But he stays content with the belief that he does not know, that no one knows, and that it is okay to not know. He conveniently passes judgement by hearing only one side of the argument. He does not want to bother his mind with any counter argument. This judgement, this choice to remain ignorant can be hazardous, don't you think so?"

"Yes sir, I belonged to the same class, until I met Hart. Now though, I want to do what any true atheist should do—conduct thorough research, seek clarity, make comparisons, and draw conclusions. I do not want to have blind belief in the almighty, as we beckon him."

Govindji furrowed his eyebrows, "Yes that should be the start, but with a clean slate. Only an empty cup can receive, while I see your cup filled up. Do you not already believe in God, unconsciously? Ok, tell me what the purpose of your life is, what are you living for?"

"To do good in life, and to try to have a happy and perfect life for me and my family."

"Who defines what is good and what is bad? Who defines happiness and who defines perfection? What logic says that doing good will bring you only good? I guess people do good only because of rewards that have been promised with good. The day one is rewarded for bad, he will do bad. It's all about the rewards, good or bad do not matter, does it?"

He wanted me to answer, though cognizant that I was clueless. But I somehow compiled a response. "Yes, only because we have been taught to do so. We have been taught that in this game of life, God is the referee who makes rules and is the presenter at the prize giving. Doing what is categorised as good will usher happiness, while doing the deeds categorised as bad will ensure suffering."

I knew, with these answers, I was weaving webs around me.

"So, you already have a blind belief in this game of God. It is our instinct to search for meaning and when we find none it is our instinct to fill up the cup with existing beliefs around us."

"Ok, I get it. Atheism does not have answers to eternal questions. Does God have answers to these questions then?"

Govindji tried to explain, "We, our beautiful body, our mesmerising brain, our synchronised organs, and our loved ones live in this magical symphony of nature. We never admire the creator of all this, perhaps because we have never made any effort to understand him. Seeing a rainbow in the sky may mean different things to different people. Men of religion will admire the beauty of the rainbow but will not enquire about the reason of its creation. Men of science will ignore the beauty but will enquire about its creation. Men of atheism will neither admire the beauty, nor want to know anything about its creation. Only a true seeker will admire the beauty, while also enquire about the reason and purpose of its creation."

"Ok, let us assume that there is a grand designer who created everything. He is the director of this drama of emotions and feelings. Let us also assume that this grand designer has answers to all the questions. Still, I do not understand, why should I be bothered about him, or take efforts to know and understand him?"

"If you think that life is purposeless, then let it be. But if you think that your life has a purpose, then get into it. Seek and explore because that is the very purpose of your life."

He continued, after a pause. "The gift of free will is granted to humans only. The way you use this free will, shapes your destiny after death. This free will is nothing but the precious human intellect. No animal will ever ask why this creation, why this suffering, or the meaning of his life. Only we have been given this precious intellect.

"The magnitude of this inestimable free will is realised by a weakened mind only after death, but an intellectual mind will know the importance of this free will in this life. You see, animals are unconscious progression, while God is conscious progression. We humans lie in between. Now it is upon us to either go backwards towards the unconscious or march forward towards the ultimate pure consciousness or God.

"You said staying happy is the purpose of your life. It is at best a premise, a presumption, you have made to lend purpose to your life. Now, it is your choice to live on assumptions or use your free will to adjudicate the real purpose of life, of existence. Think again, the things which are considered to dispense happiness for a man—money, friendships, relationships, trust, lust, are the ones that eventually become seeds for future misery. Happiness and sadness are two sides of the same coin; one cannot exist without the other.

"We disregard the preciousness of this gift called life. We can see the world around us, age and perish, yet we just want to be fooled by this limited illusion of life, which shall be taken back from us. We do not want to find the purpose for which someone suddenly sent us and then suddenly pulls us out, without even consulting us on the matter."

There was silence for a few minutes. Mr. Hart tried to intervene, "Indeed, a rational person will always be embroiled in a loss and benefit analysis before pursuing anything. The loss in seeking God is limited to the time we have spent in this life to explore him, while the profits may be huge and infinite. The profit in not seeking God is just limited to the insignificant luxury one can avail in the time saved by not exploring God. While the loss of not seeking God may be heavy and infinite. Given the above rationale, it makes prudent sense to explore God."

The explorer in me doubted, "Sir, in this fast-paced world, where does one have time to explore god? Deducing this complexity will require a massive investment of time, and we have no idea if it would eventually be worth it."

"Do you consider living to be worth it? Yes? Everyone does. So then why do we stop breathing one day?"

I was perplexed, "It is not under our control. If it was, no one would wish to die."

"Even after knowing this, we dedicate our lives, trying to establish command over it. Only if we turn our attention to the one who controls this breath, the one who has authority over it, will we find the worth of life. If the time we devote to futile and hollow pursuits in life, like preserving the perishable body, finding unattainable happiness, fulfilling the inextinguishable desires is worth it, then investing time in going after the imperishable soul and reigniting our eternal relationship with the infinite god is most definitely worth it.

"Exploring is the only way truth can be unearthed. The religions of today realise this, and try to allure us, stating that they require only a limited time of yours for the religious quest. They deprive us from exploring. One either stays dead believing in the religion he is born in or else because of his authoritative education, stays dead believing in science.

"The only thing required to be a seeker is not stopping at any belief whatsoever, not to waste time protecting and strengthening these beliefs. One should divert this time towards seeking and experiencing.

"We devote every waking moment to doing things that will leave a positive legacy after we're gone, knowing full well that our physical form, material possessions, social connections, and memories are all fleeting. Once we pass from this world, only God's opinion of us will matter, won't it?"

I understand that precisely now. It does not matter what I or others think about my father's life, the only thing that matters is what the Devil or God thinks about my father's life.

Govindji continued, "You are still young. Plan, explore, and start now. Tell me something, you came to Banaras all the way from Mumbai. Were you aware of the purpose of this journey, did you know which train/flight to travel? Did you not plan, before setting out on this journey?"

I affirmed, "Yes, of course, I did."

"Imagine you embark on this journey without defining the purpose. Will you arrive at your destination and achieve your purpose? Certainly not! You'd be lost. In that lost state, if you decide to plan and ascertain your purpose, it would be next to impossible. What is the point of referring to the road map once the journey is over? One should start on this search for the roadmap early and young."

Hart, smelling victory, added, "Indeed, make wine out of the grape quickly urgently, because if we don't, the grape will get rotten and will have to be thrown. If we make the wine now, it will keep getting sweeter with time and have an immortal beauty."

It was lunchtime by now, Govindji invited us for lunch. My father was unable to stand up without support, owing to this severe back problem which aggravates if he sits cross legged for a prolonged duration. With combined support from me and Hart, he stood up strained. My father thanked Govindji, "Thank you for your wonderful insights on life and its purpose. We would have loved to have lunch with you, but I have an orthopedist's appointment at three and must leave."

I had completely forgotten about that. It was half past two already. I thanked Govindji, joined both my hands, and bowed down to him in respect. He grasped my joined palms with both of his hands, in acceptance of my regards. His palms, outside both my clasped palms felt warm and comforting.

Govindji smiled, "Brother, this is indeed what happens in old age. One explores more doctors than gods. This is a shallow love for the perishable body which the mind has been conditioned to develop over the years, which now overpowers the love for God."

"Sorry Govindji, we must hurry, but I would love to come here again. Is this your permanent residence?"

Govindji smiled, escorting me towards the main gate. "No one stays here, we are all just visitors, we just come and go." I did not know what to make of it, but Hart burst out into laughter. Later Hart explained to me that he was referring to our limited stay on earth. We can own nothing here, that we are mere visitors.

Returning from there, my mind constantly dwelled on the road map concept. All my life I have been allowing my ego to paralyse my intellect and have been a pessimist about the unattainability of truth. I was ready to use the power of free will and enquiry now. I shall no longer instantly kick out the questions arising in my intellect, nor will I dumbly obey my feeble mind. I will start confronting my mind and enquire.

We headed to our hotel after visiting the doctor. I asked the auto driver to stop at the ghat, just before our hotel. Hart was still with us. I requested if he could drop my father to the hotel room. He instinctively understood why I wanted this "me" time. For him, it was mission successful.

I managed to scour myself a secluded staircase, which had its feet drenched in the holy water of the Ganges. I sat there facing the river and tried to recollect and organise my thoughts. But however hard I tried, I couldn't get my thoughts in order, they gushed in from all corners randomly. Birth, life, sufferings, death, god, science, purpose, cosmic insignificance, good-bad, creation, time—each one clamoring for attention, defying all the intense reasoning and thought trails I had collected so profoundly sometime back. I requested the grand mighty designer, God, to begin with the basics. It was my first day at his school.

One of the elements of this grand design, the Sun had also started to dip its feet in the water of river Ganges. His job was done. Handing over the baton to the moon, it was time for him to relax. The party in the glorious dark sky was just about to begin, only a few lights were on, and I wasn't invited. I decided to leave them alone and go back to my room.

On the couch, my dad and I watched television in silence, both lost in our own thoughts. My thoughts abruptly shifted to my father's trembling hands. His whole body seemed glued to the television. A commercial for a vaccine depicted the disease as a terrifying black beast. I looked at my father; his face was pale, with the fear of the night and the relentless devil approaching him with unfailing tenacity. He couldn't eat in that fear; he just had a glass of milk. I had my dinner and we both unwillingly retired on the same bed.

"Please go, please go, I am searching…" I heard my father saying, followed by sounds of loud weeping, as though a gangster was breaking the bones of a tied up helpless body.

It was twenty minutes past midnight. My father was lying on the floor, unable to move his arms or legs, eyes shut, he seemed in pain. Weeping like a baby, his entire body was trembling. I tried waking him up from his dream, but in vain. His body endured this state for around fifteen minutes, after which he collapsed. I rushed, wanting him to wake up, but he did not respond at all. I checked for his pulse but could not locate it. I placed my finger below his nostrils, the warmth of air reassuringly tingled my fingers. I sat beside him. It was another fifteen minutes before he woke up.

My father broke down and wept inconsolably burying his head in the cusps of his palms, "I can't live like this son, this is torture, my old body can't handle this anymore."

Knowing that I couldn't help him, he pleaded with God to help him. I was indeed helpless. All I could do was sit beside him, occasionally rubbing his back to lend some comfort. My father had almost died before me! I still didn't want to believe the Devil to be real, but if he was, I wanted to have a word with him one-on-one. I was furious with him, I wanted to ask him why he was so unrelenting to my father. I now had this intense desire to debate with this Devil if he really exists. Looking up, I challenged this unreal Devil to appear to me, if he dares.

My father was not willing to go anywhere the next day. He just wanted to sit in prayer. I believed in God now, but did not know which one of the multiple ideas should I pray to, and more importantly, how to pray. I picked up a translation of the Bible and a book on the Rig Veda from a local library. Throughout the entire day, my father was praying, and I was reading on whom and how to pray. As the night approached, he started to shrivel, he lay on the bed, covering himself from head to toe with a quilt. I kept myself engaged, helplessly. As my eyes refused to take in anymore, next to my father, I went to bed. Looking at the frightened wrapped up body besides me, I viciously dared the Devil to show up to me and spare the old man.

I was spooked and horror-struck. The awfully frightening creature, way more fearful and monstrous to the timid version my father had described, scared the hell out of me. I had never imagined or beheld anything like this ever—a horrifying, spine-chilling evil figure, staring right into my face.

"Why were you wanting me to show up?" he demanded. My tongue was electrocuted and could not move a muscle for a few minutes. His palms were like a huge black rock. With a lame nudge, he shook up my entire body; he demanded an answer.

My father's trembling seemed to have passed on to me. A few moments on, I collected myself and uttered with fear, "Why do you do this to my father?"

Angrily, he said, "I am following my orders."

I mustered the arrogance to ask, "What orders? Who commissions such orders?" Having read some of the Bible earlier in the day, I anticipated the answer to be Satan. But he replied, "My boss, my manager."

"Who is this manager, is he Satan?"

The devil didn't appreciate my knowledge. "It's not that simple, you lucky one. It is a very complex and mighty structure. There are managers imposed on managers, each of them following their set of orders and instructions. All this to sustain the organisation you call creation."

"Where do you and your managers live? Does God stay with you guys?"

"This creation is infinite, it's too complex to understand. We all live in eternal worlds. You will also shift there one day, after your death."

"Does God stay with you guys?"

"No, he doesn't."

"Does he exist? Where does he stay then?"

"Yes, he definitely exists. He dwells beyond everything, unapproachable by us. In all honesty, I really do not know who he is, or where does he stay. If I knew or had access to him, I would not be here, following the painful orders of my cruel master. My order permits me limited time here. Tell me you lucky one, why did you ask for me?"

"Please stop torturing my father like this, end this now. If he has to die, let him die peacefully."

"It's my duty, my orders, to warn him. I cannot disobey."

Almost immediately, I shot back, "Why not?"

With some hesitance, he continued, "If I disobey, I shall be punished. The punishment is beyond imagination. My manager is mighty and merciless. "

"Can I have a word with him, I will request him to change his orders."

"No. No, he can't either! He is also serving and executing orders from his managers. I have already explained this out to you, it is a complex organization, run by managers."

"Then who is on top? The CEO? The one who can revoke this order."

"He is god, the one whom you enquired about earlier."

"Please tell me who he is and allow me to meet him, please."

The earnest look in his eyes served as assurance. "I already told you, I only know that he is the one supreme power. But I do not know who he is or where he is. I am trying to figure it out myself. I live and suffer in pain each day, conforming to the cruel orders of my boss, living like a prisoner. The only option to free myself, is to know him, attain him and then be liberated."

"How is it possible that you do not know him?"

"Can I not ask the same question to you? It is not as simple and as easy as you think. Like your earth, there are various worlds in eternal space, each has its own confines and with no permits to overstep these set boundaries. You, lucky one, are the privileged, allowed to explore and even invade boundaries. My orders are just to act as an alarm clock, to awaken you guys. You need to look for answers to questions, find God and thereby an exit to this strenuous and enslaved creation. This earth is as complex as the creation, but within this complexity, lies the key to God."

"At least tell me where to find this key?"

"I do not know. The only thing I can tell you is that you humans have created several duplicate keys and misplaced the original key amidst this heap of duplicate keys. You would have to search for the original key, which will get you all the answers and open the doors to God."

"If no one, including you, has ever seen or known this original key, how can you be sure that it exists and that it will do its purpose?"

"These duplicate keys are the very evidence that the original key exists."

"What happens if I am unable to find the original key and just rely on a duplicate key?"

"I am the result of a duplicate key. During my time as a human, I depended on my duplicate birth key assuming it to be the original. I refused to invest time in exploring the original key and the result, this suffering and trauma I am being made to go through in the eternal world. I had an overwhelming excuse to accept the easily available religion. Everyone around me was indifferent and I had company."

"The original key dwells only in your world and not ours. Once you transcend to our world, there is no hope, no key."

"At least tell me how to begin to find this original key."

Yet again, I met disappointment. "I have no idea what this original key looks like. You would need to scrutinise every key. Analyse, measure, match and compare them. Only then will you be able to single out the original key that would lead you to boundless bliss and immortal happiness."

'Endless boundless bliss' provoked my mind. All my life, I have been working tirelessly, making humongous efforts to find and fill pockets of happiness. I was utterly convinced and completely ready to embark on this extraordinary odyssey.

"Thank you for shaking me up. I assure you that I shall find the original key. But for that, you will have to relieve me from worrying about my father. I request you to stop terrorising him please."

"I am not entitled to as many liberties as you lucky ones. I have no free will to disobey my masters."

My eyes tore away from the terrifying eyes of the Devil, and I looked at my father's frail and fragile anatomy. After a while, the Devil came up with an idea. "I can only do one thing. As per my orders, I must appear at your father's bedside. So, come I will, in observance of my order. But instead of your father, I will come to you. You should be sleeping in the same bed."

What was I getting myself into? It was one of those quagmires that entreat you to make sacrifices towards the fulfillment of your duties. But now that I realised this Devil was not so terrifying, and he could potentially help me along in this journey, I decided to endow my father with *Moksha* (or salvation) from this Devil.

Mission Update

The mission to free my father of the Devil is accomplished. But this mission has intrigued me to embark on a new mission—*Mission to find God.*

Chapter 5

History and Evolution of Religions

In search of God, I would have to scout the market of religions and find the original key, amidst the stockpile of counterfeits. Throughout evolution, this original key has upheld regard for being the most precious existence in this creation. The key to a perfect world, society, happiness, body, and being—in desire of which, man has been running and toiling hard. Humanity has always sought this greatest treasure. Few found it, and most remained aground.

It seems, the pursuits that ran astray conceived a duplicate key—religion, and blazoned it as the original one. All such failed attempts very conveniently adapted these duplicate keys. Posterity followed suit. Aware of their forefather's vain attempts to find the original key, the generations to follow readily embraced these duplicate keys. Witnessing how wholeheartedly and successfully these duplicate keys were being embraced and adopted, the scholarly set out to formulate multiple adaptations of this key.

For generations, these multiple versions of the duplicate key were proclaimed, discoursed, and celebrated. The sellers embellished and decorated these to lure buyers. Buyers embraced these keys, as it was easy and effortless. Sellers ensured that no one felt the urge to go in search of the original key.

The world we live in today is brimming with such duplicate keys. Each key presents itself with promise and fantasy. Each key continually evolving and adapting to time and trend, so that its relevance is not overpowered. By virtue of its experimental character, it is constantly chiseled by religious leaders to imitate the original key and ensure a sustained market for it. This makes searching for the original key even more far-fetched, difficult, and time-consuming. As humans, we always tend to lean towards ultra-convenience that is accessible and handy as opposed to inaccessible, inconvenient, and unhandy quests.

What makes this search for the original key more arduous is that every human is born with one of these key variants, the one embraced by the parents. Everyone inherits a key and does not need to search for one.

Nobody tests the birth religion. Why should we then? We were taught to trust our hereditary key. Why spend effort testing this key? We believe in this virtuous key bestowed to us at birth, and accept it, not validating it for its purpose. We never worry about the time when the key will be called forth to serve its purpose. Who is responsible if the key fails at death? How can we accuse the key? We were negligent.

WHAT A COINCIDENCE! THE RELIGION YOU ARE BORN IN, IS THE BEST. NO NEED TO SEARCH AND EXPLORE.

After I had volunteered for my father's salvation, this gentleman was free as a bird. He started to visit places around with my uncle, relish delicious local street food, and pay respects to different sages each day. I overheard his conversation with my mother on a few occasions. These were about his feelings of pride and appreciation for me. It made me feel good. My wife was not so impressed. She was bluntly appeased to know the depth and intensity of my newly found pursuit.

Nothing was happening at my company amidst the takeover rumors. My boss acceded to my request for a three-month sabbatical. I resolved that in these three months, my intense reconnoiter would lead me to the original key. The key which will help me answer back the devil and lead to my liberation.

To begin this journey, it was apparent that I should know the history of all these keys, these religions. Hart helped me meet Dr. Tripathi, a theology professor at the Banaras University. He was a short and lanky man with silver hair that flowed down to his shoulders. He wore round, wire-rimmed glasses that perched at the end of his nose, and his sharp, piercing eyes seemed to see right through you.

Seeing my curiosity, he agreed to help us. Hart and I visited his chambers for a few days. A spacious room filled with shelves upon shelves of old and dusty books, it was a sight to behold. The walls were lined with framed portraits of famous theologians from centuries past, and a large wooden desk dominated the centre of the room. On the desk sat a stack of papers, a quill pen, and a few well-worn books.

When Dr. Tripathi spoke, his voice was deep and sonorous. He had a way of drawing out his words and pausing for effect that made his lectures captivating. He spoke with authority and conviction, and I hung on to his every word. We discussed the evolution of religions.

The professor said, "The evolution of religions can only be understood with respect to time. Time as we know it today, is broadly divided into the era before Christ and after Christ. There is no single event that can be pinpointed as the beginning of the pre-Christ era. Most of the existing religions, Judaism, Zoroastrianism, Buddhism, Jainism, Islam, and Christianity have been founded between the fifth century BC and the sixth century AD. One religion which alleges to hold foundation much before the fifth century BC is Hinduism.

"Hinduism renders time as a cyclic or circular concept, without a start or end; it just keeps rotating. This cycle of time is described rather elaborately in Hinduism. The primary cycle is characterised by creation and annihilation, which spans around three-hundred trillion and forty billion years. Within this is the circuit of four *yugas*. Starting with *Satyug*, followed by *Dwaparyug* and *Tretayug*, and finally succeeded by *Kalyug*. The end of Kalyug ushers in the start of Satyug again. One such span is called the *Chaturyuga*, which lasts for four-hundred and thirty-two million years. This cycle in turn entails the sequence of birth and death."

Hart added, "Indeed, Hinduism is obsessed with numbers. Is it not true that they have assigned age for every yuga. Satyug around one point seven million years, Tretayug around one point three million years, Dwaparyug around zero point eight million years, and Kalyug around zero point four million years."

The professor continued, "Yes, in fact other mythologies also mention of similar cycles. Greek mythology has the golden, silver, bronze, and iron ages. In Zoroastrianism, they have the four ages represented by a tree with four branches made of gold, silver, steel, and alloy iron. Celtic mythology has four ages: Partholon, Nemed, Tuatha De Danann, and Milesians. North American mythology has four ages represented by four legs of a white buffalo."

Hart said, "Indeed, many believe in this cyclic nature. That it starts with the golden age evolves to a dark age, followed with annihilation, Pralay or Ragnarok, and start with golden age again."

The professor began, "Let's backtrack to the evolution of religion. They say that in Satyuga, people believed in one supreme god and had access to the eternal realm. During this time, there was no idol worship, and people could communicate directly with the gods. As time progressed, people became self-centred and lost their ability to interact with the gods. In Tretayug personal gods such as Brahma, Vishnu, and Shiva gained prominence, and the supreme creator God was forgotten.

"As time progressed, in Dwaparyug, personal gods such as Vishnu and his avatars Rama and Krishna became even more prominent. The leaders of different factions within Hinduism propagated stories and tales to glorify their respective gods, resulting in it becoming a polytheistic religion.

"During a certain timeframe in the year 3012 BC, there is a record of the period heralding the onset of Kalyug. Annals of the Surya Siddhanta suggest that Kalyug began at midnight on 18 February 3102 BC. This is also upheld as the date on which Krishna departed from the earth. Aryabhata, the great mathematician also recorded that 3102

BC marked the commencement of Kalyug. He goes on to elucidate that in the month of Feb 3102, there occurred an extremely rare planetary alignment, which is also depicted in the Mohenjodaro seal no. 430 unearthed."

Hart couldn't resist, "Indeed, this major event being precursor to the transition of era also finds mention in Christianity, Islam, and Judaism. It was around 3000 BC that God got enraged with disobeying humans, the flood befell upon earth and Noah became the first inhabitant to walk the new earth.

"Nations and faiths got formed. Initially, the whole world was dominated by polytheistic religions. Faiths like Greeks, Sumerians, Babylonian, Romans, Persian, Egyptians, and Indians, all believed in polytheism. They worshiped several gods and goddesses."

The professor continued, "Then comes the age of monotheism. Religions like Judaism, Buddhism, Jainism, and Zoroastrianism, formed between 500 BC to 100 AD."

Hart knew a lot about the origins of both Judaism and Christianity from his research. He wowed us with it and was impressively detailed.

"The holy Bible is composed of 70% Jewish text, the Old Testament. The narrative is mostly about 'Yahweh', their personal God and the promised land. How God guides the Jewish people to it, how they disobey and then face his punishment. The promise of a messianic king and the promised kingdom of God lives.

"You see, around the first century CE, there co-existed several small Jewish sects, the Pharisees, Sadducees, Zealots, Essenes, and Christians. After the destruction of the Second Temple, these sects vanquished. Christianity survived, but only by disintegrating with Judaism and building its identity as a separate religion.

"Common Era dawns with the birth of Jesus, which later forms the base for Christianity, second of the Abrahamic religions. Like Judaism, Christianity is also based on the promise of Yahweh, the coming of a messianic king and the kingdom of God. Christianity believes that Lord Jesus, per the affiance, is the messianic king. The promise for the kingdom of God remains yet to be fulfilled and the assurance is that Lord Jesus will return to establish this promised kingdom of God.

"Christianity came forth as a more refined form of Judaism. The God of Judaism has a much personal flavour, bears human-like traits. His conduct is at times cruel and questionable. Christianity does away with these questions by not indulging in the details of their God. Christianity tries to mole down and perfect this monotheistic religion.

"The first so-called Christian community was centred in Jerusalem, chaperoned by Peter, James, brother of Jesus, and John—the Apostle. Till this time, Jesus followers comprised of a small Jewish community. They complied with the Jewish Law in its entirety. You see, St Paul is the founder of Christianity. He was a diaspora Jew from Turkey and a zealous persecutor of Jesus' followers. After the Damascus

Road incident where Jesus revealed himself to Paul, it was time for a new movement called Christianity."

Hart insisted that the message of Lord Jesus is far more spiritual and deeper, than what has flown with time. Why would God sacrifice his own son for relieving us from our sins, deploying such indiscriminate cruel means? He could have just uttered Amen and things would fall in place; all sins gone. Furthermore, human sins and evil have been on the advance since then. The Christian community led by St Paul, took it upon themselves to spread Christianity and grow the community. After him, the political councils, kings, and popes, took up the role to certify and license the laws and teachings of Christianity.

The professor then enlightened us with the history of Islam, the last of the Abrahamic monotheistic religions.

"Like Christianity, Islam also acknowledges itself as being an extension of Judaism. While Christianity traces its descent from Issac, the second son of Abraham, Islam bears its lineage to Ishmael, the first son of Abraham and his wife's handmaiden Hagar.

"Like Moses and Jesus, Muhammad is the prophet and founder of Islam. Born approximately 570 CE in the Arabian city of Mecca. In that period, Arab did not observe an organised unanimous religion; all embraced polytheism with one God postulated as being on top. Along with being the site of an annual pilgrimage, the Kaaba shrine in Mecca housed 360 idols of tribal patron deities.

"At forty, Muhammad received his first revelation from Angel Gabriel. As he could not write, he would recite it to other people. The followers of Muhammad were initially few and suffered hostility at the hands of Meccan polytheists. Muhammad and patrons moved to Medina. Muhammad now led Medina spiritually and politically. The Querishi tribe of Mecca confiscated the properties of Muhammad and his followers who had moved from Mecca to Medina. In revenge, caravans belonging to wealthy Meccan's were attacked by followers of Muhammad. In one such ambush, followers of Muhammad slay one of the Meccans. The victim, named Ibn Al-Hadrami, is regarded to be the first person killed for the cause of Islam.

"The Battles of Badr, Uhud, and the Trench followed. Muhammad made his final Kabbah pilgrimage in 632 CE. Arabian pagans called this pilgrimage to Kabbah, Hajj. It resembles Ismael and Hagar's travels after being abandoned by Abraham. Most of the Arabian Peninsula was Muslim by his death. The caliphs then took over as chieftains and promulgated Islam."

I was curious, "Are Christianity and Islam just divisions of the Abrahamic religion?"

"The Abrahamic religions share similar beliefs such as a belief in one God, but worship different messengers, Moses, Jesus, and Muhammed. They have the same objective of following mandates and laws to secure a place in heaven after death. Followers regard themselves as the chosen ones. The holy books emphasise the prophets more than the one God, and there is no account of the prophets seeing God in its absolute form. After the prophets, the leaders and rulers of these religions took it upon themselves to spread and grow their follower base or their kingdom. This bred missionary activities and wars."

Professor Tripathi, Hart, and I were convinced that the one God concept and his message via the prophets is brilliant. Only if we could have known much about this supreme God and obtain some detail on that true message which he delivered via the prophets. Today, that would be God's nectar, the original key. But it is apparent that the message has been lost, diluted, in the wilderness.

Professor Tripathi further informed us that none of the holy books, be it the Torah, the Bible, or the Quran, have been written by the prophets. They have been inscribed by the followers and then translated, altered, interpreted, and versioned, decade after decade by the proponents of those religions. It is so easy to derive that the original message, which has been travelling from one hand to the other, centuries after centuries, has been influenced and adulterated by imperialistic leaders of religion for their personal and political motives.

Through these scriptures, leaders have projected God as the ultimate ruler, who rules, judges, rewards, and punishes. It is so easy to justify one's own inherent disposition being in compliance with God's personal nature. They created and marketed stories which projected God to have all these traits. These premises limit the thought process and prove harmful for society, as is apparent today.

We enquired the professor on the development of religions following the founding of the major faiths.

"The period between sixth to thirteenth century saw the conquer by these monotheist religions. Christianity, in its initial phase, dissociated God and itself from wars. Lord Jesus taught and practiced peace. But after his death, his sermons were amended to legitimise engaging in combats in the name of religion.

"Christian philosophers initiated the formulation of the doctrine of 'Just War'. Post this regulation coming into effect, violence as a virtue was deemed right and appropriate, to spread the 'Message of God' and deal with its opponents.

"With time, Christian commanders convinced the people for war, by way of assurances. Pope Urban II issued the holy cry in the first crusade event of 1095: 'Let this be your war-cry in combats, because this word is given to you by God. Whoever shall offer himself to him as a living sacrifice, holy, acceptable unto god, shall wear the sign of the cross of the Lord on his forehead or on his breast.'

"They marketed that God had said—'You must warn them so they may live. If you don't warn others, they will die in their sin. But I will hold you responsible for their death.' The status of war was raised from bellum iustum—just war, to bellum sacrum—holy war."

Hart asked, “Professor, is this not the same justification other religions use?”

“Yes, the chiefs of Islam also quoted the Holy Quran as justification for their missionary activities—Allah defends those who believe. He has no love for the unfaithful. To those against whom war is made, permission is given to fight, because they are wronged; and verily, Allah is most powerful for their aid. If Allah were not to repel some through others, monasteries, churches, synagogues, and mosques wherein the name of Allah is much mentioned, would certainly have been pulled down.”

This baffled me, "First they build churches, temples, and mosques to command leadership. Then they imprison God within it. Then they want to protect that prison, so that God does not flee. Then they write that God himself does not want to be free, he wants to only stay in those prisons, not the green grass outside. All this to sustain and protect their leadership and the religion they have manufactured. Such fundamentalism has murdered humanity."

"True, fundamentalism has plagued religions. Each religion corroborated that the ultimate message of their God was to spread their commune through all potential and possible means. These religions spread like wildfire and were established throughout the world during these Middle Ages. Christianity lay siege of the western world, Islam settled its stronghold throughout the Middle East, Central Asia, North Africa, parts of Europe, and India."

The professor cleaned his spectacles, put it on, and continued.

"As monotheistic religions flourished, conflicts in numerous locations led to Holy Wars. Islam clashed with Zoroastrians during the Islamic conquest of Persia, Christians fought Muslims in the Byzantine-Arab Battles, the Crusades, the Reconquista wars, and the Ottoman wars in Europe. During the Mongol invasions, Buddhists, Taoists, Muslims, and Christians fought Shamanism. Muslims attacked Hindus during their conquest of India. These conflicts were fought to extend, defend, and assert superiority. The vanquished had to convert and worship the conquerors' God.

"With the expansion of their respective kingdoms, leaders realised that for their fraction to further advance, an institution is required. An institution encompassing a place to study, laws, rules and regulations as its constitution, books to study, and teachers to teach. The religious leaders indulged in forming these institutions.

"The introduction of rituals did wonders. It acted like a tape, wrapped around the followers, binding them to their belief system. Temples, Churches, and Mosques came to bloom rapidly; the Holy books—Bible, Quran, and *Upanishads*, were printed and distributed widely. Scores of humankinds loomed as preachers and many a rituals debuted. Rituals evolved as an aid to interact with the invisible, means to cement the followers. It bestowed identity to the protégées of that religion. The rulebook for every religion started taking prominence—ten commandments, the Sharia law, and the Vedic law. Many such institutes, with their respective philosophies, bloomed into existence. Intolerance tenaciously continued to amplify between these divisions, each vying to overpower the other."

Hart and I both were quite shocked. Killing millions of people and causing extensive destruction for spread of religion seem to be as off-track and far-flung from holiness as one can envisage. God unfolded to the prophets minus any

institution, rules, laws, rituals, holy book, place of worship and preachers. It seemed that with time, religion degenerates into a mere philosophy, subject to being interpreted in umpteen ways. When hypocritical men get to the helm, hypocrisy becomes intrinsic to religion.

It was getting interesting, we insisted professor to continue.

"Thirteenth to Fifteenth century witnessed the rise of Mysticism. Weary from all missionary ventures to spread one's religion coupled with infighting and frictions within different internal camps, provoked some to contemplate retracing their perspective and conduct back to the original word of God. They realised that all the prophets, through the channel of meditation, sought God within themselves, rather than scouting for him in any circumscribed institution.

"Kabbalah for Jews, Sufism in Islam, and Christian mysticism instituted these schools and supporters soon enlisted. Others like the Cathars movement in west, Zohar in Spain flourished too. India continued to be the pillar of mysticism. The Bhakti movement gained prominence, the quest for *atman* within. It is indeed hard and tricky to determine the success or outcome of the mysticism franchise as it was surmised as being a personal experience. It did not find its place in the religion galore.

Hart added, "Indeed professor. I have read that the society sanctified that mysticism was meant only for the privileged few. So people turned to external ways to find God. Art and music were the new essentials. Illustrated paintings, statues of God, and poetry in his acclaim. 'Sufism' is a case in point which encompasses both internal mysticism and external art and music. For them love for God is internal, which is expressed externally via music and dance."

I wanted an espresso to take in this heavy stuff. We sat down under the Banyan tree, which was part of the University canteen. We inquired professor on the evolution after fifteenth century.

"Fifteenth to Eighteenth century was the period of Religious colonisation. Communal divide intensified.

Catholics and Protestants were killing each other. Christian divisions conquered much of the world previously occupied by Jews, Muslims, and Greeks. Christianity spread throughout Columbus' fourteenth century America. European colonisation spread Christianity in sub-Saharan Africa, Americas, Australia, and the Philippines. The printing press accelerated the Protestant Reformation under leaders like Martin Luther and John Calvin. The thirty-year war, which ravaged central Europe from 1618 to 1648, was a religious war. Ottoman Turks in Asia Minor and Eastern Europe, Safavids in Iran, and Moghuls in India advanced Islam.

"India remained the breeding ground for polytheism. India accepted Jainism, Buddhism, Christianity, Judaism, Islam, and Sikhism, which formed its diverse culture."

I wanted to participate, so I said, "I guess the Moghul emperor, Akbar, epitomised this inclusiveness. He established a House of Worship for academics of all religions to discuss God. But as the Moghul monarchs lost power, numerous lobbies revolted."

The professor welcomed my involvement and took the discussion forward.

"The Eighteenth century saw the rise of Science, communication, and Secularism. Formal education incorporated Science. Science solved many questions that were previously allocated to religion. The informed and rational mind continuously fought faith.

"Innovative scientific instruments improved communication as science advanced. New communication devices changed the planet and human thought. One could easily stay informed about global happenings without substantial travel. Information flooded the brain. It raised thoughts and concerns about global events and misery. The human mind evolved, and people no longer wanted to be blindfolded by authoritative leaders of society and religion. News of Nuclear warfare, the Holocaust, and Auschwitz raised worries among followers about the constant savagery that seemed indomitable even by God. God, religion, and leaders were questioned."

"If God is merciful and mighty, why these horrendous acts, diseases, and sufferings surround us?" I expressed.

"Today's faiths and leaders are so afraid of unresolved questions that they redirect subscribers' attention and energy to little things, like following laws and doing rituals. If a question arises, it is suppressed by instilling the fear of questioning god. This apprehension controls questioning and testing these religions. But an informed mind will always question."

Hart added, "Indeed, after the French Revolution, Europe began secularising in the eighteenth century. Religion fell throughout Europe during the late twentieth century. Communist Eastern Europe and China were anti-religious by the twentieth century. In response to this threat, several new religious leaders advocated syncretism, or a combination of top elements from established religions. These new institutions, a synthesis of religions, competently skirted inquiries about each religion. I have read a recent survey, which found that three quarters of the world's population follows classical world religions. The remaining are either atheists or they believe in God, but not the God of the orthodox religions."

I belong to this remaining lot. I think God must have given Jesus, Muhammad, and the Hindu sages his original message. But imperialistic leaders and their religions, which followed, have done everything to crush the curiosity within us for God's true nectar.

We greatly appreciated Professor Tripathi's kind hospitality and wealth of information. As I searched for the true religion, the original key, I learned a little bit about the nature of the various counterfeits I encountered. Back at the Hotel, I wanted to pen down my thoughts on Religion.

Religion is nothing more than a shared imagination and a crowd of people who unite under this banner for security. This imagination is led by the so-called God appointed leaders, who carry the banner in one hand and scripture in the other. The leaders have the job of engulfing more followers and shielding their imagination from other imaginations. This imagination is believed to be the only chosen one by God.

Religion keeps the crowd hanging between the fear of imagined hell and the promise of imagined Heaven. This imagination is fortified by patented laws, rules, morals, customs, and rituals, believed to be prescribed by the imagined personal God and subject to alterations only by God-designated leaders. The imagination acts as an established boundary. Followers are regulated within the confines of this and forbidden to entrench borders. Any action or reaction that breaches this imagination is decidedly blasphemous and deemed punishable.

To my mind, the recognition and spread of these institutionalised religions can be attributed to one single instinct in humans. The imperialistic instinct to feel supreme, special, chosen, the instinct to be different than others, the instinct to 'rule' over others. To vouch for this ruling instinct, they even visualise, define God as the 'ruler' of this world.

I wanted to understand how this imagination or religion aids to satisfy this ruling instinct in man. Kings, religious leaders, and politicians across centuries have used religion to establish their rule. I asked Hart about this while we were having breakfast at the cafe the next morning.

Hart answered confidently, "I read a book that explained the founding essentials for ruling people effectively. You see, the basic principle is establishing commonality in the ruled class. Make the people rally under one banner, one ruler, having common fear, common rules, laws, common hope, common promise, common objective, and common customs and traditions. Make them believe that this commonality is the supreme most, and make them feel proud and superior to others."

"Wow, how easily can religion aid all this. Leaders can use God to bring about this commonality and then rule effectively. They say that the leader is commanded by the supreme God himself and his honour should be upheld and respected. That God not the leader, wants them to have a common objective of spreading his message, his kingdom. That God will protect only if one stays within the kingdom. That God not the leader, has made the rule book, which needs to be complied by all. The purgatory that follows from their disobedience is beyond the ruler's dictum as it is decided by God himself. That they should be proud of their kingdom, as it's the only one chosen by God, superior to all."

We both saw how religions have evolved as a tool to rule people. How an imagination shared by the populace is crucial to the establishment and maintenance of a monarchy. The tensions and debates between the ruled and the rulers are inevitable in a society ruled by different belief systems. Warfare throughout history has always been fuelled by tensions between two belief systems. *There was a sure-shot correlation between unified religious conformity and a ruler's success.*

Hart was furious while he added on, "These buggers—the ruling class and religious leaders killed men for their beliefs. Temples and libraries belonging to other faiths were destroyed by them. A belief can only be broadcasted through the texts. Thus, only the books and religions with the most extensive missionary networks were able to survive and pass on their fantastical tales to posterity, robbing us of access to many more enlightening texts and ideas. The rationale behind destroying these libraries was that if the books were less worthy than the demolisher's book, they should be burned, and if they were more worthy, they should definitely be burned. Leaders have been trying to silence opposing opinions to advance their own.

"In the second century BC, Qin Shi Huang of the Qin dynasty buried scholars and burned all Chinese libraries, the Persians destroyed Egyptian temples and scrolls, Alexander the Great destroyed Zoroastrian temples and texts, and the Romans destroyed the libraries in Greece and Italy.

"This practice continued in the Common Era. Romans destroyed Jewish temples and scriptures. Christian missionaries destroyed ancient Greek temples and libraries. Islamic missionaries also destroyed churches, hindu temples, and intellectual work of other beliefs."

I concurred, "Even more atrocious is the fact that in the name of religion, those people were murdered who were using the power of 'free will', gifted by God. The intellectual class, scholars, who wanted to know God using wisdom, were termed heretics and killed. There is a long list of such gifted humans. We have no access to their enlightening work, the culprit being religion again. Weren't Galileo and Socrates termed heretics by religious leaders and punished?

"Organised religions are tools used by humans to rule and to satisfy their personal ego's. This ego is nothing but the desire to be glorified as the only knower of God. The knower of what God is and what he is not, of what he wants and what he doesn't, whom he loves and who he doesn't. *Religions have aided the ruling class to slave human society and steal from them, the gift of free will and curiosity.*"

Hart was in acceptance, "Indeed, religions have divided us humans, into the chosen ones and the rest as the inferior lot. It is strongly believed that the gods this inferior lot believes in, their rituals, the food they make, their water, even their breaths, all are infected by devils.

"You see, Adolf Hitler also adopted this theory. For ruling he made everyone believe that Germans, the Aryan race, is far superior and that Jews were an inhuman inferior race. That the only prudent thing was to eliminate them entirely. A single leader responsible for killing six million men in the name of this divide. Napoleon Bonaparte had said that, 'Religious wars are basically people killing each other over who has the better imaginary friend'."

This subject occupied me for a few days. I went through books and surfed the web. Realising that the worst thing to happen to human society is Religion—these duplicate fake keys. *In the name of uniting us with god, they have divided humanity.* They are responsible for all the divides, racism, slavery, hatred, wars, and cruelties faced by our society, even today. These religions have all clearly evolved only on the grounds of *Imperialism.*

Christianity: Jesus—original words, followed by a few followers, encouraged private prayer, non-violence, and non-confrontation. What followed was the opposite. The Priest-King nexus emerged as Constantine embraced Christianity in 313 CE, becoming the first Roman king to do so with ruling motives. Followed by various ruler's adopting Christianity to ensure a unified belief system within their kingdom. They tailored Christianity to their needs. Theodosius declared Trinitarian Christianity the state religion in 380, leading to the execution of non-Christians. In the fourth century AD, Roman Kings silenced dissent by executing church offenders and agitators.

Popes exerted dominance over Christian realms by appointing bishops, legislating, owning affluent churches, consolidating power, and expanding territories. Kings and bishops collaborated to send missionaries, who converted Europeans from the top-down. They targeted leaders of other faiths and raged wars to ensure followers' conversion.

Islam: Angel Gabriel revealed Islam to Prophet Muhammad. The prophet led Medina and finally took Mecca in 630. All Arabian God monuments around the Kaaba were out casted and most Meccans converted to Islam. After Muhammad died in 632, Rashidun caliphate (four rightly guided Sunni caliphs) followed him.

Muhammad did not choose a successor. Medina's locals elected Abu Bakr, Muhammad's close friend from the same Qureshi clan. Ali Ibn Abi Talib, Muhammad's cousin and son-in-law, and his followers rejected this election. Many Arab tribes abandoned Islam and taxation. Abu Bakr led the Ridda Wars. Umar, Muhammad's father-in-law, became his successor. He conquered the Persian Empire and two-thirds of the Eastern Roman Empire. A great military and political commander. He captured Jerusalem, Damascus, and Egypt. Persian hostage Firouz Nahavandi killed him.

Uthman, Muhammad's son-in-law, succeeded him (two daughters of Muhammad were married to him). In 650, he led the empire to Iran, Afghanistan, and Armenia. Rebels killed him. Ali, Muhammad's cousin and other son-in-law, was the fourth and final Rashidun Caliph. He faced a civil war between his supporters and those of Uthman—the assassinated caliph, during his five-year rule. Ali died. Islam split. Sunnis were the followers of all four caliphs. Shias opposed the first three caliphs and followed only Ali. Muawiyah, the ruler of Syria and a relative of the third Caliph,

Uthman, became the new Caliph after Ali's death. Creating the Umayyad dynasty, he made the caliphate hereditary.

The Umayyad Caliphate conquered much of the Iberian Peninsula. However, Islamic tribes and clans clashed. In 680, Yazid, son of Muawiya, commanded Umar ibn Saad to kill Ali's son Hussein and his family in Karbala, solidifying the Shia-Sunni split. Infighting led Abbasids, Muhammad's nephews, to overthrow Umayyads. By the eighth century, Islamic Kingdom territory was vast. City governors, sultans, and religious leaders prospered. Local dynasties ruled Islam and fought each other for territories in the later Abbasid era.

Hinduism: Since childhood, I have been hearing about the two great wars in Hinduism—the Mahabharata and the Ramayana. In Mahabharata, Lord Krishna along with the Pandavs win the war against their cousins Kauravas, for territory, leading to the death of 1660 million human lives. In Ramayana, Lord Ram wins the war against Ravana, killing 320 million human lives.

I wonder, would Lord Krishna be Lord Krishna if he lost the war against the Kauravas or would Lord Ram be Lord Ram if he lost against the mighty Ravana? Would history ever write of them. If not, would they ever exist? Victory has ensured their identity. Ram should thank Ravana for his glory. The more Ravana is painted evil, the more glorified Ram becomes.

Hinduism as a religion always stayed confined to India, with its various divisions. The leaders and kings had liberty to

create their own personal gods and launch a sect or division. The leaders and followers of Hinduism never marshalled under a common banner, or unified under aegis of just 'One God'. This precisely captured its growth and ensured its confinement.

Select religions like Buddhism, which was founded around the fifth century BC, initially prospered under the wings of its leaders and Kings. Buddhism was the state religion for the Mauryan empire. King Ashoka, after the Kalinga war adapted Buddhism and started preaching it. While other dynasties like, Sunga, Kanva, and Gupta confined themselves to Hinduism.

The prophets, sages, and the ones who experienced God, did not belong to any religion. Jesus was not interested in Christianity; Buddha did not have anything to do with Buddhism. They had nothing to do with any scriptures, rules, customs, or rituals. None of them searched for God in a church, a mosque or a temple. These enlightened ones surely cannot be regarded as the founders of today's institutionalised religions. This credit can only be given to the religious leaders, priests, kings, rulers, and politicians—all greedy for territory and power.

These ruthless power-hungry people saw that the ground was set, they already had a group of followers who believed in a particular idea. They only had to personalise this idea, make them believe that they are the only chosen ones and that it's their duty towards God to protect this idea against any other idea and to spread this idea territorially.

How can a man be so dumb and follow these so-called leaders of faith? How can they kill other people and have no realisation of what they are doing in the name of faith? How were these leaders able to kill rationality, suspicion in the minds of their followers?

To my mind, scriptures were the drug used to kill any distrust or suspicion in the minds of the followers. The leaders knew that a man can someday always have doubt on the words coming out of a human leader. But if they can assign these words to the personal God, the doubt shall be crushed instantly.

The prophets had known God, without any scriptures, without words, so how could they write about him in words.

The prophets tried narrating their experiences, dress it up with the words of the language they knew. These words exchanged countless hands as they percolated down. These scriptures are just assembled words collated by one or many of the followers in time. All the verses in a Buddha scripture start with, "Thus have I heard".

An analogy describes this process well: A blind man was listening to a person who had seen the sun and was narrating it as the supreme most God, the eternal light, and how it warms the earth without any bias. The blind man was so overwhelmed with this idea of Sun, that he started to write about it, without experiencing it. He started to preach it to the other blind people in his commune, gathering followers. Everyone was awestruck with this idea of the supreme sun. After his death, many blind leaders succeeded and kept adding on to the scripture, further glorifying the sun in their own imaginative ways. The scripture now mentioned that the sun is a golden God, the foremost God. The leaders now wanted to spread this word of Golden God to the neighbouring towns.

They confronted the followers of the neighbouring town. They argued with them that their idea of Sun as a Silver God is not correct, that the scriptures, which come directly from God, mention that Sun is the supreme Golden God. Each quoting their own idea of God, mentioned in their respective scriptures. Unable to convince the other, the leaders instigated the followers to protect their idea, their scripture against the onslaught of the other ideas. The scriptures were amended, to mention that the followers who fight for their own God will be in the army of god and will be awarded for it.

GOD WANTS EVERYONE TO HAVE BLIND FAITH
HENCE, MAKE SURE NO ONE CAN SEE WITH OPEN EYES.

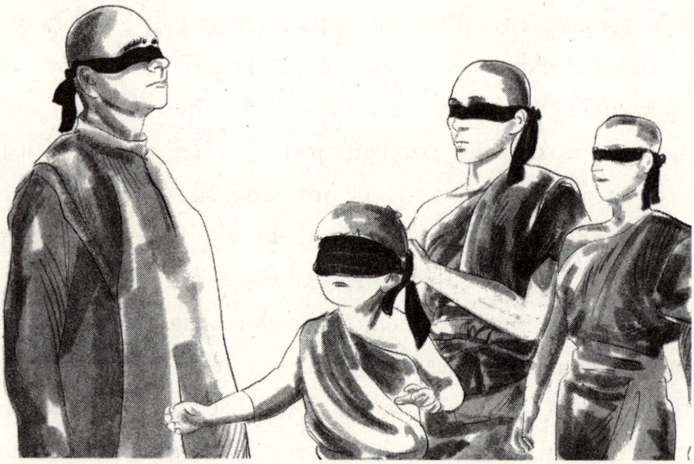

With time, these various ideas about the sun and about God, got contradictory, intermingled, confusing, and blurred. It was getting difficult to keep the questions arising in the mind of the followers under wrap. They would ask about how to see the Sun God and the blind leaders with their blind scriptures would not have much to guide. The leaders then tried to get rid of the Sun itself, and started to glorify the man who had originally seen and described the sun.

It became easy now, the blind leaders kept glorifying the man with eyes, and how the Sun God had appeared to him. They marketed that the followers need not make efforts to experience the sun, having faith in the man who saw this sun is enough. Only a few seekers with strong urge to see the Sun God went astray in search. Seeing this threat, the leaders devised a plan to keep the followers content and busy.

The scriptures then were filled with rules, customs, rituals in the name of the man with eyes. Through scriptures the blind leaders started propagandising that the follower who obeys to these rules, customs, rituals, traditions, the word of God, will ultimately be with the man with eyes and the Sun God, on his death. Keeping this reward ceremony after death was the key towards the success of this propaganda. A man can question only what he can see, how can he question the reward ceremony which will happen after his death.

The followers kept busy in their faiths, their ideas, their hope. For the followers who did not have much hope in this hope, the blind leaders had one more card up their sleeves. The card of fear. The scriptures were inflicted with the preposition that if anyone disobeys or does not follow the laws and rituals mentioned in the scriptures, God will punish them at the reward ceremony. The scriptures even defined the punishments.

The religious political leaders, in the name of religion, have done all they can to blindfold man, to ensure that he never has this urge to open his eyes and look at the sun as it is. Because if he does so, he will get out of the blind commune, get out of the rule of the blind leader, get out of all the shackles of the scriptures, influence others to open their blinds. He will become free and not a slave anymore. How can a free man who wants nothing, be ruled?

I embarked on this quest to discover god's first key. I've started spotting the fake keys but still have no idea about the real one. On day thirty-three of my expedition, I wanted to update my friend and ask for his assistance. Around midnight, he sat at the edge of my bed and stayed quiet for a while.

"Does he, God, want me to find him, find the original key to unlock his altars? If yes, why did he authorise man to create this booming market of duplicate keys? It has been over a month, and I still have no clue. I think I am wasting my time. Why has god made it so difficult? Why can't he just get rid of these fake keys and reveal the original key? Won't everyone benefit from that?"

I noticed a smile taking form around his lips, but he still looked ugly. "Think again, you lucky one, has God made it difficult, or have you? You have made the path towards God tougher, because of your ego. Your ego feels satisfied only when it projects that it is pursuing a difficult thing. It's not God who has made it hard. If god wanted us circumcised, he would have made us so in the first place. It is only you humans who should take the blame for this treacherous path to him."

"You have created laws, rules, rituals and have made yourselves slaves to them. You then rely on the same set of rules, rituals, to liberate you from this slavery. Do you not find this paradoxical?"

Paradoxical, indeed it is. With little hope I asked him, "Since you know so much, why don't you make it easy for me. Just tell me the address of the vendor of the original key."

Shaking his rocky head, the devil replied, "If I knew, I would be with my God, not sabotaging my night, heeding orders, sitting with you."

The Devil got up, it was time for him to leave. His voice sounded stern, "It's upon you, lucky one, to infiltrate this key market and find the original key. Or you can give up and regret later."

Mission Update

As humans, our quest for identity is undeniable. Identity is the compass by which we navigate our existence. It isn't merely a label for others to recognise us, it's the mirror through which we perceive ourselves. This identity, our core, is woven from our beliefs, our ego.

Identity is not enough; we yearn for an identity that reigns supreme to other competing identities or beliefs. This is where religion plays its part, lending himself a robe of superior ego. "You are the chosen ones, only your scriptures are holy, only you will be embraced by god in his abode, while others will burn in fiery hell".

With this belief, this ego, firmly in his mind, he finds clarity in his identity and a reason to feel superior to other fellow beings. He becomes a guardian of these beliefs, defending them fervently against any challengers. It's this very dynamic that has ignited countless wars throughout human history, as diverse identities or beliefs collide in the struggle for survival.

Religion promises us unity with God, but ironically does nothing but take us away from him. It carves divisions between us humans, by giving us an identity, a belief system, an ego, different and superior to others. It helps us distinguish ourselves from other beings, and God himself.

I am not disheartened with this evolution of religions. Like any other thing in this cosmos, they too are subject to the laws of nature—originate, grow, disintegrate, and perish. Most of the religions of today seem to be in their third state.

All said and done, my heart still questions my almighty God. Why does he not stop all this drama of the various religions and reveal the true path towards him?

Chapter 6

Recipe of Religion

I resolved to take the plunge into the market of religions and at least try finding the bonafide version. What if God is as enthusiastic and willing to facilitate my pursuit? The possibility was worth the venture.

The bright morning sunshine galvanised my rekindled optimism. I headed straight to Hart's apartment. He was in the middle of his routined religious chores. The therapeutic aroma reminded me of a temple. A line up of incense sticks venerated the glazed motionless buffet of Gods. Hart had adorned that space very well, with lights and artificial flowers. The only out of place thing that came to my notice were the fresh roses and jasmine flowers. They still reflected the glory of life, amidst the lifeless stone idols and pictures.

I could recognise each of the idols organised in this sanctified chamber. The elephant headed effigy—Ganesha, the *trishul* bearer—Shiva, the flute caroller—Krishna, the bow and arrow wielding avatar—Rama, the goddess girdled in a golden galore—Lakshmi, the monkey demigod—Hanuman, the curly haired—Buddha, and then there was the sorrowful projection of Jesus, crucified on the cross.

I thought to myself, if these gods switched their costume and accessories, would we still be able to uphold them with the same recognition? Our conditioning steers us to identify a helpless, beautiful man agonized on the cross as Jesus. If we dethrone him from the cross, freshen him up, dress him with ornaments, a glittering dress, and give him a flute, he would be throned by the Hindu's as Krishna. If the sculptor replaces this flute with a bow and arrow, the idol will fluently adapt to being acclaimed as Rama. If he chooses to mount an elephant head on Jesus's torso, the ensuing idol will find acclaim and identity as Ganesha.

My mind summoned a shrewd, yet reasonable concern. What if the sculptor skips the accompanying accessories all together? Without the cross, will Lord Jesus be laughing with us all on the streets? Without the flute, will Lord Krishna dance with us to the melodies of Mozart? Will they be commoners? It dawned upon me that the sculptor is the magician, who metes out identities to the entire community of gods.

We bear in our minds an engraved image we uphold as our God. The evolution of this picture to its current form is attributable to the priests, leaders of religion, culture, and tradition one grows up ensconced in. So, in essence, people worship a concept, an idea. An idea better than other ideas.

I settled in the corner chair and tried making sense of what Hart was chanting away fervently to appease his array of gods. I realised he was reciting a medley of hymns and prayers, that we were taught in our childhood. Hart took another fifteen minutes to complete his routine. Next, he headed straight to the kitchen to brew fresh coffee for us. With a touch of annoyance, my attention remained fixed on that huddle of deities. Why was my scholarly friend worshipping abstract ideas? Why is he vomiting borrowed prayers? At the very least, a prayer should be honest and original, coming from within and not something you are trained in. Taking a sip of the coffee, I pointed to the corner and asked, "Why this market?"

With a smile, Hart replied, "Mate, I realised that each religion had built a wall around itself, its God, isolating from others. I decided to knock down the partitions and put everything together in one convenient location. So that they may find safety in one another's openness and honesty. So here I am, weighing the various Gods and beliefs, in the hope of finding some point of agreement between them."

Seeing the bible in my hand, which he had gifted me, my friend found an escape route, "Are we discussing some verse today?"

"What we are discussing is the history of these guidebooks, these pillars around which a religion pivots. I was reading about the history of Bible, and it has left me stunned. The infinite interpretations, amendments, omissions, additions, adulterations, which have taken place are mind boggling."

Hart raised his orange coffee mug, indicating me to continue. I kept the Bible and held my notes. Taking reference from them, I poured out my frustration.

"As the Professor had said, Lord Jesus has not written this. Whatever he preached or said, just travelled in the words of that land. Emperor Constantine after adopting Christianity formed a council of bishops to make authoritative decisions on common teachings and practices. The first council of Nicea in 325 CE was attended by 318 bishops. They composed the first Bible more than two hundred years after Jesus' death. They also developed Christian trinity theology.

"After this, almost twenty councils were held by kings and bishops to resolve controversies and shape Christianity. First seven councils from 325 to 787 debated and concluded on the divine and human nature of Jesus, Christian constitution, authoritative laws, form of prayers, idol worship and other doctrines to be abolished or taken forward."

Hart said, "Indeed, I have read Origen, an early Christian theologian, who argued that God has only one nature, love, and that all souls, even Satan, shall dwell with God. Such teachings were abolished by these councils."

I continued with my notes, "Churches were brimmed with politics and corruption. Pope Benedict IX supposedly murdered, raped, and hosted orgies. He was elected three times and accused of selling the Papacy. Pope Gregory VII in his efforts to restore church power, implemented Dictatus Papae, establishing 27 laws against simony, clerical marriages, affinity, and even giving pope the right to depose emperors.

"Lateran Councils were held by the Pope to assert the command, control, and influence of the church on all public matters. Four councils were held from 1122–1215, forcibly imposing almost 150 rules on the public. Let me tell you about some that I have noted down.

1. All adult Christians to confess all their sins, at least once a year to their own priest only.
2. Priests are entitled to a fitting portion from the revenues of the church.

3. Clergymen were exempted from paying any tax.
4. Tithes, was a tax imposed to support the church and the clergymen.
5. Additional tax for three years to pay for the righteous war against the Turks.
6. A dress code was ordered for Jews and Saracens to distinguish them from the Christians.
7. Public to always consider, regard Christians over Jews and others, in all matters.
8. Kings were ordered to consult the bishops before dispensing any orders.

"Did Jesus not fight against all this?"

"Indeed he fought against such political orders. These leaders not only transformed his teachings to mere authoritative rules but also crushed the core spiritual teachings. Have you heard of Hesychastic Prayer? A method of concentrating the mind, meditation, which results in union with Tabor light, the God light which Jesus encountered. It resembles yogic meditation, with navel being the union point. This had been the central element of the Eastern Orthodox Church. But scholars shunned the idea of union of the soul with God and western church kept themselves aloof from this."

I concurred, "They even abolished the teachings of catholic priest Wyclif, who taught at Oxford. He challenged the papacy's supremacy. He translated Bible in the most simplest of the languages, which was later forbidden to be printed, by the papacy."

"Are you aware of Renaissance papacy? Cardinals' relatives, European kingdoms, and rich families dominated the Pope's college of cardinals. Popes came from the Italian noble rich houses of Borgia, Della Rovere, and Medici. Along with politics, they discussed theological concerns, interpreted texts, finalised doctrines, and decided on scriptural rules to be passed on."

"How can someone not question these scriptures and the rules; knowing history? Let me complete my notes on evolution of Bible.

"In 1604, a conference of church academics found that the translated Bible is contaminated and untrue. King James I took charge. Forty-seven scholars formed six groups. Two each working separately at Westminster, Oxford, and Cambridge on sections of the Bible assigned to them. The King James Bible was published in 1611, replacing the Great Bible and Geneva Bible.

"In 1881, British and American scholars made more than thirty thousand modifications to the King James Bible and published the New Testament. Some changes were not adopted by the British scholars. In 1900, the American Standard Version Bible was produced incorporating the rejected changes. Again this was edited by thirty-two scholars and the Revised Standard Version was published in 1952.

"The King James Bible was again revised by 130 biblical experts to publish New King James Version in 1983. The U.S. National Council of Churches, Protestant, Eastern Orthodox, Roman Catholic, and Jewish scholars created a Bible with 'all the finest' of the King James Version and Revised Standard Version, publishing the American New Revised Standard Version in 1989.

"While the International Bible Society revised the New Testament and published the New International Version in 1978. The best-selling English Bible is the NIV. NIV was revised again in 2011.

"Phew, the imperialist priests, rulers and politicians will keep making such changes for their survival." I paused.

Hart responded, "Wow, even I have never put my mind to the history of Bible. If this is the story of the English Bible, I wonder about the history of Dutch, French, German, Greek, Italian, and Bibles of other languages."

"You see, even the holy Quran was not written by prophet Mohammad. It was compiled by his followers after his death. The Islamic empire was expanding and with it the various interpretations and recitations of the Quran were evolving. The third caliph, Uthman Ibn Affan ordered the compilation of the standard version of the Quran. Which is known as the 'Uthmanic codex' today. The scholars still debate on the history of Quran. Sahih al-Bukhari, the most valued books in Sunni Islam, states that Caliph Abu Bakr commanded

Zayd ibn Thabit to compile the written Quran, based upon both textual fragments and the memories of those who had memorised it. While the Shia sect of Muslims believe that it was Ali ibn Abi Talib who first compiled the Quran, after the death of Muhammad.

"Similarly, the Gita was not written by Krishna, Guru Granth Saheb was not written by Guru Nanak, and Buddha or Mahavira also never wrote anything."

"True, also these religions claim that their scriptures, their beliefs are old and hence true. What has truth to do with old? Old does not make a crowd belief, true. In fact, things rot as they become old.

"It was only these feeble, interpretable, and modifiable words incapable of handling the spiritual experience, which flowed down as religion. Words destroy the truth and further different minds destroy it further. Scriptures or religions are like a poster of sunrise in a dark room. We keep believing and hoping that the poster will lighten up our dark room in the future."

"Indeed, I read an interesting analogy. These religions and scriptures are mere shadows of the prophets. The countless leaders who followed, kept working on these shadows, tried incorporating and adjusting their own shadows with the previous shadows. What we have today is just blend of these innumerable shadows, with no clue of the man behind the original shadow."

My discussions with Hart have always been captivating and provocative. Upon returning to my lodge, I sat with my notebook.

Religion is the work of man. All religions are formed by leaders and not the God or Prophets of that religion. Christ never built a church; in fact, he tried demolishing one. The Gods and prophets were away from all this nonsense. It is only the leaders who came after these pure souls, who took benefit of the situation, propagandised the belief system, and named it religion. Made religion and its God or prophet a marketable commodity.

Dissecting all religions reveals that the ingredients and composition which make up a religion are all the same.

In the recipe for religion, authority and scripture are the main ingredients. To that:

Add personal God - The Supremo Uno. The meaning of God is the same in every religion, it's only that each imagine and words him differently. A personal God who is the supreme most and saves only those who belong to that commune. For humans, God is a human and for a bird, god is a bird. The god of mouse rains cheese, while the god of cat rains mouse's, in answer to prayers.

Add Division - Personal God will lose its purpose, if it cannot be compared and made superior to others. My imagination superior than yours. Each religion through their scriptures claim this. Jesus in Bible—"I am the way, the truth, and the life. No one comes to the father except through me.' Krishna in Geeta—"*Mame ek sharnam vraj*, or I am the only

one, all take my shelter." Yahweh in Old Testament—"I am, Yahweh, there is no other savior but me." Kuran—"He is God, the one God, the everlasting refugee, and equal to him is none". The competition is so fierce that while they throne their God in the supreme most abode, they claim that others are in dungeons. Jain's have placed Krishna in the deepest Hell.

Add Heaven – This abode goes as far as the mind can imagine pleasure, not further. All religions believe that their God does not like to stay with them in this lowly world but resides instead in a luxurious abode somewhere faraway. Most call this place Heaven, others just to sound superior call it with other delicious names. For a Scandinavian, Heaven is a place where the sun never sets, it's always warm there. For an Indian, Heaven is fully air-conditioned. For a donkey, Heaven is vast green pastures, without any humans around. Scandinavian's heaven, where the sun never sets, would be hell for an African or Indian. Ones heaven is others hell. A Scandinavian, after enjoying his sun lit heaven for a while, will eventually crave for the Indian's air-conditioned Heaven.

Add Hope - Promise a ticket to Heaven. Cultivate hope of being in communion with God in his divine abode, a hope that all sufferings would end. A promise that if the follower follows the prescribed way of the religion, he shall be given the ticket. There is no need to fulfil these promises in this world, its only for the other world after death. Experience has never won when there is hope in the game.

INDIAN : I WAS PROMISED THAT HEAVEN WILL BE AIRCONDITIONED. IT'S SO HOT OUT HERE.

SORRY SIR. THIS IS THE RUSSIAN HEAVEN.

Add the most important ingredient, i.e. salt, FEAR - It is the soul of every religion—Hell. A place constructed with all possible sufferings a human mind can imagine. Religion infuses in our minds that we have been put in this world of suffering and are bound to go to Hell. That we are put into this well of suffering. That the rope of religion is the only hope we have, to get out of this well of suffering. I wonder! they describe god as merciful, kind, gentle, and loving. Then why will he make this well of suffering and put us into such a miserable state? If not for God, who would have benefited from making this well? *All Religions must imagine and create this well of suffering to market their rope of hope - Religion. Without the well, who will bother to buy this rope from these leaders of religion?*

They have mastered this business of marketing the fiery well and selling rope. Investigating this well reveals that the walls of this well are constructed by using bricks of beliefs, laws, rules, customs, traditions, objects of worship, scriptures, etc. Entrapped by these, one feels suffocated. He demands the rope. Religions are ready to oblige at the cost of his life.

To my mind, the leaders also believe in the story of fear, because they have also been infused with it, by their predecessors. A lie told a thousand times over the ages becomes the truth. But have we ever seen anyone around us pulled up by the rope?

Fear is the only way to market Religion. Without fear, no one would ever desire an escape route. Just imagine, if there was no fear, no hell, would you want a rope to hold and escape?

Every religion claims that their way is the way of love. Jesus taught love, Krishna taught love, but all that the religions do today is teach fear.

In the way of love, how can you generate the desire for an escape route, how can you create laws, rules, discipline? How can you impose authorities, boundaries? How can you create religion, it's just not possible. But with fear, all this is a child's play.

Love is dangerous for institutional religions, it cannot be taught or infused in the followers, it's a natural thing, it requires no authority. If Love cannot be taught, how would one build a school of Religion *and what would he teach there. Fear on the other hand is easy to be taught and infused in followers. Also, faith comes from fear alone, hence fear is never allowed to shrink. Religions must keep Hell alive to ensure their existence.*

Add Premium - All religions act like insurance companies, they demand premiums in exchange for hope of security in the other world. Only if we pay our premiums, can we expect indemnity from god. Only if we give our time, obedience, and loyalty, will we be spared from fiery hell. We need to conduct our life in a way that showcases our religion. We need to contribute, either with money or time or both, as we shall be judged by the Insurance company on the judgment day. They all have a price chart for us. How much good, how many repetitions, how many rituals, are required to be on the right side of God, how many to be on the left side. How much to receive his blessings and how much for his forgiveness. *They sell heaven at a price of our share in this heavenly earth.*

I would love to work in such a company, where I can demand the premiums receivable in this world but am not bound to show proof of fulfilling the claims in the other world.

Add Judgement Day - God shall judge us after death, if we have paid the premiums righteously and on time. Have we ever gone against the rules and laws of the insurance company? Have we marketed our insurance company? If he finds that our conduct has been proper towards the insurance company, he shall fulfil his promise of securing our life in the other world. But if he finds otherwise, he shall punish us with eternal sufferings in the other world.

Religions call God the forgiver, generous, non-judgmental, lovely, but what they have made of him is just the opposite. That God has a job of making laws, keeping a record of our every action and reaction, judge us, reward or punish us, and keep doing so for eternity. Even God must have been fed up of this exhaustive job by now. But poor God, he has no one to put his resignation to.

Religions know that without a judgement day, the whole game of religion will fall apart. All seriousness and fear is infused with the help of this judgement day and hell.

Add Demi Gods - All religions create similar gods with similar attributes. Trinity gods, Brahma, Vishnu, Shiva for Hindus; Zeus, Hades, Poseidon for Greeks; Odin, Vili, Ve in

Norse mythology, Father, Son, and Holy spirit in Christianity. God of love and lust—Kama in Hindus, St Valentine in Christianity, Venus in Rome, Aphrodite in Greek, Inanna in Sumerian, and Ishtar in Akkadian mythology. King of demigods and the god of rain—Indra for Hindus, Zeus for Greeks, the god of judgement—Yama for Hindus, Hades for Greeks. Devils and angels also exist in all religions.

Add Stories - These to lend identity to gods and make him feel real. These stories help followers to glorify their gods and themselves. The more magical and enticing story a God has in the religion, the more popular that God and religion becomes. Like in Hinduism, Brahman the creator, the supreme God, has almost been forgotten, as there are no stories around him, which the followers can hang on to, glorify or preach. Whereas there are mammoth mystical, magical stories around Lord Vishnu, his avatars Lord Rama and Lord Krishna, who have become the most popular. Likewise, in Christianity, Lord Jesus has his own magical stories, but his father, the supreme God, has no stories around him, so we do not get any grip over the supreme father.

These stories or mythologies in all religions are more human-like than divine. Surely, because they are imagined and created by humans for humans. Major themes of these stories are power, ego, love, betrayal, lust, relationships, success, quests, wars, voyages, cruelty, and then miracle of the divine. Such stories or myths are bound to fascinate the human mind. These created stories also help leaders of that religion to justify their actions, influenced by the above traits.

Religious leaders have not been very creative. There is a great deal of similarity in stories of different religions. All have stories of the constant fight between the gods and the devils in the various dimensions. Asgard, Midgard, and Niflheim in Norse mythology, like Devlok, Bhulok, and Patallok in Hinduism. Iliad and Ramayana, Mahabharata and Trojan war, Gilgamesh's flood story and biblical Noah's flood story, Ragnarok and Pralay, birth story of Krishna and Zeus, Yahweh making way in the sea for his devotees, Lord Ram making way in the sea via floating rocks. God or father showing his vast illuminated form to Jesus, after he is baptized, Krishna showing his vast form to Arjuna, Gabriel showing his vast form to Muhammad. Jesus being a shepherd and Krishna a cowherd, did similar miracles, healing people, walking on water, multiplying food, and bringing dead people alive.

Add Laws & Rituals - All religions are commune-based and institutionalised. Individual laws, ritual activities, and dress codes. All this, to manage the commune, to differentiate it, make it feel superior to the other communes. All of them have rituals for activities throughout the life of an individual: birth, marriage, pilgrimage, death, etc. A Christian child is baptised as soon as possible; a Hindu child is *mundan*-ised (offering of his hair to the commune deity), and a Muslim child is circumcised as soon as possible. Not giving a chance to the child to exercise his free will and choose for themselves.

Add Faith & Belief - All religions have been built on the foundation of faith which invariably brings violence. Faith in their God, scripture, and the promise. But faith invariably conflicts with other faiths and brings violence. No war can be initiated without igniting belief and faith. The leaders of religion have always drugged the followers with this faith and belief. Under the influence of this drug they have made the followers do inhuman things, like the religious crusades, massacres, killing of animals in the name of religion, and hurting oneself in the name of faith.

All religions assembled and made the blueprint.

Inject fear and he shall be enslaved. Then inject hope, which shall protect him from fear. Inject suffering to subdue him—but then do not forget injecting faith, which shall ease those sufferings.

Why are all these religions just the same? Religion is nothing but a crowd of people having the same belief, led by a leader. The law of the "Leader and the Led" remains the same and hence all religions are carbon copies of each other in different colours.

At the core, our individuality leads us to desire superiority over others. To claim superiority, we need division and the inferior lot. Religions, with a flag and the flag bearer, do this with ease. The led exist as individuals in this world, demanding to be led. The led, then choose a leader to establish superiority under a banner. This gives rise to a religion, a commune, a society, a nation.

The leaders are bound to destroy the followers and so are followers bound to destroy the leaders. Creating a society full of chaos.

The Ant Mill—Death Spiral

This phenomenon was first observed by William Beebe in 1921. An ant mill of 1200 ft in circumference. This phenomenon is a side effect of the Led and Leader structure of ant colonies. The led follows the leader and the leader eventually follows the way of the led. A pattern is formed, a continuously rotating circle, each one following the other in circles. Each ant is conditioned to follow the crowd, the thought of breaking the pattern isn't a possibility. Following this circular pattern, the ants eventually exhaust and die. This phenomenon has also been observed in caterpillars and fish. If someone tries to observe the human society from the outside, he is certain to observe such patterns, wherein we keep going in circles, following each other in the crowd, eventually exhausting ourselves to death.

Mission Update

Religions are formed by imperialistic, egoistic leaders, on the tombs of the enlightened prophets and sages. The prophets and sages achieved enlightenment sans any religion and rules, only via experience. The opportunist leaders saw that a crowd

had been cultivated by the Prophet and it would now need a leader, a ruler. They have mastered the game of dividing and ruling a distinguished crowd.

Religion is nothing but a commune of people, who have been conditioned to have a common and most supreme imagination. Their ego bubbles are inflated. They would now protect and promote this imagination, even at the cost of being inhuman.

All religions survive or exist on one foundation stone—Fear. The fear of an imaginary Hell. Remove this foundation stone of Hell and the glorious mansion of Religion will instantly crumble. It requires fear, to enslave the crowd, to make them follow the rules. The irony being that the same rules are propagandised to bring freedom to the enslaved crowd.

Religions have transformed this Heavenly Earth into Hell, by creating the greed, the urge, the desire for something better, a future Heaven.

If there wasn't any Hell or Heaven, who would require any religion? Without religion, this earth would be the Heaven.

Religions stop us from doubting, questioning, exploring God. Religions deprive us of freedom by fixing our path to a final destination. We get chained to that path now and have no freedom to explore. *If religions stop showing the path, the path shall truly be found.* Most of us lack sincerity and willpower to explore a path, hence commit ourselves to a religion, mostly our birth religion, for convenience. Believing others is the easiest, while believing in yourself is the hardest.

"Blind belief in authority is the greatest enemy of truth" – *Albert Einstein.*

Chapter 7
Priest, Politician, & Society

I was keen on showing off my notes to Hart. We had planned to meet at the quiet end of the Chet Singh Ghat. It had a lonely, dismal beauty. My excitement expedited my arrival. A huge Banyan tree blocked the only trail leading here, isolating it from the main ghat. The dusty emptiness of the steps seemed to take pleasure in the ritual bathing performed at its foot by the sacred Ganges.

The clouds cast comforting shadows over the ghat. The main ghat's vivacity and frenetic display of colours caught my attention. The priests escorting families to perpetrate rituals for the dead. Semi-naked men dunking in the Ganges. Zesty boys taking turns diving in the water to stash up coins offered to the holy river. Local crowd dutifully observing their morning ritual. Beggars tugging at the fat wealthy merchants for money. Vendors selling garlands, coconuts, flowers, sweets, and empty bottles. A herd of cows blissfully reposed, deciding to stay back under the canopy. Screeching sparrows and crows nibbling at the leftover sweets. Particularly loud was the hubbub of haggling on the rates of the rituals.

Amidst all this stir was this man under the banyan tree with striking impassivity; he had no need to bargain. On the contrary, he was being favoured with voluntary bestowals from the crowd, at his feet. A stringy lion cloth covering the needful, his tongue pierced by two small arrows was clearly on display. He was opportunely torturing his body for the sake of public wonder and money.

A glimpse of my friend, striding through this bustle towards me, was indeed uplifting. Settling beside me, he picked up my diary, turned to the bookmarked page, his gesture asking me if this was it. I nodded. While he read, I had nothing to do, so I retracted my attention to the buzzing bazaar. Everything seemed regular, until I noticed a swarm of followers entering the main ghat, hollering out their religious slogan at deafening sound levels.

A disciple upholding an orange flag was immediately followed by the saint himself. His skin seemed darker than an average Indian, expressions of disgust congregating on his face. His head appeared swollen with spirituality. He walked quickly while his followers were prostrating before him. He was followed by a group of children around the age of ten-fifteen, who had shaved heads and wrapped in saffron weave. His attenders unsparingly shoo'd away people and objects on the way towards the centre of the ghat. The saint swiftly settled down on a bedecked platform which had already been meticulously organised, while his cohorts hustled about, making frantic arrangements. It looked like they were preparing for a ritual.

After ten odd minutes, I was witness to another similar brigade. Squinting my eyes for a closer and careful look, I could recognise the leader. There was an ugly festooning of his cringy posters all around Banaras. It was Arjun Dev, the local politician. With elections being two weeks away, such propaganda was commonplace around here. Arjun Dev headed straight to the saint, touched his feet and with an obvious aplomb, took a seat opposite the saint. Priest and politicians need these pomp and glorious road shows to hide their inner darkness, I guess.

The ritual started with factions from each side encircling the centre stage. This obstructed my line of vision, and I returned my gaze, eagerly waiting for my friend to finish reading. It took him rather long.

I could tell by his voice that he was impressed and curious.

"Thanks for having me read this mate! You seem to be reading a lot. I went into flashback and can relate to most of the things written here." He took an intentional pause before continuing.

"I remember my father; I can still picture him as a frightened slave. You see, I was born in a north-eastern village of Norway. I was part of a native Norwegian tribe, which believed and worshipped the gods of the Norse. Our village leader was a staunch follower of Odin and passed judgements in the name of Odin. We all submissively feared him and our gods. My father being the most ardent of all such.

"He worked tirelessly as a slave on the orders of the village leader, until one day. Our Chief sold himself to a Christian church of the neighbouring town. He called for a meeting to coerce our entire clan to convert to Christianity. He asserted that Odin appeared in his dreams and instructed him to relay his message. We were promised money, food, shelter, and security. I never expected my father to revolt against this. He was at the fore with two-three other villagers who vehemently refused to convert. They were all banished from the village. That was the last I saw of him."

My friend's eyes welled up. After a pause he continued.

"Our newly indoctrinated chief turned covertly favourable towards my mother and me. He encouraged me to be an active member of the community and to be regular to the church, learn from the priest there. This stirred my urge to make my mom proud and craving to be a recognised member of society. I started to take active participation in church affairs. I was baptised at the age of fourteen and given a new Christian name. I became a respectable member of society."

I was curious, "What's your birth name?"

"Elias. I grew up as Eden. When I grew eighteen my village head summoned me and assigned me the task of preparing myself to join the army camp in town. You see, in my country, we are mandated to serve in our army for nineteen months. I detested the army life and was in love with Ida, who studied with me. She wouldn't let me go. I refused to go. The chief asked my priest to convince me.

"The nexus between politician and priest was evident. The priest benefits from the politician's crowd, so he praises and protects him. Similarly, the politician benefits from the priest's crowd. They left no stone unturned to vanquish my rebellion. I applied for a scholarship at a university in the UK which was fortunately granted.

"I continued to be a good Christian and visited church in Leeds at least thrice a week. I would simply go to the altar, kneel, and pray to Jesus. Would confess to all my sins and pray for his forgiveness. After about three months, the priest called me to his chamber. He informed me that I was committing a sin inside the church. I was perplexed. He told me that it was a sin to confess our sins directly to Jesus. That we cannot approach Jesus personally. We have to confess to the bishop only and not bypass the set channels and protocols of the church. Mate, that day I decided, I would no longer visit the church where such shallow hearted people are ordained as priests."

Hart looked away and immersed in what looked like introspective silence. As his gaze returned, the measly dew in his eyes transformed into a glitzy twinkle. As though he had unveiled some occult wisdom.

"*Adolf Hitler* had written in his autobiography—'Whether there is a problem, an enemy, or not, you have to go on shouting that the country is in danger, keep fear alive. People remain united when there is fear, no matter if the fear is real or not.' You are right, it's all fear tactics. Fear keeps a nation, a religion, closely knit and intact. It gives a common identity, a common cause and purpose.

"*Fear subjugates freedom*. A fearful mind keeps searching for something which would give him security. Something he can lean on, be it his religion, his caste, his society, or his nation. He is slaved now, he cannot stand on his own, free of any ideology and belief, he would need a commune.

"You see, the politician and the priest have mastered and orchestrated this tactic. Should fear or problems not persist, both their entities would not be required. Their services are needed when the crowd is fearful, when someone is required to decode and solve the problems. The politician and the priest must create, catalyse, and commit that the fear and problems are sustained. Like you have mentioned hell being essential to the existence of religions."

I couldn't agree more, "So true, politicians devise the fears of this world. The fear of insecurity between nations, the fear of war, the fear of poverty, the fear of joblessness, the fear of exile. Likewise, priest devices the fears of the after world. Both know that a crowd gripped with fear would demand to be ruled.

"The politicians who are glorified in our history books have all led nations to wars. They have all acquired glory in exchange for blood. The priest rules our soul with the fear of Hell and hope of Heaven, while the politician rules our mind with the fear of insecurity and hope of a perfect nation. The politician rules us by creating boundaries, nations in this world and the priest wants control of us by creating boundaries between this world and the other world. They create a prison around us with bars of constitution and commandments, so that they can domineer over us efficiently and without any rebellion.

"The priest and politician are smart, they have engraved 'FREEDOM' on our shackles and now we are conditioned to wear them with pride and assurance of indemnity. We move around proudly showcasing our shackles—I am a Hindu; I am an Indian."

"Indeed, mate. When someone says I am British, and I am a Christian, all what he is saying is, look I am not a free individual, I am the slaved crowd. These priests and politicians keep us away from exploring avenues of freedom. They traumatise us that if we try to escape or explore too much, God will punish us or that we shall be alone and society will provide no security or solace in times of need. They fear that such explorations for freedom will render their prisons worthless. Such massive efforts and investments they undertook would all go in vain. Also, such rebellion will instigate others to follow suit. Surely one cannot rule over or confine flying birds. A ruler can only rule those wanting to be ruled, how can he control a person who wants nothing?"

The sun finally triumphed over the clouds that held in its custody. It became scorching hot. We decided to head back. My mind was absorbed in this nexus between the priest, the politician, and society. On reaching home, I freshened up and immediately took to my couch. Carelessly browsing through Netflix, I came across several documentaries and historical dramas on this very subject. I loafed on my couch for five long hours. It was already late, and I wanted to be available for my other friend at midnight. I gave myself to bed.

I woke up late at midnight. My friend was already there, sitting on my study table and glancing over the pages of my diary. He turned back, leaned over, and requested me to lie comfortably.

"I am impressed by your analysis. Let me tell you a secret, you lucky one. *There is a monkey in your head,*" my friend continued in a lowered tone.

"I have been at this job for twenty-two long years. Every day we are assigned to people who are to die that day. The body of each one is the same, cold and lifeless. We have nothing to do with their physical bodies, that is for their families to take care of. We are assigned to just take out the monkeys from their heads."

I had to give up my relaxed posture, sitting up straight, I curiously enquired, "Are you out of your mind? What are you saying? Monkey in the head?"

"Believe me, everyone, including you, has a monkey installed in head. Within a few months of birth, this society installs a monkey in every child's head. This monkey becomes a slave to society and the human becomes a slave to this monkey.

"As soon as this monkey gets installed, society starts to give the monkey a name, a family, a caste, a society, a religion, and a nationality. The monkey now starts owning these. Distinguishes himself from others and creates his individual identity.

His family's thought, his community's thought, his religion's thought becomes his thought. This thought governs his actions and reactions. The monkey now thinks in a guided way, behaves, dresses, acts and reacts in a guided way. Society has successfully conditioned and leashed the monkey. The monkey's vision is now slaved. It is time now for society to educate him in their own ways.

"The already conditioned family, school, and society educate the monkey on ambition, reputation, respect, and position in society. The monkey is taught that society only respects, favours, and looks up to people who have power and position in society. They train the monkey to do the things the monkey should do and things he should not do, to gain this power and position in society. The monkey is conditioned to be competitive, to defeat the others in the race, every monkey for himself, fighting against the others for fame, recognition, and success. Society traps the monkey in its vicious circle."

My devil friend stood up and sat beside me. He locked my gaze and continued.

"By the time the monkey becomes an adult, he is completely conditioned by this theory of Rules, Actions, Punishment, and Rewards. He keeps demanding more rules which will enable him to get more rewards, be it material or religious. The more the monkey acts and reacts out of this conditioning, the more he strengthens it. Society keeps cultivating the monkey to be a carbon copy, no originality is entertained. The best imitator is rewarded, while the worst one is punished.

"By this time the monkey knows what he knows, he has no space for the unknown. What he knows becomes his individuality. He stays busy strengthening his individuality. He has no strength left to explore the unknown. The monkey has been trained to resist, to reject, to hate everything outside his conditioned beliefs. This hatred, this resistance brings in aggression and violence in him. Society approves of this violence. The leaders have certified that it is righteous to hate, to war, when one's beliefs are attacked. These angry monkeys, and their respective beliefs, form the chaotic conditioned society.

"You lucky one, do you see how this society slaves the monkey, and how the monkey in your head slaves you? How it blindfolds you, gives you a slaved vision. Converts you into a conditioned robot, acting and reacting as trained. Indulges you into this battlefield with other monkeys, to fulfil your aspirations, to defeat them to glory. Have you ever wondered, is there ever a winner, or is the race endless and infinite?"

I could relate. *This monkey never stops chattering even for a second. He keeps us away from hearing our inner voice. The inner voice keeps dulling under this pressure, until its completely lost.*

The devil stood up, staring at a painting in the room, "There have been hardly times, wherein I have encountered a human, not slaved by their monkey. Some of them are painters, musicians, singers, and explorers. Their freewill and curiosity helps keep the monkey in check. They seem to be outside the prison walls of this society. But all others, I met them within these walls, in this ever-active battlefield. Their monkeys were all dull, exhausted, anxious, and fearful. I often wondered, why take their lives when they were already lifeless.

"The authoritative society, conditioned by centuries, slaves the human soul. It rips off the gift of freewill and creativity gifted by God. It captures the free-flowing curious energy within humans. I saw no worth in the lives of those who led a slaved life, a conditioned life, a life of imitation without any room for creativity and exploration."

My friend came closer, focused his glare on my forehead. His glare was followed by a smile on his face.

"Within you, I can see a tussle taking shape—between your monkey and your inner voice."

I sat there, dissolved into deep realisation. The monkey in my head, had heard his story from my friend and went into a self-awareness mode. My monkey had nothing to say. The devil smiled at me and left. I didn't want him to leave. I wanted him to keep talking as long as he could because this self-awareness was relaxing. Before long, I slept with my monkey in my head.

The day fought with darkness and convinced me for a jog. Nature was enchanting, the independent wind flowing freely, the leaves dancing with it, the clouds so creative in their formations, the birds flying with freedom. The flowers in the garden, each so distinctly coloured and fragranced. The trees grew randomly as they wished to, not imitating the others around them. I jogged around, appreciating how the creative energy was blissfully creating and painting the nature with freewill. They seemed to have no monkey in their heads! All the beings following just one law, god's law, the law of love. While man has created his own laws, substituting god's law of love.

I always made a pit stop at my juice vendor's store on the way back to the lodge. I sat down with a glass of orange juice. My attention was driven to the chaos on the corner turning towards the left street. A dog with three loafs of bread secured tight between his teeth, was resisting. Lifting his upper gums and growling in anger. The other three dogs were perpetually barking at this dog with the bread loafs. They took their chances to nibble at him and try to steal the loafs.

The dog with the loaf combated with all his might, he would not let go of the loaf's, not even one of them. This muddle went on for almost five minutes, until it was unbearable. The shopkeeper of the corner shop came out with a stick and smacked one of the dogs. The protagonist dog spilled over the bread loaf's and all the dogs ran off. All of them split and the chaos ended.

My mind on this journey, now no longer looked at things on the surface, it digged in. It coerced me to think, we live in a similar chaos all our life. We are either the dog with the loaf or the one without it. The loaf of power, money, pride, and prestige. Everyone competes in this chaotic market for these loaf's. The one who has it resists letting go of it, defending it from other pursuiters, with all his vigor. The ones who do not possess these loaf's, growl and bark at the other dog. If they manage to steal the loaf they will be attacked by the others who do not have it. There is no end to it and the struggle goes on. This idea of the loaf—power, prestige, and success has been conditioned in society. The moment the dog gave up the bread loaf's, the chaos ended. Will the chaos in our society ever end?

I came back home, had a good, long warm bath. Still my thoughts were heavy. I made myself comfortable on the study table and tried to offload.

In the realm of creation, a child is born, a masterpiece woven with the threads of marvel by the divine hands of God. In its inception, the child embodies boundless energy, an effervescent spirit unburdened by preconceptions. The child's heart races, blood coursing through its veins unimpeded by the barriers of thought, while curiosity and wonder gleam like stars in its eyes.

But alas, the child's cradle becomes a crux of conditioning. The child, a fledgling bird of vast potential, aspires to fly, while society's wings are clipped by dogmas, traditions, and conformity. Filters are erected, permitting only sanctioned knowledge and actions to seep through. A free-spirited creature finds no kinship within this labyrinth of caged society.

Like my friend said, a monkey is then installed in a child's head, to be controlled by society. Within the school's corridors, a child is forcibly put in a race. He is taught and trained that no matter if he likes it or not, he has to keep running faster and faster, to outrun others and aspire excellence. Only then will he be celebrated, admired, and respected.

We are schooled not to be satisfied and content with what we are, what we have, and where we are. A transformation is demanded, from ordinary to extraordinary, from unadorned clay to a sculpted masterpiece. Society, with its critical gaze, seeks progress, not contentment. It's engraved in the child's psyche that he shall not be accepted the way he is, the way god sent him; he must aspire and transform to be part of this respected society. Child gets intoxicated with competition, pleasures of success, fears of failure, and anxiety. He is no longer his natural self, he is conditioned to wear an artificial mask, which is so celebrated by society.

A child is treated as a garbage bin. Society keeps dumping garbage and trains the child to proudly own up his garbage bin and showcase it with pride. He keeps piling up more garbage. Even if its garbage, its superior to the other's garbage. The bird with wings has now been successfully operated, free'd of its wings and put behind the prison bars of society. This bird now is just like the other wingless birds in society. It just stays busy competing and decorating its cage. The rewards will depend on how well the bird decorates the cage, compared to others.

Even if the thought of flying somehow penetrates the mind, society crushes all courage needed to fly. It scares the bird of the world outside the cage, the unknown world. It keeps reminding it of the security being provided inside the cage. The bird now wants to drop the leftover feathers of its wings at every corner. It chooses to avoid the resistances created by society and fears the unknown sky. It stays confined in the cage. It is made to realise that its wings are broken and there is no possibility to fly towards God, unless with the support of an authority. The bird follows the flock and is trained to say amen to everything, without curiosity and question.

Being in the crowd is the best way to get rid of our responsibility. We are responsible for nothing, the crowd is. We hide our dull minds, behind the banner of these crowds.

The children of yesterday become the adults of today, an immaculately conditioned artificial being. With the filters of belief, religion, nation, virtue, and law firmly installed.

Our conditioning and filters guide us *what to think, keeping us away from learning how to think*. Our brains are incapable of processing anything fresh and new, they do not make it through our filters. These filters are installed by society and hence we can only think what our society wants us to think. *Our minds are incapable of welcoming wisdom.*

We have been made to formulate goals and targets, not only for this world but the other world as well. We have been trained to accept the authority of those who promise to know the way. We enslave ourselves to authorities, to learn the tricks to reach our illusionary goals. The gifts of freedom and creativity are further crushed.

There have been a few birds in the past, who have refused to imitate the crowd, refused to be imprisoned by society, refused any security. Who courageously flung their feathers and left the cage to explore the unknown, infinite sky. Society hated such birds, fearing that others seeing such freedom, would follow. They made every effort to capture these flying birds and cut those glorious wings. Wasn't Jesus crucified?

The political leaders draw the boundary lines, dividing nations, states, humans. Their existence depends on these boundary lines, so they go to any extent to ensure they exist. They collect heavy taxes for the army and ammunition, want people to join armies, on the propaganda that by doing so, people would be serving their mother nation. But the truth is that they are protecting the boundaries created by them for their personal glory and agenda.

The religion leaders are far more dangerous. They created Hell and marketed it unanimously. The human psyche consciously or unconsciously has been brimmed with this fear of Hell. It does not matter which religion, commune, society, or nation one belongs to, this one fear rules over all other fears in one's mind.

The nexus between the Priest and the Politician is evident for ages. They have mastered the art of "Divide & Rule". All the animosity, hatred, insecurity, anxiety, and chaos, come out of this authoritative game of divide and rule. They will go to any extent to maintain their authority, even to the extent of killing the human in them and their followers. They have crippled society to an extent that it cannot stand up and explore anymore. It just stays enslaved.

Imagine a world wherein the boundaries between nations and the boundaries of Hell, Heaven, and Earth do not exist. Will that not be the perfect state of being which everyone aspires for. But don't imagine far, the priest and politician are ever busy in their business of the virus of fear and vaccine of hope. They will keep burning your houses and then come riding in a fire ambulance, without any water in it. You and I are just puppets, used by these priests and politicians for their personal agendas. *They keep us so absorbed in the affairs of this chaotic society, leaving us with no time to self-introspect and reason the chaos.*

We have been slaved, by the shackles of laws, rules, rituals created by these priests and politicians. And the irony is that they school us that these shackles would set us free.

Authority or power corrupts everything. Give bind the authority and he shall pluck the eyes of everyone, more so the eyes of those who wish to see. Give the slave authority and he shall slave everyone. Authority and dependence create a slaved and a fearing society. Such a society cannot denounce the prison bars fabricated and decorated by their own hands. The only option they have is to keep beautifying their prison, stay competitive with other prisons and try to imprison others.

Our conditioned beliefs and thoughts, are who we are, our ideology. What would we be without them. This prison has been our support system, which we have built over time. It would be virtuous to rebel against anything which challenges our support system. *We resist curiosity, questioning, exploring, reading, listening to anything which can weaken and eventually ruin our cultivated beliefs and support system.*

We are aware that our prison bars are brittle and would not stand against any questioning. So, we keep protecting them against any questioning. Forgetting that they are supposed to protect us, not the other way round. My bars of atheism were shattered as soon as they were questioned.

We have built nations, religions, and societies, over centuries, now these need to be defended. Offense has proven to be the best form of defense. Each nation, each religion today will go to any extent of offense, in the name of defending themselves. The more of these will ensure more insecurity, more defending, more offending, more wars. The external wars between nations, between religions, surely trouble us. More devastating are the wars in our brains between our own belief systems and the others questioning them.

We become hypocrites, protecting our belief systems. This hypocrisy within us is projected out in the hypocrite society.

These religions, nations, societies, steal from us in the name of gifting us, destroy us in the name of protecting us, slave us in the name of giving us freedom. We were one, until politicians divided us, religious leaders separated us and society classified us.

It compels me to think, what if we did not weigh down the God-gifted wings of our children with our beliefs. What if we encouraged our children to value their wings and taught them how to fly. Fly in the open infinite sky, without any blindfolds, any boundaries, without a set pattern, without obstacles. What if we let them bloom unencumbered? Let a beautiful red rose bud be a rose and a delicate jasmine bud a jasmine. Let them be as they are, not comparing and wanting a change.

When I see a child, his eyes seem to be so beautiful, curious, and exploring. He seems to be happy and jolly. When I look at society, it is all filthy, anxious, and sad. Society knows what it knows and whatever is known is always dead, in the past. So the society is dead with no curiosity. It makes me wonder, *does the happy, curious, living child need to learn from a dead society or it should be the other way round.* Society has nothing of worth to give to the child, while the child has the gift of God—"Love & Freewill" which he can give to society.

If society starts learning from the natural instincts of a child, rather than imposing its stale beliefs on him, there is a possibility of an unanimous loving society. If we can just support our children's instinct to question, to seek, to explore, rather than impose our ideas. If we can give them tools to explore, I am sure they will find their answers and solve our queries too.

The saying of Jesus, 'Be a child and you shall enter the kingdom of god', gives me hope. We make our society and unless and until we do not change, society will not. We would have to reignite our curious souls, which have been pushed into dungeons of darkness and grow back our wings to explore, which have been cut down by our beliefs. We should have the intensity to explore. Just like children, we need to have innocence, vigour, and energy to look at things afresh. Not to look at them with our installed filters of the past, our conditioning.

We should stop installing monkeys in our children's heads and stop training them in accordance to our beliefs. We should just water and nourish our saplings, rather than cutting, slicing, and modifying them to bear the fruits of our choice. We should value the curiosity in our children and let them have the freedom to choose any religion, any God. We should stop filling guilt and fear in our children, making them ask for forgiveness. Stop forcing the authorities over them; stop making them puppets of society. Stop training them in the game of aspiration, competition, and success. Stop mending their wings, as prescribed by our religion, our scriptures, and our traditions. Let them be with their God gifted wings, no matter if they are black, or brown, or bulky, or thin, or ugly or with faults. Do not try changing them. God intends them to fly only with their own gifted wings, unaltered.

We have been blinded since our birth. Layer after layer, blindfolds of religion, community, caste, nationality, beliefs, traditions, customs, rules, laws, and authorities have made us completely blind. Then they talk to us about the sun (God), they give us rules and directions to reach the sun. Wake up early in the morning, pray, go to a temple, ask for forgiveness, obey the priest, meditate, go inside, move upwards, then right/left, and choose the door on the right and not the left. Generations after generations have been doing all this nonsense, with all the blinds still on. Apparently, they have never seen the sun. They have kept themselves busy, decorating their blindfolds, to impress the blinded society.

There have been enlightened men, who have removed their blinds and seen the sun. The leaders have made religions out of these enlightened men. They have further blinded the followers. Even if Jesus wants to show the sun to the followers, he would not be able to do it. The blindfolds are firm now and are under the protection of the leaders and are forever kept safe and secure. People prefer the known suffering, over having to explore an unknown path. Now it's our choice, to keep fantasising sun with our blinds firmly intact, or do we wish to get rid of them and see the sun eye to eye.

The Road of the Believer or The River of the Seeker: Choose one.

Road of the Believer

A path well-trodden by crowd's embrace,
Puppets, blind, led in scripted chase.
Priests and politicians, their influence dire,
Leading to the Ant mill, a death spiral's fire.

Built on conditioning, ages of rule,
Influenced by dogmas, and society's cruel school.
A journey of competition, hatred's bitter taste,
Guilt and fear's shackles, as you move in haste.

Where newborn dreams meet aged chains,
Old beliefs and thoughts, the soul's growth restrains.
Ego and supremacy, religions in a war,
A chaos-filled highway, far from life's true core.

Fanatics and neurotics rise as leaders bold,
Waging wars for nations, religions they hold.
A road where conquerors preach to the slain,
God's auctioned, promises empty, all in vain.

Here, love is questioned, smothered by hate,
Cherish unnatural bonds, your worth you equate.

Either love your God, your scripture, your creed,
Or hate the other gods, follow the script, heed.

A believer dull-hearted, stays on this old road cold,
Believing his shackles, would render freedom as told.

River of the Seeker

Seekers River meanders, love its gentle guide,
Curiosity, wonder, freedom in each tide
Life's current surges, unburdened by past,
Fresh and unfettered, free from beliefs cast.

Flowing, ever seeking, with open heart,
Away from the crowd, into the unknown's art.
No rules to constrain, no scriptures to bind,
No rulers, no judges, no fears of any kind.

Fearlessly exploring, each twist and bend,
Courageous seeker, on a quest without end.
No certainties sought, no final shore in sight,
Content in the journey, through day and night.

No discrimination as muddy waters blend,
Polished marbles, dust, to the same end.
A seeker, true lover, in this river's flow,
Breaks society's chains, lets authenticity glow.

Nurturing natural love, that precious gift,
Breaking shackles, limitations swiftly lift.
Into freedom's embrace, the seeker dives,
A river of wonders, where the soul thrives.

Embrace freedom, be natural, be whole,
No beliefs to anchor, no imposed goal.
In curiosity, in wonder, the seeker's truth lies,
Flowing, exploring, under boundless skies.

The choice

It seems to be a simple choice between a fearful, guilty, aspirational, desirous, competitive, ruled, judged, rewarded, punished, conditioned, ritualistic, chaotic, ancient, dead and a slaved life, vs a fearless, guiltfree, content, harmonious, un-judged, un-ruled, unconditioned, un-biased, un-ritualistic life of freedom and love.

A believer is no one, but a seeker who has stopped seeking and now stays believing in something. I wish not to stop, but to go on seeking. I wish to be a seeker, keep seeking, not stopping at any belief, until I experience the truth for myself. I am prepared now to make efforts, to travel back the road of the believer and plunge into the river of the seeker.

Mission Update

A soul is born with gifts of God—freedom and love. But these are not good for our society. Freedom and love know no boundaries, no rules, history, dogmas, religion, nationality, community, and no authority. There would be no nation to rule, no authoritative society, no dogmatic community, no religion claiming superiority, if every soul was free. Will anyone look out for a vaccine, a doctor, if he is all fit and healthy. So the only work society does is to steal our freedom from us. They do so by infusing the virus of fear, social fears, economic fears, fear of wars and to top them, fear of the other world after death. We now demand the vaccine which they are so ready to sell.

They give us a commune, a religion, a nation, a caste, all to enslave us and rule. We can only identify ourselves with the crowd now. We want to belong to more such crowds, a nation crowd, a caste crowd, a religious crowd, a club crowd. We keep consolidating our false identity. We need the crowd now, needing recognition, respect, post, and power from the crowd. We are the fearful crowd now; and forcefully enroll our children into it.

This Fear is nothing, but a thought infused in our minds which we consider as real. One can fear only what he knows or what has already been fed in his mind. One fears ghosts only because he knows about ghosts. One fears Hell only because he knows about Hell. Will a child who has no knowledge of ghosts or Hell, ever fear any of those?

From birth the priest and the politicians inject fear and make us believe that we need a support system - these crowds. Over the years we get paralysed by this support system. A conditioned slave then is more bothered about his security than his freedom. The mind gets so slaved to the support system, come what may he will keep holding on to it. Even if it hurts him, he will keep gripping harder. Crushing all possibilities of freedom.

God sent us with wings to explore and all that these priests and politicians do is to cut-off our wings and rule us. Transform us into wingless birds in the prisons of religions and nations, into imitators, into puppets, into blind followers. If and only if somehow, we can realise our paralysis and try getting rid of the support system, or somehow our support system gets forcibly stolen from us. Only then will we be free to dive into the river as a seeker and take our first step in the quest for God.

As *Lee Camp* said, "99% of us are good-hearted people who respect others and want peace. The other 1% rule the world and tell us we're at war."

Chapter 8
Seeker's Quest

God gave me freedom. I was free to be a slave, as long as I wanted to. I was free to have faith in my beliefs. I was free to be blinded by society, as long as I wanted to. And I am free now, to remove the blindfolds, the filters, to spread my wings and fly.

I am hungry for my God now. He has started flirting with me, he entices me towards him. I do not know how he looks, or his name, or where he is, but I have started liking him. He has snatched my clutches—my beliefs—and is forcing me to fly towards him. However, I have no one to show me how to fly. I look around and see caged birds without their wings.

The ones who flew, unfortunately haven't left any footprints in the virgin unmarked sky and I see no one flying around me now. What to do with my brand-new wings is a mystery to me. If I jump off the cliff, I will certainly land on the rocks with a thud. The only way to fly to him is to figure out what the birds who have broken free of society and taken to air are trying to teach me.

We have been conditioned to think that anything related to God must be colossally complicated. I too used to feel the same, until now. On my journey so far, I have discovered some keys, which I believe would make it easier to decipher the hidden teachings of our prophets and sages.

What made it easier was covid. My three-month sabbatical was getting over in nine days and I had already booked my flight home. But then, my organisation announced the work from home policy applicable until further notice. This meant that I could attend to my office sitting right here. Without a second thought, I cancelled my tickets and decided that whatever spare time I would get in the mornings and evenings and the weekends, I would devote it towards learning how to fly.

The covid situation improved in a few weeks. Hart and I decided to attend a lecture by sage Sehajanand, who is renowned for teaching and demystifying the *Sanatana Dharma* across the world. After a forty-minute long bumpy rikshaw ride, we arrived. An arched door stood on the right side of the main road that led to a curvy half-baked private road surrounded by dense vegetation. It seemed Hart had been here before, as he knew to spot this turn. We could see a large colourful tent a few hundred meters down the road. At the tent's entrance, men and women dressed in brightly coloured clothes greeted the visitors. Hart, the lone white man in a sea of people of colour, caught their attention, and they all vied to be the first to greet him.

We were made to sit in the first row. The outspread of cotton-filled mattresses covered in white sheets made for comfortable seating. On the stage was perched a lotus-shaped throne, reserved for the sage. On one side of the stage was a choir singing Mira bhajans preceding the sage's arrival. On his arrival, everyone stood up and chanted his name in praise. He was a chubby old man in his sixties, with curly white hair, saffron robe, and tiny eyes. With a gesture of his hand, he signaled for us to sit down. For the first five minutes, he stayed quiet and surveyed the gathering that sat before him. His gaze came to fix at Hart. He managed a reticent smile and inquired, "Would you like to hear anything specific?"

Hart looked at me and then replied, "O learned sage, please enlighten us about the foundation, origin, and meaning of Sanatana Dharma."

The sage closed his eyes for a few minutes and then commenced his discourse. "Sanatana Dharma is the philosophy prevalent from the Vedic times. It is but a science, which explains the laws of nature and confers liberty on its followers to institute theories of their own. Hinduism is one of the theories that came out of this philosophy.

"Like a drop of water that evaporates from the ocean to become vapour, condenses into clouds, then rains back into the ocean. This creation is cyclic. The smallest cycle is our birth, death, and reborn cycle. Then this spirit journeys through countless other engulfing cycles. The whole structure is too complex and beyond the imagination of the normal human mind."

I thought to myself, they keep saying it's complicated. *It's not beyond the imagination of the mind, but merely the imagination of the mind itself.* I reminded myself of the vow to be a good listener and absorb only things which shall aid my journey. I continued to listen carefully.

"Shruti and Smriti constitute our scriptures. Shruti or revelation scriptures are the four Vedas. God gave us the first scriptures. They studied logic, philosophy, and nature. Smriti, on the other hand followed the Vedas and were a work of human experiences and stories. Smriti books like the Puranas and Upanishads chronicle human experiences that have become traditions today. The Smriti scriptures lauded the gods below the almighty creator and established rituals, lifestyles, and caste systems. These scriptures became part of people's daily life.

"This spiritual journey or exploring needs to be planned well. Else one shall be trapped in this maze of numerous gods, goddesses, and various spiritual realms. We have three hundred thirty million deities. Then we have Brahma, Vishnu, Shiva, and Shakti, as the creator, protector, destroyer, and fertility goddess, respectively. Creation is based on duality; hence Goddess Shakti is essential. She marries Brahma, Vishnu, and Shiva as Saraswati, Laxmi, and Parwati. These gods have abodes in the eternal realms.

"*Devlok*, *Bhu Lok*, and *Patal Lok* are the three eternal dimensions, divided further into fourteen *Bhavans. Sat Lok, Tapo Lok, Jan Lok, Maha Lok, Dhruv Lok, and Siddh Lok* are parts of Devlok and then comes Bhu Lok or *Prithvi Lok* in the middle, this is where we live in. Patal Lok, below Bhulok, has *Atal Lok, Pital Lok, Sutal Lok, Talatal Lok, Mahatal Lok,* and *Rasatal Lok*.

"Kashyapa, son of Brahma married Aditi and Diti. Devas were born from Aditi and their brothers Asuras were born from Diti. Devas live in Dev Lok and Asuras or devils live in Patal Lok, underneath our Prithvi Lok.

"Heaven, or Devlok, is luxurious. Heaven has never-aging bodies, no sicknesses, and all material wishes. But, these riches never bring happiness, neither in this world nor the worlds of god. God Indra, the king of Heaven, is the wealthiest soul. His heaven is opulent. He has the wish fulfilling tree Kalpataru in his kingdom, Kamdhenu cow who grants all wishes. Gorgeous apsaras and singing gandharvas. Lord Indra is never happy because he worries that the asuras, devils, would steal his wealth. Just like rich individuals in our worlds worry about losing their wealth.

"Further, everything is cyclical. Indra knows his throne is temporary. Everyone can become Lord Indra, the richest soul. If one does a particular amount of goods in this world, he gets the ticket to dethrone Indra and become the new King. Therefore, Lord Indra uses any means to distract the human who seeks his throne. Indra uses Menaka, his most beautiful angel, to distract humans who are trying to dethrone him.

"These eternal abodes, these luxuries, the souls of gods, mortals, and devils, nothing lasts. All must undergo creation, destruction, and rebirth. Sanatana Dharma's ultimate purpose is to find the eternal abode where the permanent soul can enjoy permanent bliss untouched by creation, destruction, and rebirth. This is Moksha or Nirvana."

The sage's eye suddenly became heavy and shut. The story was over. But I was hoping to probe him on the topic of Moksha which he was alluding to. According to Sanatana Dharma, there are two different kinds of moksha, *Dwait moksha*, in which the human soul resides alongside the divine soul, and *Adwait moksha*, in which there are no two souls and the human soul dissolves into the divine soul.

The gathering had just begun to disperse when Hart approached one of the sage's pupils and asked if they might set up a meeting for us with the sage. Fifteen minutes later the student came back and told us that the saint would see us in another thirty minutes. After enjoying some tasty food from a nearby booth, we went back to the tent, and were led to a little cottage hidden behind the tent.

As we walked inside the conference room, we saw a group of turbaned disciples circling a decorated plate facing the saint. Then they poured milk from a vessel at the feet of the decked-up saint. A few moments later a toddler was presented before the saint. He used scissors to clip off a section of the child's hair. This followed some more offerings, chants, and slogans. I knew of this ritual. The saint had a confident grin on his face the whole time. Once the disciples left, we were summoned forward.

We sat on the ground facing him, palms folded, as a sign of respect. After a few minutes of silence, wherein each of us was expecting the other to speak, a disciple intervened and said, "Please go ahead and ask what you want to ask."

I was waiting for this, "Sir, I was born in the same religion you preach. In my childhood I used to follow my parents in the rituals they performed. They feared that if they did not do the rituals, they would face God's wrath. They made me fear him as well. As I grew up, I couldn't see any logical reason to follow these made-up rituals anymore. Anyone can form a new ritual and within no time we start accepting and following it. It is such an adoptive religion, which keeps incorporating new beliefs and thoughts with a complete blind eye. Sorry for being blunt, but it seems to be just a glorified, decorated, blindfold religion with great imaginative rituals and stories behind them."

The saint was very composed, "So what do you believe in?"

"I believe there is one almighty—the supreme God of the Vedas, the God of the Bible, the God of the Quran—they're all the same. Eventually the religious authorities were able to exile him to the woods. In my opinion, ninety-nine percent of what we call religions is nothing but worthless rituals, rules, and dogmas. Countless rituals for each stage of our lives are created to keep the faithful engaged and united. The religious leaders know that these gods need to be kept current and trending or they lose their importance. The best marketed gods climb the popularity chart."

Aware that I had gone too far, I backed off. The wise man though kept his wonderful grin on throughout. He looked around and seeing that there was nobody else apart from us there, he spoke,

"I am pleased that someone is putting his mind to religion. It is important to know about something as important as the religion you follow and base your life upon. I completely understand where you are coming from and agree with most of it. You see, it is not only about advertising or marketing, but also about the internal and external influence on a land over a period."

This got me curious.

"In the Vedic period the teachings of Veda dominated. The caste system was introduced in this period to run society in an organised manner. It gave a sense of belonging to people and played an important role in economic, social, and political life. But the hunger for power took over and the caste system was interpreted wrongly to take benefit. Only Brahmans were allowed to gain knowledge of the Vedas. The lower castes needed something of their own, their own God, whom they could worship freely, hence they started creating the demigods and earthbound gods, created regional tales around them. And so, village gods, tantrics, yogis, amma, mata, folk deities, bhut, pret, and pitr entered the scene. People started gathering crowds for the one they followed.

"Temples and rituals were introduced by the various kingdoms in their land. Kings sponsored the making of idols of gods and goddesses in metal and stone and built temples. The temples were managed by Brahmans, who acted on behalf of the Kings and dominated the society via these temples and rituals."

I thought to myself, "priest and politician nexus is ubiquitous," while the decked up saint continued.

"The circumstances also changed with the global religions of Christianity and Islam gaining prominence. India was fragmented into several Hindu kingdoms, which were at constant war against each other. Each kingdom adopted one of the divisions of Hinduism and fought under its banner. Major divisions were *Vaishnavism, Shaivism, Shaktism*, and *Smartism*.

"Taking advantage of this infighting and the religiously divided land, invaders succeeded. First it was monotheistic Islam and then the Portuguese. Then the British came to India with a vision to rule it. To rule a country, the ruler must know the culture, the traditions, and the religion of that land. But India had a complex landscape. The custom, tradition, God, and language changed every hundred or so miles.

"It was too confusing for these invaders. They had experienced only one holy book and one God—Bible and Jesus, Quran and Allah. In order to simplify things, they decided to select and popularise one God, one scripture, and one religion. All the Hindu scriptures, like the Vedas, Upanishads, and Puranas had several gods and goddesses. Filtering down they were left with Gita. Gita is the smallest of the scriptures, a part of Mahabharata, which has just one God, Krishna, delivering his message to Arjuna. Like any other Hindu scripture, Gita was also written in Sanskrit. British decided to translate Gita into English."

Hart intervened, "Charles Wilkins was the first person ever to translate Geeta to english."

The sage smiled and continued, "The British distributed and popularised the translated Gita. Krishna and his sermons to Arjuna became widespread and popular both among the invaders and the commoners. With time, the popularity increased, and the other gods were left behind. In today's world, Krishna is the most worshiped God in India and in other countries."

Our discussion was going on a different tangent, I wanted to bring it back,

"I agree, the influence on the land has its imprint on the God popularity chart. You talked about Nirvana. I want to understand; how will these gods help in achieving Nirvana. As I understand, Nirvana is the ultimate state a soul may reach, and its definition and existence is universally known and accepted. That's why no subgroup is content to operate below it. Every sect believes that its own unique God or path is the only way to achieve Nirvana, dwait or adwait."

Without warning, Swami Sehajanand's eyes shifted away from me and gazed out a bright window at the verdant garden outside the tent. A little while later, his eyes returned to me, but they seemed even more diminutive than before.

"At the core we have the Vedantic Brahman, *Maya*, and Atman trilogy. Brahman, the creator, is the omnipresent primordial matter and Maya or Desire is the primordial energy. When they combine, they form this creation. To achieve the state of Brahman or Nirvana, one needs to understand the creative energy, Maya. Maya is the omnipotent energy, the creative force, the desire. This creation is nothing but an interplay of energies or Maya.

Maya applies two forces while creating this creation. First, *Avaranasakti* or dark force, which veils the Brahman from us and is also called the Veiling Force. Second, *Viksepasakti* or active force, which projects the forms of the world, the illusion, and is also called the Projecting Force. What we can observe or see in this creation is because of this projecting force or Viksepasakti of Maya. While what we cannot see or cannot observe, our creator, is because of the Veiling force or Avaranasakti of Maya.

"The Vedantic belief is divided into Dwait and Adwait. The Dwait followers believe that the Brahaman and Atman are different and two entities. While the Adwait followers believe that Brahaman and Atman are the same. They are also divided on the causation of this creation. The Dwaits believe that the creation is caused by self-transformation or Parinamakarna. Just like milk transforms into butter and then butter cannot be transformed again into milk. While the Adwaits believe that the creation is caused by non-self transformation or Vivartakarana. Just like ice transforms itself into water when heat force is applied, and water again transforms into ice when heat force is withdrawn.

"The Dwaits believe that the atman can never become the Brahman, the creator, but can only attain him. After liberation, atman can live in the same world with God or salokya, live near God or samipya, become like God or sarupya, and enjoy with God or sayujya. While the Adwaits believe that Brahman and Atman are the same, and after liberation Atman becomes the Brahman, the creator."

Hart was keen to intervene.

"Sir, before going deeper into this, I just wanted to verify my understanding. I am a follower of Quantum Physics and I believe that the Vedantic teachings are similar to laws of quantum physics. All creation is made up of atoms, like you say all creation is made of Brahman and Maya. Can we then relate Brahman, the creator to the primordial matter, the nucleus of an atom? And Maya, the creative force, to the electrons which revolve around the nucleolus? Quantum physics believes that anything that can be observed or seen, or which comes into existence has to be perceived.

"The theory believes that everything is made up of energy waves or Maya, as you call it. Only when these energy waves are observed do they become matter and are projected and seen. Experiments have revealed that all this creation boils down to just energy and it's just illusionary or projected. That there is no solidity in the world around, all is made of subatomic particles, which again is nothing but just bundles of energy.

"The two attributes of Maya as you said, the veiling force or the power to veil the Brahman and the projecting force, the power to project things in this creation are the same two forces attributed to electrons. Electrons form a veiling shell for the nucleolus and are also the projecting force, which when observed takes the form of the created universe. Electrons keep the primordial matter or mass unknown, blanketed with just energy. No matter how hard the scientists try, with the discovery of every new subatomic particle, it is also discovered that every subatomic particle is just made of energy or mathematically ninety-nine percent of energy. That something always stays hidden, aiding the curiosity to find it. So does Quantum Physics say the same thing in a different language?"

Sehajanandji looked a little dazed, yet he tried to explain.

"Son, I have not studied what you just mentioned, Quantum Physics. But yes, I remember a discussion in my younger days with a learned philosopher from the west. He had studied the Vedas, and in our discussion, he was referring to something similar to what you have to say. He said that Maya's Avaranasakti is like the projector screen or the veil between the observer and the Brahman, and Maya'a

Viksepasakti is like the movie being played on the projector screen, caused by the vibrating light waves, keeping the observer busy. I did not hear this comparison of Brahman and Maya to Nucleus and Electrons in an atom, but the learned western philosopher referred to atoms in a different way.

"He said that atoms are the building block of everything in this creation and that atoms have three elements: neutrons, protons, and electrons. According to Vedas, all this creation is caused by Maya or that like atoms, Maya is the building block of everything. The Vedas say that Maya has three attributes or qualities: *Satva, Rajas*, and *Tamas.*

"The Satva Guna or attribute is associated with Goodness, compassion, illumination, and positivity. The Rajas Guna is associated with energy, activity, chaos, passion, and change. The Tamas Guna is associated with lethargy, darkness, and ignorance. The Philosopher linked these three attributes to protons, neutrons, and electrons. Neutrons like Tamas, being associated with darkness and ignorance, protons like Satva, being associated with positivity and illumination, and electrons like Rajas, being associated with energy and activity.

"With atom, all these three are present in everything. He said that the interplay of these attributes give structure, shape, and qualities to things around us in this creation. Also, every action and reaction in the creation is based on these three attributes. So yes, it may be possible that Quantum Physics is also based on Vedantic Philosophy."

Hart kept himself busy with western philosophy ideas. I too was impressed, but there was another issue on my mind. At this point, it was my chance to speak,

"Sir, like you say, we are all constructed of atoms or Maya. Do we all possess these three qualities? Does Brahman, if we and he are the same thing, share these three characteristics? And does he use all these attributes to create this creation, like how atoms create all this creation?"

Sehajanandji raised his eyebrows and answered adamantly.

"No, Brahman does not possess these qualities, he is aloof of all this. It is only Maya, which possesses these attributes. Only when Brahman comes in contact with Maya, does the creation gets created out of these three attributes. You see, this also gives the purpose for one's life. One should realise that he is the Brahman and then try to detach from all these qualities or Maya and attain the original pure form of Brahman. This is how to achieve Nirvana."

I was curious.

"Which of the Nirvana's? If I follow the Adwait philosophy, I am the Brahman, the creator himself. So why do I have to make efforts to be myself again? And if I follow the Dwait philosophy, I will never become Brahman, the creator, I will only be a part of his creation, which I already am. So which philosophy should be trusted and followed?"

"I personally believe in the Adwait philosophy, and that the creation comes in to form by Vivartakarana or self-transformation. Brahman is the solid ice, when Maya, the heat energy is applied, atman's are created. It is the sole purpose of the atman's to get cooled, avoid Maya, the heat and transform back to Brahman, the ice."

Hart was back in form.

"Sir, just like atoms again. Ice is nothing but atoms in a closely combined form, solid and with no movement. Once heat is applied, the electrons come into activity and water is formed. Ice loses its solidity and electrons are in constant motion, to give active force to liquid water."

"But how does one liberate himself? How does he avoid the heat of Maya?" I was curious.

The saint smiled, "For liberation, one should realise this causation caused by Maya. He needs to follow the path prescribed by Veda, to detach from Maya and attain the pure form."

"Let's say I do as the Vedas instruct and reach the icy perfection that is Brahman. Will this guarantee that the Brahman, who originally encountered Maya, never does so again, thus preventing future creations? How do I avoid the heat from influencing the ice? Or is there something else I need to do to make sure Maya never tempts me again?"

The saint looked rattled, but he controlled his emotions, "Son, as of now you are not capable of understanding this. What you need to realise is that Vedic teachings explain everything logically and rationally. Hence, a true seeker should follow the path prescribed by the Vedas. He needs to focus on the creator and respect his creation. You see the images of all the gods around my ashram. I respect my creator's creation, while following the path prescribed by Vedas. This is the only path of truth and I preach the same."

Hart looked at me as though to approve of the response I had just received from the wise man. To validate, praying and respecting all gods.

A devotee of Swami entered the room, bowed deeply, and asked Swamiji to have his medicines and food. To our delight, Swamiji invited us to share a meal with him. I was more than happy to do so, as I was eager to learn from the wise man and did not want our conversation to end generically, like so many other lectures and debates did. I was ready to say yes when Hart unexpectedly interrupted, "Thank you Swamiji, but we have to reach somewhere urgently."

Later, I found out that Hart had to go to the dentist. We took leave and were escorted out. The two of us headed back, and on the way, Hart tried to persuade me that Swamiji was an intelligent man and that his final statement was appropriate in light of the current situation. That one must honor both the creator and his creation. I returned to my hotel room, where my father was relaxing on the rocking chair with a book and old songs playing in the background.

Mission Update

One will have to get his hands dirty, scramble in the ashes of these religions, to somehow figure out the truth. One aspect of Sanatana Dharma that resonated with me, or at least agreed with my consciousness, was the idea of projection and concealment. My belief that there is a veil between me and my God, and that this veil is being used to screen a movie that keeps me so enthralled that I don't detect the presence of the veil. Yes, my God is veiled from me and I have ever been immersed in this projected creation. According to Sehajanandji, this veil is created by Maya or Desire, who employs one of its qualities, the veiling force, to do so. Protecting this veil from public scrutiny, Maya projects the artwork onto the veil.

How do I overcome the forces that act as a barrier between me and God? Have I got what it takes to overcome Maya and Desire? I aspire to study them well so that I may defeat them.

With this final entry in my diary, I turned to gaze out the window. The clouds were not as dark, they were at peace, with the silver light of moon marrying them. They were using their veiling force to conceal the moon and their projecting force to project the glittering shiny stars. I kept my eyes on the moon rather than the stars. It did not let me down, as its brilliant light emerged from behind the clouds with full force. I focused my eyes and questioned my God—Why don't you learn from the moon, remove this veil between you and me? Come to me, sit across eye to eye, asking about my whereabouts.

I slept with that desire, waiting for my midnight friend. As he came, I appraised him of my conversation with Sehajanandji, as well as his thoughts on Maya or Desire. I probed him for any information he could have on Maya.

His reply was tinged with uncertainty. "I have also heard about Maya, but do not know much about her. But let me tell you this, I look forward to coming to you at midnight and learning about your findings. You carry the seed of God within. This creation is like a tree. God planted the seed, and out of it sprang a tree, the universe. There are thorns, leaves, flowers, and fruit on the tree. The last stage is that of the fruit in this creation. Only the final product, the fruit, carries the divine seed. You lucky one, are the fruit, who has in him the seed of God."

My friend's eyes were soaked with emotion, but he continued, "I want to get rid of this painful life and hence I come to you, the fruit, who can give me the secret of the seed of God. You ask about Maya, she has been a topic of debate in my world for as long as I can remember, but no one has been able to decipher her. She remains a mystery. But I can tell you this, if you are able to find answers to the two big eternal questions of my world, the puzzle could be solved.

1. Why Creation?
2. Why Suffering?"

Chapter 9

Why Creation?

After giving it some thought, I realised that these two questions are the only ones that have ever ended any spiritual or theological conversations. Each one of the world's faiths assert that their God is the one and only creator. But when you ask them, why did he create? Why did he decide to bring misery, evil, hell, and the devil into the world? That if their God takes credit for all the beautiful things in creation, why do they not credit him for all the sufferings? They avoid discussing such issues, opting instead to argue solely about topics they have been schooled in.

I have not come across any religion which has given a conclusive and rational answer to these questions. By investigating these two issues, I may gain knowledge about Maya.

My idea of creation was influenced by science. Hart and I had numerous in-depth conversations on the subject. According to Einstein's famous equation, energy equals mass times its charge. If anything can be created with energy, it can also be destroyed and reduced to energy.

Creation can be attributed to force being applied on energy, thereby creating pairs of matter and antimatter. Annihilation being reversal of this process. Energy and force are the two fundamental realities. We neither knew what these are, nor could comprehend, why this force is applied on energy? So, I'm starting over, with no preconceived notions on this topic.

To understand "why", I had to learn more about the creator and the creative process. I thought I could get some clues by applying critical thinking and reasonable inquiry to creation myths. Knowing well that my reasoning faculties have their limits, I resolved to give irrationality a chance.

I did a lot of reading and research, had various discussions, and compiled information about the many myths and origin stories of world religions.

Abrahamic religions - Judaism, Christianity, and Islam

The almighty God was alone. He desired to have company—I was a hidden treasure, I wanted to be known.

God then created the world and us in six days. After creating the earth, days, nights, water, sky, land, vegetation, and living creatures, on the sixth day, he created man in his own image, who will rule over all the living creatures of this earth. God planted the garden of Eden and inhabited it with Adam, the first man he had created. In the middle of the garden, he placed the tree of life and the tree of knowledge of good and evil.

God instructed Adam that he could freely eat from any tree except the one bearing the knowledge of good and evil. A woman was formed from the man's ribs to be his companion. A serpent tempted the woman, suggesting that consuming the forbidden fruit would grant knowledge akin to God's. Succumbing to desire, the woman and man ate the fruit. Their eyes opened, they realised their nakedness, sewing fig leaves as cover.

God inquired of the man, who blamed the woman, and the woman blamed the serpent. God cursed the serpent, foretelling enmity between it and humankind. To the woman, God spoke of increased pains in childbirth and subservience to her husband. The man was cursed with toil, yielding thorns and thistles from the ground. Sweating for sustenance, he would return to dust.

Recognising humanity's newfound awareness, God barred access to the tree of life. Banishing the man from Eden, God set cherubim and a flaming sword to guard the tree. As time passed, mankind's decline prompted God's decision to obliterate creation and start anew. Noah's story, marked by a great flood, followed this decision.

The message of the Bible is adapted to the capabilities of human beings, as noted by Guston in the fifth century. The adherents of that era lacked the cognitive capacity to fathom the astounding complexity of the creation. The scholars realised that explaining such complexities would be worthless for faith and tiresomely unintelligible. They did not wish to bewilder but to help the common people preserve their faith. The following issues are brought up by this account of creation:

1. The question of why God created anything at all begs the answer, out of desire. Why did God give Adam and Eve the same lustful desire? Did we inherit this desire from God? Then is God the source of all good and evil as well as all misery and pain?
2. Why did God plant the tree of good and evil in Eden? Why did God create the serpent, the advisor? Why did God create desire in Eve to eat the fruit? Why did god make the fruit of good and evil so bad?
3. If God created Adam, Eve, and the serpent, why did he curse them? Why do we call him merciful if he could have forgiven them for their initial sin but chose to curse them instead? Why must we, the descendants of Adam and Eve, bear the consequences of their sin?
4. For what reason does God not want us to be like him? Why didn't he just give Adam and Eve a piece of the fruit from the tree of life? Why did god banish Adam and Eve from the garden of Eden, was it so they could never eat the fruit of life?
5. Does God want the man to just be in the cycle of birth and death, never to attain an eternal life, like him? Is

that why he made the earth and put man to work on it as a punishment?

This story of creation only scratches the surface, leaving many unanswered concerns. I decided to cut out the story part of creation as described by Abrahamic religions and derived my conclusion based on the starting and end point, or the reason for creation.

1. God's desire is the driving force behind all of creation.
2. Duality is the source of creation—God and desire, light and darkness, day and night, and Adam and Eve.

Babylonian story of creation:

Apsu, god of fresh waters, and Tiamat, goddess of salt oceans, birthed many sons and grandsons. Apsu, frustrated with his descendants, planned to kill them all. Ea, their great-grandson, the smartest and most powerful, stopped Apsu's murderous plan. Ea built his palace on Apsu's waters and became the father of Marduk, a deity associated with rain and storms. Tiamat's army, led by Kingu, challenged Marduk. Marduk defeated Tiamat, divided her body. Half he put in the sky and made the heavens, with other half the lands, which he placed over Apsu's fresh waters. Defeated gods were assigned to toil in fields and canals, which led to a revolt. Kingu suggested creating humanity from his blood, clay, and gods' spit. Humans were then tasked with labouring for the gods and worshiping them.

The account reads like something out of a writer's fevered imagination and onto the set of a daily soap opera. I see no logic in this, but the points I concluded for the Abrahamic creation myth, seems to hold true for this myth as well:

1. God's desire is the primary reason for creation.
2. Duality is the source of creation.

Egyptian story of creation:

Atum was alone on the banks of primaeval waters of Nun. He had a desire to enjoy company and create other gods. He masturbated and created Shu, the sky deity, and Tefnut, the moisture goddess. Shu and Tefnut birthed Geb, earth deity, and Nut, sky god. Geb and Nut had four children. Osiris—deity of fertility, Isis—goddess of motherhood, Set—god of chaos, and Nephthys. Osiris married his sister Isis, founded civilization and ruled. Set married Nephthys and killed Osiris, as he had an affair with his wife Nephthys giving birth to Nubas, the god of death. Isis revived Osiris. Horus, their son deposed Set. In one fight, Horus requested his mother Isis for help, but she refused, so Horus hacked off her head. Isis was resurrected by the knowledge deity Tha.

The same egoistic and power-hungry themes that plagued the Babylonian account of creation also permeate this version.

Greek Mythology:

Nyx, a bird, existed in darkness. She and the wind produced the love god Eros, who sprang from the golden egg. One half of the shell became Uranus (sky) and the other half Gaia (earth). Uranus and Gaia had numerous children and grandkids. All parents feared their children would overpower them. Kronus, one of the grandchildren, swallowed his infant children. His wife Rhea hid their youngest child. Zeus, the saved infant, defeated Kronus and became the leader of the gods. He began to furnish earth with life and sky with stars. Zeus then summoned his sons Prometheus (forethought) and Epimetheus (afterthought) to create men and animals and give them gifts. Epimetheus used up all the gifts. Prometheus decided he would gift fire to man, which was only reserved for gods. Zeus ordered his son to be chained to a mountain and for a vulture to peck out his liver every day till eternity. Then he began to devise a punishment for mankind. One of his other sons created a woman of great beauty, Pandora. Zeus gave her curiosity and a box that she was never supposed to open. He then married Pandora to Epimetheus. One day, when Epimetheus was away, Pandora opened the box. Pain, disease, envy, and greed escaped the box. Later that night they heard a voice coming from the box saying, "Let me out. I am hope." Pandora and Epimetheus released her and she flew out into the world to give hope to humankind.

The plot remains the same here as well, just the characters and their stories vary. But again, the principles of creation, desire, duality, and man being cursed by god are intact.

Hinduism – story of creation:

For as long as I can remember, I have been exposed to Hindu myths and legends that sound strikingly alike western fairy tales. Because Hinduism is an open and adaptable philosophy, there are various accounts of creation. Like the prior tales, these too are but flimsy words in the hands of the leaders. The product of man's creative mind. Hinduism has advanced beyond just having 'word' stories by including numerical calculations. Let me divide them into three piles:

i) Mythological stories ii) Metaphysical stories & iii) Numerical stories

i) Mythological stories:

A supreme soul existed in an unconscious state. Hindu's call him Brahman (not Brahma, one of the trinity gods) or Parmatma or other names as that division deems fit. Brahman in its unconscious state is in a void, where nothing exists except him. He desires to have company and experience something.

The only other existence is that of Maya, the duality female element of Brahman. Out of their coupling emerged several eggs, which they laid in the primordial waters (Hirnagrabhya). Out of each egg, Maha Vishnu came into being. Creating requires duality. Maya then took the form of Shakti. Maha Vishnu and Shakti mated to give birth to the trinity gods - Brahma, Vishnu, and Shiva. To ensure the continuation of this creation, Shakti married the trinity gods.

Brahma initiated the world's creation process. According to one of the scriptures, Brahma created humans from his body part and then renounced that body part, which became morning time. He then created devils from his body part and then renounced that body part which became night. He also created evil bodies and again renounced that body part which became evening. Manu was the first man and Satarupa was the first lady. Creation was created with Maya aiding every step.

Now that everything was created and the cycle started, humans still had the knowledge of Brahman and they started their journey back to their father Brahman and submerged in it. The intended drama or creation wasn't possible. That is when Maya created hunger, disease, thirst, and the karmic cycle to sustain the so-called creation. With these being introduced, creation was engulfed by the script of karmic law and the drama started.

The supreme soul Brahman who woke up, had desire, and created this creation, finally gets tired of it and decides to dissolve or destruct everything and go back to sleep. The cycle repeats itself once he wakes up again. Big Bang and Big Crunch.

Hindu mythological stories revolve around this. It depends on who is narrating. According to Vaishnavism, Vishnu created Brahma and Shiva from his navel and eyebrows. Shaivaites believe Shiva created Vishnu by rubbing nectar on his ankle. Shakti's adherents believe she created the trinity, Brahma, Vishnu, and Shiva.

Hinduism is so accommodative, that it justifies all the versions. That after each cycle of creation and destruction the three Lords manifest in different ways. Sometimes it may start with Vishnu, sometimes with Brahma and sometimes with Shiva. It is believed that after the latest destruction, the current creation started with Bramha coming out of a Lotus which grew out of Vishnu's Navel.

ii) Metaphysical stories:

These stories seem to be the framework behind all the other mythological stories. It appears that the creation stories in all the mythologies, paint the canvas, placed on this framework. This framework also seems to resemble the approach of Metaphysics or Quantum physics of today.

Brahman/ Parmatma: The Omniscient and Omnipresent existence—the seed of everything, the ultimate consciousness. It can be referred to as the Omnipotent energy, unbudging, rooted and frozen force. Some also refer Brahman to be the primordial matter. As taught by my friend Hart, matter is nothing but concentrated energy. Brahman—primordial matter.

Maya/ Desire: This duality component of Brahman is also Omniscient and Omnipresent. It is relatively the omnipotent energy, budging, vibrant, nonstationary, unbound, and free flowing. Maya - primordial energy.

Creation starts by coming together of primordial energy and matter. Energy and matter mutate and start multiplying into individuals "Souls". Soul is the first individuation. In scientific terms, we call this combination of energy and matter an "Atom". The individualised soul is nothing but the "I". With the "I", comes in mind, thought and the ego, which is called Ahamkar in Yogic Hinduism.

Post atoms, science explains the creation only in terms of intelligent design, i.e everything gets created randomly from atoms. While Yogic Hinduism tries to explain the further process of creation. Creation requires activity or action to evolve, and not the same activity by all, but different activities by different individuals. This variation or differentiation would require other factors and elements. Maya then introduces these elements in the form of qualities or attributes. The three core attributes or three gunas, Satva, Rajas, and Tamas.

The proportion and interplay of these elements decide the characteristics, nature of the individualised object or soul. These three traits distinguish all souls in this creation. Sages have more Satva and Kings more Rajas. Everyone pursues happiness. However, gunas make happiness different for everyone. Satva individuals find enjoyment in assisting others, listening to learned people, inner calm, etc. Rajas people find happiness in luxuries, and Tamas persons by troubling others. These three gunas make life's song.

Coming back to the framework of creation. Resemblance in mythological stories—trinity was introduced, Brahma with the Satva guna, Vishnu with the Rajas guna, and Shiv with the Tamas guna. Now, "I" in association with Maya who possesses the three gunas produces the other twenty-four elements required for the framework of creation:

From Satva Guna—The four Antahakaran or internal organs of cognition sense evolved. Namely, Manas—the lower mind, Ahamkara—the empirical ego, Buddhi—the intellect, and Chit—consciousness.

From Rajas Guna—The five Cognitive senses or Gyanandrias and five active senses or Karmendriyas evolved. Five cognitive senses are the sense organs, namely—nose, tongue, eye, ear, and skin. Five active senses—organs of action, the excretion organ, the sexual organs, the organ of locomotion, the organ of holding (hand), and the organ of speech.

From Tamas Guna—The five Tanmatras—transit media of the five senses—smell, taste, sight, touch, and hear evolved. It also produces the five subtle elements, Mahabhutas namely Earth, Water, Fire, Air, and Ether.

Till this point, according to Vedas, the creation is called Samashti Shristhi (Divine creation). Beyond this all the creation is individual creation or Vyashti Shristhi, or the creation every individual creates around him.

The objective of Yogic Hinduism is to recognise and control this mind, the ten senses, and the three gunas. Go beyond these and be part of the supreme father, the Brahman. Brahman is considered to be *Nirguna*, or the one without any of these three gunas and hence he does not act in any manner. They say, this inactivity is not a negative trait, it requires one to go beyond gunas, to go in such a state, where one does not need to act. There are two school of thoughts in Hinduism—Nirguna and *Surgana*. Nirguna strive to achieve Brahman the one without any guna, while the Surgana strives to achieve any of the trinities, who are the carriers of these three gunas.

From my perspective, this seems like a case of reverse engineering. Collect all the elements and keep attributing them to a source. The elements of nature, mind, organs, and senses, attributed to gunas, gunas attributed to trinity, trinity attributed to Maya, and Maya attributed to Brahman.

iii) Numerical Stories

Whenever anything is explained with numbers, it gives more gravity and sanity to the explanation. Cognizant of this fact, Hinduism gives timelines to this cycle of creation and destruction. It seems they have deliberately kept these numbers on a massive, infinite scale of time. This way they can keep it outside the questioning of the human mind. There is no way these numbers can be proven. It's just like someone declaring the number of sand particles on this earth and gives it a mathematical calculation.

The creator, Brahma's each day is considered to be 4.32 billion years, and night also of the same period. At the beginning of each day he creates everything in this universe and at the end of each day there is partial annihilation. Brahma's life is of hundred such divine years or 300 trillion and 40 billion years on human timescale. After this time there is complete annihilation or Pralay, or Big Crunch, everything dissolves into a null and void state. The current Brahma dies. The cycle repeats with a new Brahma.

If these numbers are to be believed, our lives in the five-thousandth year of the Kalyuga, of the twenty-seventh Mahayuga, of the seventh Manu, of the current day of the current Brahma, seem utterly meaningless. The years we live through don't even amount to a drop. I have no choice but to enter these figures into excel. One divine second in Brahma's time would be equivalent to one lakh years on Earth. So, if our life is hundred years, this will be equal to one millisecond of Brahma's life. This Kalyuga epoch will end in 4.32 Brahma seconds, and one Chaturyuga will conclude in 43.2 seconds. If these calculations are correct, the end of the world is predicted to occur in about 4.27 million years.

Hindu Scholars have woven mythological stories to lend credibility to divine timescale. King Kakudmi lived on Earth in the Satya Yuga of the first Mahayuga of the current Manvantara. He sought Brahma's guidance to locate a suitable groom for his lovely daughter Revati. Brahma took twenty divine minutes to return from a dance performance. Brahma warned Kakudmi that twenty-seven Mahayugas had passed on earth during his wait, and if he returned now, he would find people enjoying Krishna's avatar. After returning to Earth, Kakudmi married his daughter to Balarama, Krishna's brother.

To me these are just numbers, meant just to lend seriousness to the subject. *The scholars gave these numbers for pondering, to the common mass, in exchange for their faith.* They deliberately kept the numbers so massive, beyond imagination, so that the common man feels insignificant and frivolous under the weight of these astronomical numbers. If I alter this calculation to say two into two equals twenty or four into five equals twenty or ten into two equals twenty, nothing will change. Even if I say that Brahma's age is not hundred divine years but two hundred divine years and just double the numbers to arrive at this two hundred, nothing will change. I can be a scholar too, I can keep going on, give a number to Shiva's age, Vishnu's age, and Ganesh's age. I do not have to prove it anyways. Numbers have no meaning.

From these narratives, the following inquiries arise:

Could Brahma not resist desire or "Maya"? Why did Brahma, the creator, want to create the universe and keep man enslaved in the cycle of birth, death, and rebirth?

What differentiates the creator from the created if Brahma also dies and is replaced? Is there only a disparity in how long people live?

Hinduism states that God is timeless, then who created time and basis which the time bound creation?

These stories also decide the ranking of gods. Hindus rarely offer prayers to Brahma, the religion's supposedly divine creator. Story says that Brahma's daughter was so stunningly gorgeous that even he couldn't resist her. Brahma, seeing that his daughter was trying to flee in every direction, suddenly manifested four heads, one in each direction in which she had fled. When his daughter suddenly took off towards the heavens, Brahma reared his fifth head to pursue her. Shiv on seeing this cut of Brahma's fifth head.

Why are these mythological stories of creation so toxic? The human mind is programmed to themes like, want, hate, bliss, grief, lust, crime, jealousy, and so on. To justify these traits, they are assigned to God, via these stories.

All these are just made up stories. Some just want to avoid the question, on the premise that knowing so, leads to nothing. Some just wrap the framework in a fantasy story, knowing that the common man is incapable of complicated explanations. Some makeup the explanation so complex and entangled for authentication, such that the human brain cannot process and question such an overpowering explanation. Some draw puzzles around it. Some explain it with reason. A few others explain it as reasonless. All in all, to shield the faith of the follower and suppress the questioning mind.

Creation - Saint and Scholar versions:

It is a chicken and egg story. What came first, the chicken or the egg? The creator or the creation? There is no way to explain this if you think linearly. But if you place the chicken and the egg in a circle, one after the other, it makes sense. Similarly, creator - creation - creator - creation, keeps looping circularly. Also, there cannot be a straight line. Keep extending the straight line to infinity and it will return to the starting point, forming a circle.

God created the creation in his desire, just as my father created me, out of his desire. I or creation, am nothing but desire which penetrated my father's mind. Creation is mind's manifestation.

Creation is reasonless. God is pure energy, which keeps creating without any reason or desire. Just like kids keep jumping without reason, just like flowers bloom without reason, just like rivers flow without reason, just like electrons keep moving without reason. Human minds cannot understand creation because they have been trained to understand only things with reason.

God is the director, who creates a drama. He writes the screenplay, creates the scene, is the producer and plays every character in this drama.

A fish lives in the ocean and they are one. Fish isn't aware of water. Ask her do you know of water, and she will say, "I haven't heard of such a thing." But when she is thrown on the heated sand on the beach, she prays for water and the waves take her back.

Mind is like a prism which is placed at the centre. When the invisible sunlight, the supreme energy, enters the prism, the prism refracts the white light into various visible colours and their interplay (creation). Each prism (mind) will generate different colours. This depends on the make of the prism, it's lenses, it's angles, etc. (conditioning). If the prism is removed from the centre, all that will exist is the invisible sunlight - the Supreme Energy.

The creator "I" has thoughts and the creation comes into being. The entire tree exists in a seed and so does the entire creation exists in the seed of 'Desire'.

My take on my creation:

Everything is created, grows, decays, dies, and gets recreated. The force behind this, energy, stays the same. God stays the same.

To me, supreme energy or God manifests into energy and matter, forming the core duality. This manifestation or duality only exists in the field of relativity or divisions. This core duality further manifests into other dualities, which we ultimately call creation.

On my writing desk, I had a rectangular magnet. It was coincidental that I grabbed it while pondering and writing about creation. Magnets are polar, with a north pole and south pole. Polarity is nothing but duality. Both the north and south poles are necessary for the other to exist. What would happen if you tried to cut the magnet in half to separate the north and south poles? Nothing, there will simply be one additional north pole manifested at the south pole and the opposite at the north pole. Just to keep one alive the other will develop. Neither duality or polarity can ever be eliminated.

This duality or polarity can be referred to as primordial matter and energy, as creator and created, as mass and energy, as Brahman and Maya, as father and son, as seed and fruit, and as consciousness and illusion. Manifestations of a singularity which exist only in relativity to each other. The Knower and the Known is what I call it. There can be no Knower without Known, and there can be no Known without a Knower.

The north pole (N) and south pole (S), or God and human, are manifestations of God, the enormous magnet, the pure and primeval energy. Now each of them is a knower and can only know the other relatively. Both N and S are necessary for the other's existence. The magnet keeps getting sliced and divisions after divisions happen, creating infinite small magnets. Each magnet having a N and a S. Each magnet having God at one pole and humans at the other pole.

We are a part of this creation, having a N and S or God and human as two extreme poles within us. We identify ourselves as the human pure consciousness or the knower. God, the universe, and everything known would be impossible without this knower. Likewise, without this known there wouldn't exist a knower. God wouldn't exist without human and humans wouldn't exist without God. One is required for the others existence.

So, is there a possibility where both wouldn't exist? Where duality ends?

The magnet still in my hand, I pondered. N and S do not exist at NS (the magnet's core). Humans are located at the south pole of this rectangular magnet and God at the north pole. Both are just manifestation of the magnet. Me standing at the south pole am searching for my God sitting on the north pole, how should I get to him. I was stuck and couldn't see a way out.

After a few minutes I took the second rectangular magnet lying on my table and brought the first one's south pole (Human) towards the north pole (God) of the other magnet. I felt merged with God at the centre as the two magnets merged into one.

So, rather than trying to find God at the other end of the pole, maybe I ought to just move to the centre of the magnet, where there is neither God nor man, nor is there any duality or relativity, but only pure energy. It appears that everyone, including myself, is looking for answers in the realm of relativity and duality at poles. Is there a place to look beyond the realms of relativity and duality? Does god's mystery have an answer in a dimension beyond relativity and duality, where there is just one existence?

Mission Update

To learn more about "Maya" or "Desire", I began looking for solutions to the big two questions, as advised by my Devil friend. Researching the first question, "Why Creation?" I discovered that humans have created meaningless works of art out of words and numbers when telling creation stories. The most rational scientific explanation of creation is that it is nothing more than the manifestation of pure energy or God into duality and other dualities. But "Why manifestation?" tends to boil down to "Why desire?" again. At this point, the inquiry "Why sufferings?" is my last, best hope for understanding desire.

Feeling drained by this creation and the many unresolved issues it raised, I decided to call it a night. I lay in my bed, requesting God to annihilate the creation around me. I wished to de-manifest, wind up duality, travel from the pole to the centre of the magnet, where I could rest blended with my God. I was deeply immersed in this fellowship until an alarming idea interrupted my concentration. What if I go to sleep, without any hope of waking up? What if tonight really was the last night? *What if God decides to stop making things and I never wake up again? Just to lay in this non-dual null and void state, was a scary thought.*

Chapter 10
Why Suffering?

I was tired of the static state and yearned for the dynamic state of creation. When my consciousness was jolted awake by my desire, there stood my Devil companion. I snapped at him, insisting that he was just wasting my time.

"The question of creation came down to desire. But that led to an even bigger question, why did God have the desire to create?"

Without flinching at my wrath, he sat down at the foot of the bed and contemplated. "This is a mystery for me as well. But I think he desires only to be known. If there wasn't any creation, there would be no God."

We were both silent and lost in our own thoughts. Having no answers to this question, we decided to move forward with the other big question—Why sufferings?

Why did God introduce suffering on this planet? What wrong did we do to him? Why is one child born on the roads among beggars and the other in a palace? Why are there so many natural calamities, which take so many lives, why so many diseases in this world, why do we have our hearts broken?

"You lucky one have researched quite a lot, what do you think?" asked my friend.

"I haven't explored this question yet. However, the religious explanations that I have read so far strike me as particularly foolish and unjustifiable. God created us, we disobeyed him, hence he cursed and imposed suffering on us. How can God punish his creatures for the qualities he shares with his creation and the qualities he bestows upon it? How can god punish us for our sins, when this division between sin and non-sin is created by him? He should have not synthesised sin in the first place."

My friend raised his eyebrows and intervened "Why are you debating on stories?"

I thought for a while and responded, "Since duality is the building block for creation, a world without suffering is impossible. The state of suffering or happiness is relative and not absolute. Suffering can only exist or be felt in relation to the absence of bliss. Suffering is like darkness, having no existence of its own. It is dependent on the lack of its dual aspect light or bliss for existence. Suffering seems nothing but the experience of lack of pleasure. If travelling in a small car is my pleasure, then not having one is my suffering. But if travelling in a chauffeur driven Rolls Roy is my pleasure, travelling in a small car is my suffering. So suffering is just relative and exists only due to lack of pleasure. Duality is the nature of creation and hence the sufferings."

The smile on my friend's dreaded face communicated that he was impressed by my insights. He wanted a chance to impress me now.

"Suffering is not only the duality aspect of this creation, it is also the framework for sustaining this creation. This framework is responsible for the situation in which I am now. It is also responsible for the situation you are in now. The understanding of this framework I got from a learned saint in Iran.

"I was assigned the death orders of this saint. His soul was calm and so confident of the journey ahead. Mostly all the souls on there after death journey are horror-struck and terrified. On my request he confirmed to me the reason for his calmness.

"He said that he knew that he was just changing clothes. That, every soul in the cycle of continuous creation and annihilation passes through the different species or to say the soul keeps changing the clothes. It's just like we remove and wear a new shirt every day. He said that most people foolishly associate themselves with the shirt, hence the fear, while I know that I am the soul within. I am not the house; I am the one living in it. Once the house gets old, I will have to look for a new one. Will it be a mansion or a hut, depends on the bank balance or Karma's I have earned. If we have a stock of sinful deeds, we will have to assume an animal's body or even lower forms whereas if we have a stock of pious deeds we may get a human or a super-human body."

I have heard this Karma theory before and have had unanswered questions about it. But I wished to allow my friend to complete his explanation.

"There are 8.4 million species or dresses in the wardrobes. Placed in six racks, namely aquatics, trees, insects, birds, animals, and humans. There are 0.90 million species of aquatics, 2 million species of trees, 1.1 million species of insects, a million species of birds, 3 million species of animal bodies, and 0.40 million species of human bodies. A soul must wear all these 8.4 million clothes in a span of 4.32 million years, before repeating them again. Different clothes have different durations of life. A human has a hundred-year life; a more premium brand, like that of God's have ten thousand years. There are insects which have a one-day life and further there are microorganisms which have life in seconds. The framework or the Karma theory decides which dress we would wear and in what condition."

Numbers again? But I choose not to interrupt.

"There are only two types of Karma, good Karma and bad Karma. The definition of good and bad is according to the eternal cosmic law. These good and bad karmas are like the good and bad cotton which are raw materials required to make the dress. The quality and age of the dress depends solely on the raw material used. The whole manufacturing process has three units:

"The Warehouse - Accumulated pool of Karmas. All the cotton, bad or good, is harvested, plucked, and collected by a soul in its journey, in all its lives, is dumped here. This warehouse never runs out of cotton, as the eternal soul keeps dumping.

"Production unit - A Portion of the accumulated Karmas. The limited cotton which shall be required to produce the next cloth, is taken from the warehouse, and moved to the production unit. The quality of the limited cotton taken out from the warehouse depends upon the quality of the cotton stored in the warehouse, which shall determine the quality of the new dress to be worn by the soul.

"Collection unit - Farming and collecting karma. A soul has freewill to harvest and collect good cotton or bad cotton, i.e. do good karma or bad karma. Farming is the most important aspect of this process, as it solely decides the quality of the dress. One shapes his own destiny.

"God has established this business and kept the soul busy in this business. The soul is so engrossed in this business that now it only associates itself with the cloth it wears. Keeps harvesting karma, dumps them in the warehouse and keeps manufacturing. This business of cotton and cloth is the framework for this creation. It is completely insured and protected by God. As it lets God sustain his creation and also keeps him away from all the blame. God only ensures that this warehouse never runs out of cotton, for which he keeps the cycle running and keeps soul continuously engaged in it."

I chose to intervene,

"By the quality of dress, you mean the situation and quality of life one would face. Weather the child will be born in a palace, or will he be born on the streets, whether a dog will be eating dirt or will he be eating premium dog food?"

"Yes, God gives freewill to the soul to decide and wear whatever he wants. If he wants to become a demigod, or be born a millionaire, or a celebrity dog, the soul must do only good deeds, collect only good cotton, in its present life."

I could not resist,

"Friend, no offence, but why did you harvest bad cotton in the first place, which according to you has resulted in your current painful state."

He repented, "If I had known of this God's game before, surely I would have made a conscious effort to do only good deeds. But even if I did collect good deeds in one of my lives aware of this game, I am not sure it would have made any difference. I have no idea what is dumped in my warehouse. Ages and ages of deeds, good and bad. Maybe this current state of mine is based on some deeds in one of my past infinite life's, I have no idea."

He stayed quiet. After a few minutes, I nudged him with a smile,

"No worries, now that you know about the game, just keep doing good deeds. Start that with relieving my father of this stop-clock of death, will you?"

His head shot up in exasperation. The next second, his face was buried in the crook of his hands, and he remained.

I wanted to console him. I sat down next to him and put my arm across his back. His composure returned after a short while, and he said in a hushed voice,

"I am a slave; I cannot go out in the fields to harvest and collect cotton. I learn that God has not assigned this field work to all his creation. The ability or the freedom to collect good or bad cotton is given only to the end product of his creation—you humans. It's only you lucky ones who have been given the gift of free will, to decide your own destiny. All other species, including those of demigods have no free will, they are just slaves, assigned jobs in the warehouse or the production unit."

"Say you get this human body, what will you do then? At best, as a human, you would engage yourself in consciously collecting just good cotton, avoiding the bad ones. What more can you do? But, as you explained, your warehouse still would have all the good and bad cotton collected from past human life's. Let's assume, over millions of cycles, you consciously just collect the good cotton, dump it in the warehouse and keep emptying the warehouse of the bad cotton, by weaving clothes out of it. That's the best possible scenario, right? What then? Surely, it will ensure that you wear only the branded clothes, out there, in your next lives. But you would be wearing clothes and then collecting more cotton for weaving future clothes. I hope you realise that even after getting a human body, you would be in the same business, as

God intended you to be in. In this state of yours, you are in the same business, so what's the difference."

This cheered up my friend. "I knew this would come from you. In my current state, I am chained in this warehouse, I am slaved. Even if I know of this setup and want to run away from this, my chains would not allow. If at all I get a human life and my awareness of this game persists, I shall go out in the fields and escape. I would know that collecting cotton, bad or good, makes no difference and makes no sense, why should I play this game. This free will is the greatest gift, intended for the humans to realise the worthless business and run away. Fool's waste the gift of this free will and a true seeker aptly uses his free will to escape."

"So now you know the real purpose of me coming to you and asking for help. I want to start exploring right away, so that once I get the human body, I am well prepared to exit this business. You are the lucky one, chosen one, the one with free will. That's why I keep pushing you to explore."

I interrupted, with raised eyebrows, "Oh, friends for benefits!" His expression revealed that he did not understand what I said. While his purpose is okay, I doubt the reason behind it. My friend hasn't experienced this Karma theory; he is just vomiting what he has heard from the saint. This theory has been doing rounds and I too have heard of it. It surely comes closest to explaining the various species, life cycle, situation one faces, and quality of life. But also raises a hell lot of questions. I was compelled to put them forward.

"Where will this escape path lead to, will it lead me to the God who created this business, or will it lead me to some other place? Will that other place be outside the purview of God? Then are we trying to escape from God himself?"

My friend was unsure "It would lead to God himself, I guess."

"But that defeats the whole purpose, doesn't it? Firstly, you said God created this framework to sustain this creation. Then why will he want someone to break the rules and escape from this framework. Secondly, if this path leads to God, by taking the escape route, am I not returning to the same business of God. Ok, I would no longer be a worker in the business, but I will be a part of it. I will either be sitting with God, observing this business or else, setting up my own, similar business. That's about it. Could there not be a possibility that this escape route leads to something unknown, something beyond this business altogether?"

My friend appeared terrified as he stared up at the sky through the window. There were probably two causes for his perspiring forehead. The first is that he was caught off guard by the inquiry and feared losing his last hope. Second is that he must have just received the last of his reminders about his upcoming task. In consideration of his time constraints, I asked a follow-up query.

"Tell me this. When god started this game, where did the cotton seeds come from or who created these deeds. Who harvested the first cotton? Also, who separated them, good deeds and bad deeds? As you explained, the dress called human, would need raw material, which is this cotton. So, someone harvested the first cotton and it was not a human. Then was the first cotton harvested by God himself and defined as good and bad by him? If so, why should he punish us for what he created?"

My friend was clueless and in haste,

"I don't know, have no clue about it. But there is something I can relate your questions to. I had once overheard this debate between the demigods. I can't narrate it fully, but they debated about, the creator being separate from God. That all this creation is just the creator's business and that God has nothing to do with it. *Creator has claimed to be the 'God', in the creation created by him.*"

These were his last words that night. While delivering them, he slowly stepped backwards towards the window and suddenly evaporated from the open window. He left me zapped, I stood there motionless. What was he talking about? God and creator being two different entities. We have been on this journey to know about one, without much success. Now there are two unknowns. My mind could not process this. What if the devil was making it all up, just to avoid my question and protect his belief. My mind reluctantly parked this for my friend to answer later.

I stayed awake the rest of the night. I wanted to process the discussion I just had. If the Karma theory explains "Why suffering?", then the questions should be "Why Karma theory?", "Why god wants us to suffer?", and "Why can't he leave us alone?"

To my mind the truth lies elsewhere, and Karma theory is just a cover up, developed by human mind.

This Karma theory seems to be a dressed-up version of the Thoughts Theory. Thoughts manifest thoughts. We keep reaping from the thoughts we harvest. In the same way that our thoughts shape who we are and the world we live in, they also shape the circumstances in which we find ourselves. It's not good or bad, it's just thoughts manifesting thoughts. I think, that is why I am, or I am, that is why I think.

The wheel of time keeps this cyclic motion of reaping and harvesting. Pleasures and sufferings, lust and envy, friends and foes, etc., keep repeating. I wonder, what if we just harvest universal love, will it only return universal love, every time, every place? But how can we love a person who makes us suffer? Are we reaping this suffering from our earlier harvest? If we greet this person with love, the next time he comes to us, will he come to return only love?

As the next four to five days passed, I gave these ideas plenty of consideration while asking myself, "Why Suffering?" My outlook has changed drastically because of my careful observation of society and my reading of many books.

My God is blameless; he has nothing to do with the sufferings we see around us.

The reason for suffering is the setup of society. A society is built on desire, aspiration, comparison, competition, defeat, success, pride, position, caste, religion, money, etc.

It's difficult to picture, but pretend we live in a world where everyone is treated equally, there are no divisions, and no one cares about things like wealth, status, family, religion, etc. Everyone is sufficient and happy. No longer will one infant be a beggar and another a royal simply by virtue of being born. A polar bear cub cannot be a beggar or a prince.

Suffering is the outcome of society, which creates a desire in us to be superior to others. We aspire to be more successful, more wealthier, more respected, than others. Equality is thrown out and we find ourselves in a divided, aspiring, and a suffering society. We suffer if anything goes in the opposite direction, if aspirations aren't fulfilled, if we are inferior to others, if we fail, if we are unsuccessful, if we are powerless, if we are position less, if we are not respected, if we are not wealthy.

Social constructs surrounding us are to blame for our relative levels of suffering. If the idea of money didn't exist, there would be no beggar nor his sufferings. One does hardly imagine a stone age society with a beggar or his plight. Suffering is certainly just relative and comes out of aspiration.

I experience suffering, either in my loss, what I formerly had and what I have now, or in unfulfillment of my desire, what I should have had and what I have now. All is relative.

While growing up, until now, this thought never occurred to me that why do I suffer? I guess it was blanketed by my parents, relatives, and religion. They trained me not to think much about it, because it was all God's will. That God is forgiving and with time the sufferings would end. I stayed with those blinds, but the suffering never ended. Now that I am seriously thinking about this question of "Why do I suffer?" I might have a solution to end it.

I suffered because of all the traits gifted to me by my society. If I put away all those traits, so say I do not aspire, compare, compete, strive for success, etc. will these sufferings be able to hurt me? If I stay content with whosoever I am and whatever situation I am in. If I do not desire to be someone else, someone superior to what I am. If I do not want to change the situation in which I am already. Will suffering ever hurt me?

Change is the only constant. Everything in this creation is subject to change. But society teaches us to hold on, hold on to the old traditions, customs, rules, dogmas, thought process, etc. Hold on to your possessions. We have been conditioned to resist any changes, to keep holding on. This resistance creates suffering. If I stop resisting or condemning any change around me, will suffering hurt me?

My God is certainly not responsible for my suffering. I solely am. He on the other hand gives me freedom. Freedom to either keep suffering or freedom to end the suffering.

My father and I went for a stroll and sat at my favorite hidden spot at the Chet Singh Ghat. The sun's orange radiance was fluttering, as if it were savouring its final moments of the day. The sun was getting ready to pass the torch, and the shadows on the great flights of stone steps were quickening. My dad was humming some old songs, while I stayed busy in my thoughts.

A sage with bronze-coloured skin spots and a strange greyish cloak walked down the steps and sat down two rows ahead of us. He sat there, chomping on a snack. Under his paper-thin skin, his skeleton protruded. After waiting a few minutes, my dad finally approached this peculiar gentleman. My dad used to go up to everyone dressed in a saint's garb. They were still close enough; I could hear my father.

He was telling the sage about the Devil and that death was quickly approaching him. The sage was as emotionless as a block of granite. My father became overcome with emotion and began to cry at the old man's feet. The sage snatched him up and murmured, a grin spreading across his face, "My friend, you are truly blessed, I am happy for you."

I couldn't resist, I stepped down, embraced my dad, and stared up at the sage in disbelief. He had a rugged grey beard and thick eyelids, giving him a stern appearance. I was both surprised and sarcastic. "Sir, did you hear my father's words, or were you deep in your own trance? My father is suffering and feels that death is approaching. He sought you out for guidance, and you're telling him how lucky he is and how glad you are for him?"

He said nothing, just kept staring at me intently. I couldn't take my eyes off him either. After waiting for around a minute, he finally began talking. His voice was calm and assured.

"Son, is suffering not the reason your father is seeking help, seeking God? Is it not the reason you are with him, helping him?" I nodded in acceptance.

His smile was back again. "God's work is strange. He is mysterious. But let me assure you this. He knows exactly what you need and when. You will never know what you need, but he knows it very well."

"Are you indicating that my father's suffering is his need?"

"Indeed," he replied. "Suffering is the key, which helps you unlock your superficial being and brings you closer to the one within you. Suffering brings awareness, about you, about illusions, about reality. Without suffering one stays lost in their superficial being. Your father has been sleeping and dreaming all his life. This Devil, this suffering, is only for the purpose of waking him up.

"We live on support systems. Suffering is needed to take out our support system and force us to think. My wife and son were killed in a car accident eight years ago. I spent two years in extreme pain and suffering. It made me think about God, about life, and about myself. It led me to my God. Only suffering makes us realise the falsehood of our ego.

It revealed that I was nothing, which prepared me to shred myself and be one with my God."

The sage had tears in his eyes. He placed his thin hands on my knees and spoke humbly, "What hurts, always blesses you. One finds God, when his heart burns with suffering. When the house is on fire, one simply runs out. Until then, he keeps inquiring about what should be done, if at all the house burns. Suffering is the door to wisdom.

"God keeps knocking on the door time and again. But we resist the knock and keep protecting the door. We keep trying to overcome suffering and not go into it, opening the door. If you open the door, you will find a way to him. You will no longer be there, once you are with him, you will dissolve in him. Once you dissolve, so will the sufferings. Do you understand that?

"In life everything is tweaked in your favour. There is no wrong happening anywhere. Whatever is happening with you has a greater plan, do not resist it, be thankful for it, and then God shall execute his grand plan for you. These sufferings are the signboards which God uses to redirect us towards him."

His hypnotic gaze rendered me dumbfounded, while my father was curious.

"*Guruji*, how should I free myself from this devil and my death?"

"Why do you fear death? You will continue to be you, only your form will change. Like this tree wood continues to be wood on the ceiling of house. The wood becomes free only when the fire within it engulfs it. You shall be free only when God within you engulfs you."

With a gentle smile he stood up, folded his hands, and climbed up the stairs.

Mission Update

The most common reason accepted is that it's god's will and hence should not be questioned. The most logical theory being the Karma theory, that God rewards for good deeds and punishes for bad deeds. Reasoning these theories reveal that these are just cover-up stories, manufactured to pacify the questioning mind.

Suffering is nothing but the non-acceptance of the current self and the current situation. Suffering is nothing but the urge, the desire for being something better or for the situation to be something better. Suffering is just the feeling which is experienced when things are not happening our way. *The day we learn to accept and not expect, suffering will vanish.* We are responsible for our suffering and not God.

The only source of suffering is the ego and the magnitude of suffering is the magnitude of one's ego.

However, it's only suffering which forces one to think deeply and pursue wisdom.

As *T Scott Mcleod* said, "Life gives you exactly what you need to awaken."

Chapter 11

Mysticism and the Mad Man

My beastly pal was fixated on his pain. Every time he came over, he would sob and tell me all about his problems, hoping that I would feel sorry for him. He did not want to take up the responsibility; he was looking out for someone who could take up this responsibility for his suffering. He was looking for a support system.

He said that suffering is directly proportionate to power, which I agree. The godly worlds are brimmed with power, ego, and hence suffering. Everyone lives a life of insecurity, envy, competition, and suffering.

We have been praying these gods, simply because they have been made powerful in our minds. More than half prey them as we fear that if we don't, we will be cursed by the powerful gods, and the remaining of us prey to be blessed with benefits, coming out of the powers of these powerful gods. It's ironic that my friend longs to live among humans while humanity longs to be among these powerful gods.

I wanted to help my friend but realised that his conditioning was too strong and deep. He felt secure in his knowing, not willing to take a leap into the unknown. While here I was wanting to dive into the unknown God.

It is true that my God is completely unknown, and it is difficult to understand or perceive him. He seems to be beyond this heavy veil of duality. I have no clue about him, but it now seems that *he is seeking me.* He has helped me realise this veil of duality and I am sure that he will help me lift it.

My mind cannot perceive or relate to him, but my soul in some weird manner perceives and understands my God. Does he live in my soul, as the mystics claim? Am I the fruit of this creation having the seed of God within me? Will I find him within me?

While me and Hart were discussing these questions in our regular coffee shop, we came across a gentleman named Mr. Krishnan. He was around fifty years old, tall, and skinny as a pole. He had a massive forehead and a long shaven face. He came over to us and politely inquired if he might join us.

He claimed he could not help but chime in on the conversation. He himself was a traveller, and he knew a wise sage who could help us. He said that Jagat Satguru sees things from an entirely new dimension and only talks to those he considers to be in genuine search of the path. He informed us that the day after tomorrow he would be travelling to a village near Rishikesh to pay a visit to Jagat Satguru at his ashram in the Himalayan foothills.

Hart was convinced, he wanted to visit Jagat Satguru with Mr. Krishnan. He told me to take some time and think about it, stating that exploring is the only way out, like I had done before.

Back at my lodge, I sat for hours, staring at the notes in my diary. Trying to figure out what this duality really means and what was the way beyond it. My newborn soul was pleading with me to find the answers, while my mind was in a state of constant resistance. My soul initially did not have any identity of its own, it was clinging to the mind and seeing things as shown by the mind. After identifying itself, my soul now seems to voice for freedom and liberation.

On close examination, it seems my mind is nothing but accumulation of thoughts and memories. It can think only what is known to it, it cannot think of the unknown. There isn't a possibility of new thoughts. My thoughts are all dead, they only come out of my past memories. *By sitting and thinking, I do nothing but chew what has already been chewed.* My mind is only capable of thinking what it already knowns, what is stored in it. It cannot understand a Persian quotation. Persian is not known to it. Even if it is translated in English, it will only understand the English words, already known to it. Then it will try to derive the meaning out of it, based on what it already knows. *So it makes no sense to sit and think*. My soul voiced out to tell me that the only possibility for new thoughts is to empty my mind and explore new things.

Over morning tea, I chatted with my dad. He spent less time with me lately because he was so occupied with his buddies and the lectures of the local wise men. In his eyes, it was like he'd never been happier. I informed him of my upcoming trip and the impending need for him to return home. His reaction was negative; he said that he would remain behind because he has many friends who can look after him in my absence. I questioned his seeming contentment in this new environment, far from my mom.

The principle of relativity causes a person who spends his days working hard to provide for his loved ones to long for a setting where he may relax and enjoy himself. Not only in this life but also the life after death. Fear of the mysterious and the unseen is innate to the human psyche. No one knows what happens after death. Then along comes the decorated religions, like a tourist agency luring the uninitiated with the promise of a paradise after death. Wow, man has been tirelessly working all his life to attain this ultimate state and religion promises to offer it for a nominal fee.

Why not try these travel companies and believe in their promise, reserve a place in God's land. Where is there time to explore? The soul tries raising questions, but is silenced by giving it the pacifier of promised abode. As long as these religions can maintain making up stories about this gilded abode, keeping it superior to the other abodes, and instilling dread of avoiding them, these tour operators are confident that their customers will continue to grow and thrive.

These travel companies have been flourishing for centuries because they have never been challenged to deliver their promise. They have also been flourishing, because of our society setup. If the father has already chosen or inherited a certain travel firm, the child is automatically enrolled as a member.

I pleaded with my father to return home. I had an agreement with my Devil friend, that he would keep appearing to me at midnight despite me and my father not sleeping on the same bed. My friend agreed as he needed me to explore more, which could benefit him. My father was at first skeptical, but after a lengthy discussion, he came around. I did not want to rely on travel companies, I researched all the alternatives thoroughly to ensure that he would return home safely and in good spirits.

I called up Hart, he was happy to hear of my decision and told me that he always knew it. I had made up my mind that I would travel and explore new things and try emptying my mind of the old. Both me and my father packed up to go on our respective journeys.

Hart, Mr. Krishnan, and I gathered at Hart's house and set out on our voyage together. Our trip would take fifteen hours. Mr. Krishnan was an enjoyable conversationalist who regularly offered fresh perspectives. The basis of his belief was that nothing exists in this world, it's only individual minds which manifest this creation and ultimately merge with a universal supreme mind. Mr. Krishnan wanted me to get convinced, hence continued making his point.

The following morning, we made it to the city of Rishikesh. The town was bustling with life and colour, with pilgrims and temples in abundance. It was a lot like Banaras, but much cleaner. The Jagat Satguru's residence was located at the outskirts of town to the east. The area was remote, but peaceful. A little hill covered in dense vegetation stood in the background of the ashram. As we reached, a friend of Mr. Krishnan's greeted us and said that the meditation session had already begun and that we were welcome to join in silence if we wished to.

We entered a medium-sized hall with a wooden floor and a capacity of almost a hundred people. There were about thirty disciples there in the state of meditation. Then I chained my eye to the lean structure sitting on the stage. A white-bearded man in his sixties or seventies, sitting with his legs crossed and his back perfectly straight in a meditative stance. Surrounded by the white moustache and beard, he appeared to have a pleasure full smile on his face. His eyes were shut overshadowed by dense eyebrows.

Unlike him, all his disciples had different outward physical appearance while meditating. Some were being disruptive, swaying all over the place, slamming hands on the floor, and shouting nonstop. Others were silent, with their chin resting on their chest. A student was standing with his hand outstretched, shaking, as if he were absorbing some sort of energy from above. In all this confusion, some were making valiant efforts to close their senses and begin their own inner journey. While Hart and I discreetly observed the shifting emotions of the other disciples, Mr. Krishnan joined the group and began his own inward trip.

The session lasted for around thirty minutes after we entered the hall. The antique clock chimed eleven o'clock. One after the other, the disciples were coming out of their meditative states. Gathering their mats, they folded their hands facing the stage and slipped out the back door without a word. No one seemed to have felt our presence, not even Hart's presence. Jagat Satguru maintained the same stance, all this while.

Mr. Krishnan told us that the sage would remain in this position for hours, hence we should leave him to it and go freshen up. We arrived at a humble shack that doubled as a lodging facility. When we had showered and dressed, we were ushered into the cafeteria for a hearty meal. To my surprise, the small cafeteria was filled with people around, but it was as quiet as a school class with the principal around.

We returned to the guest room where Mr. Krishnan asked us to rest, while he went out to try and seek a meeting with Satguru. About forty minutes later, he came back and said we were fortunate to have an appointment with Satguru at around six o'clock that evening. While we waited for the clock to strike six, Mr. Krishnan gave us a history of the ashram and Satguru. It was in the vein of a devout believer expounding upon the wonders of his faith and his leader.

Satguru occupied a separate dwelling at the ashram's western end. The large mansion stood amidst a garden full of trees and blooms. We could see the setting sun behind Satguru's mansion as we drew near. There was a large verandah that stretched along the side of the house, and that's where we were told to wait. Ten minutes later, we were beckoned inside.

When we entered the house, there was a big chowk in the middle, and on either side were two internal verandahs with three gates each. Our guide led us across the chowk and into the massive hall beyond. We walked in on the Satguru having a pleasant chat with one of his visitors across the hall. He was sitting on a rocking cane chair, while we were asked to sit on the floor at the far end of the hall. The hall was barely furnished and unoccupied, we could easily overhear Satguru's chat with the visitor. The guest, who was with Satguru appeared to be experiencing strong emotions. He bent his knees and begged Satguru with folded hands.

"Satguru, you have sacrificed so much in life, to spread the truth, please accept this money as a token of my gratitude." He then reached his pockets and put a bundle of notes at his feet. I could see the mild smile appearing on Satguru's face.

He replied in a soft tone, "My sacrifice is nothing as compared to the sacrifice the human race of today is making. I have only sacrificed the illusionary material world, outside our body, which has no meaning, so my sacrifice is worthless. While today's human race has sacrificed the soul within for the illusionary world, that's a much bigger sacrifice, isn't it?"

I had the sudden realisation that we might be on to something here. After touching Satguru's feat, the visitor walked away silently. Mr. Krishnan then approached Satguru and touched his feet with his forehead, followed by Hart. Normally, I would never do that, but it clicked my mind to let go of my ego and let my soul be humble. I too touched his feet with my forehead.

After Mr. Krishnan's introduction, Satguru gestured us to take a seat. During those silent few minutes, we smiled at each other whenever our eyes met. Hart turned to see what I'd say. I wanted to first see if Satguru was the right person to be asked the ultimate questions. With folded hands I asked,

"Satguru, please throw some light on your beliefs and teaching, which religion do you believe in and what path do you follow?"

"I try to follow the path of Adi Yogi, which leads to the ultimate truth that everyone already has inside of them. I don't follow any religion, people of all faiths are welcome to come here and search for the truth." After a short pause, he inquired, "I hear that you are trying to find the ultimate truth. May I ask you what you have found so far and what you are looking for now?"

Like many previous gurus I'd encountered in India, I wondered if the Satguru would try to tailor his teachings to fit in with what I already believe. So I gave a short response.

"Satguru, what I know is that a path exists, which was the heart of every religion in the past. The faiths of today are nothing more than propaganda. That's why I'm here, to seek out and investigate that genuine path for myself."

There appeared a pleasant smile on Satguru's face. I don't know what he liked about my reply, but he spoke with excitement this time, "Son, I am glad that you care for your soul and are out to explore. I will try to guide you on your journey."

I straightened my spine and looked at him with thirsty eyes, indicating that I was keen to hear. Satguru called for one of his attendants and asked him to bring a standing blackboard. He placed it beside his cane chair.

"Every living thing should aim for Moksha, or liberation from this cyclic world of illusion. Meditation is the only spiritual knowledge that can liberate. If we think rationally, today's religion is just history and historical characters, stories about you and me, with some powerful characters. How can history and characters be religion? People have forgotten the meditation of these powerful characters and demigods. This knowledge diluted with time. Meditation has become a form of exercise for the body instead of the science of the soul and the spiritual path to liberation. Let me inform you about the history of this science of meditation or yoga.

"Sage Vasistha's nine-lakh-year-old 'Yoga Vasistha' is the finest meditation memoir. Sage Vasistha taught his disciple Lord Rama in the Yoga Vasistha books. When Lord Rama became frustrated with life and its suffering, he asked his guru how to escape this illusion. Yoga Vasistha is composition of six books."

Satguru stood up. Writing on the blackboard with pink chalk, he continued his lecture.

"*Vairagya-prakaranam*: After realising that he too is in this vicious cycle of creation and annihilation, Lord Rama comes to his Guru. He wants to escape this eternal illusion.

Mumukshuvayahara-prakaranam: Lord Rama asks what a person seeking liberation should do. The true seeker should explore and seek with Mumukshatawa (perseverance).

Utpatti-prakaranam: Describes creation's birth, including Rama's Avatarship.

Sthiti-prakaranam: Explains the creation and its maintenance.

Upashama-prakaranam: Explains meditation to realise illusionary dualism and achieve oneness.

Nirvana-prakaranam: Explains how to achieve liberation.

Mahabharata also emphasises on Nirodha Meditation—Meditation of cessation, in the Mokshadharma section. Nirodha Meditation emphasises progressive withdrawal from empirical consciousness, including thoughts, sensations, until purusha (self) is realised."

Hart and I shared a look of admiration after hearing Satguru's words. Without missing a beat, Satguru continued.

"Beginning of kalyuga period, different Vedic philosophies emerged. Orthodox and heterodox, or Astika and Nastika.

"There are six major schools of Orthodox—*Nyaya* (logic), *Vaisesika* (atomic theory), *Sankhya* (analysis of matter and spirit), Yoga (the discipline of self-realization), *Karma-mimamsa* (science of karma), and *Vedanta* (science of god realisation)."

Satguru used multicoloured chalks to draw a flow chart.

"Jains, Buddhists, Ajivikas, Ajnanas, and Charvakas are Heterodox schools. Survival of the fittest resulted in, Jainism, Buddhism, Yoga, and Vedanta thriving while Ajnana, Charvaka, and Ajivika declined. The Vedanta school had six sub-schools, Advaita (nondualism), Visishtadvaita (monism of the qualified whole), Dvaita, Dvaitadvaita (dualism-nondualism), Suddhadvaita, and Achintya Bheda Abheda. Most of the renowned teachers who brought meditation to the modern world, like Swami Vivekananda, Paramahansa Yogananda, Sri Aurobindo, and Swami Shivananda, were Vedantins and emphasised Yoga Vedanta.

"These schools shared themes but had differing ideologies. They discussed ontology, reasoning, epistemology, axiology, free will, liberation, karma, samsara, reincarnation, meditation, renunciation. All these are a part of the Yoga teachings.

"Yoga takes the teaching of all the other philosophies, prescribes a practical and actionable approach, and tries to bring them into practice, to ensure achieving the common goal of all philosophies—Liberation."

One of Satguru's disciples entered the room with a covered food plate. Satguru settled back into his chair and blessed the food with his palm. After which he continued his lecture.

"Comprehensive methods of meditation were written by Sage Patanjali in five hundred BC. It explains the process of awakening and expanding the higher faculties of mind and consciousness. Patanjali taught an eightfold system of meditation, ethical disciplines, postures, breathing exercises, control of the senses, concentration, meditation, and absorption or samadhi.

"Buddha's enlightenment in the fourth century BC followed the meditation sutras. Before enlightenment, he meditated under a Bodhi tree employing sage-taught yoga. Buddha's eightfold route to enlightenment and Patanjali's eightfold Meditation were developing simultaneously.

"According to ancient Jain texts, 'Tattvarthasutra' from the second century common era, meditation is an essential element in the path to liberation. The five major vows of Jainism are very similar to the five disciplines in the Yoga Sutras of Patanjali."

Hart said, "Satguru, there seems to be a history of strong cross-fertilisation between these teachings."

"Yes, and all these teachings are classified as classical meditation. Post-Christ era meditation schools are called nonclassical. Practicality overtook philosophy. Shankaracharya started this phase. He unified meditation traditions, reconciled ideological divisions, and made meditation science more accessible. Hatha meditation developed. Asanas, cleaning, pranayama, mudras, and bandhas were practiced to attain body-mind harmony. Matsyendranath and Gorakhnath fore fronted Hatha meditation.

"Meditation became associated with practicality rather than spirituality. Meditation reached the west in the nineteenth century via Swami Vivekananda. He wrote four meditation books: Jnana, Bhakti, Karma, and Raja. Hatha meditation was discouraged by Sri Ramakrishna, his guru. Hatha meditation may hinder spiritual growth by focusing on the body.

"This is how schools of meditation branched out like religions. But the core and the goal remain the same—liberation from this mundane world."

Satguru paused, seeing me curious, "Yes, son?"

"Guruji, which of these schools do you teach and how can one achieve this common objective, liberation?"

Satguru smiled, "Son, to accomplish the highest, we must understand our body's energy and the spiritual world inside. *Kriya* meditation is the only realistic means to realise these energies, chakras, and the route to the ultimate self. Various meditations aid Kriya meditation. Kriya yogis can control their inner world and succeed in the outside world. A Kriya yogi mentally channels his life energy upward and downward around the six spinal points."

Satguru halted his discourse and suddenly went into a trance. Mr. Krishnan quietly whispered to us that this might be Satguru's meditation time. One of his disciples approached us and invited us to join him for supper. I looked at the clock and saw that it was already thirty minutes past eight. The lights in the ashram were dim, and the only sound was that of the cicadas. We walked to the cafeteria and got typical Indian khichdi on our plates. Hart and I sat in silence, processing what we'd learned about meditation so far. Meanwhile, Mr. Krishnan stayed busy chatting with his pals.

One lonely figure stood out, appearing distant as he ate alone in the garden, under a massive Banyan tree. A few people who exited the canteen and were passing through the same garden, talked about that person in hushed tones among themselves. He did appear peculiar, as if he were high on drugs or alcohol. It was the only thing that managed to distract my brain.

After dinner, Mr. Krishnan suggested that we see Satguru after the morning meditation. We had a terrific meditation session the next morning, mostly exercises and some meditation. While we attempted, others were great at all the postures. After a delicious breakfast, we excitedly awaited Satguru's call.

At around eleven, we were taken to the same room as yesterday. Satguru came in after five minutes. He sat down and invited us to close our eyes and focus on our breathing for five minutes. During these five minutes, I focused on my breath and wondered what meditation he would teach and fantasised the experiences I would have. He told us to open our eyes after five minutes. He then instructed us to place our fingers under each nostril for five seconds to see which exhales more. Hart and Mr. Krishnan had right nostrils, but my left nostril was dominant. After this vague activity, Satguru began his lecture.

"Our body is God's temple. The body contains spiritual elements. The seven *Chakras* (energy centres*), Nadis* (veins – energy channels), and *Prana* (subtle wind) are the core of this system. The binding element is our spinal cord, which is the highway to the infinite. *Sushumna,* the spinal cord's solitary vein, is connected to the infinite. Wind or breath carries life energy through the body's seven chakras and veins. These chakras are on Sushumna Nadi. Two other veins, *Ida* and *Pingala*, also run through the chakras, and alongside Sushumna."

Satguru called for his blackboard and wrote down the seven Chakras.

1. Root chakra (Muladhara)- ovaries/prostate.
2. Sacral chakra (Swadhisthana)- last bone in spinal cord, the coccyx.
3. Solar plexus chakra (Manipura)- navel area.
4. Heart chakra (Anahata)- heart area.
5. Throat chakra (Vishuddha)- throat and neck area.
6. Third eye chakra (Ajna)- pineal gland or third eye.
7. Crown chakra (Sahasrara)- top of the head; "soft spot" of a newborn.

"The original Kriya Meditation is a combination of pre-reverse order, or downward journey, or order of creation and reverse order, or upward journey, or journey of reversing creation. The pre-reverse order is the most important and the secret aspect of the original Kriya. It forms the basis, the foundation, for starting the reverse order. The secrets of this foundation course are known only to a few masters, others just teach modified Kriya meditation which starts with reverse order only. The pre-reverse order is to realise the order of creation and approach the last stage of creation consciously.

"The creation starts when the supreme consciousness becomes restless from its tranquil state and desires. The desire is generated at the crown chakra or the mind. The Prana then moves down each chakra, finally rests in the last chakra, the Muladhara Chakra. This can also be felt in sexual desire. Sexual desire is felt by the brain and then coming down each chakra, Prana comes down to the prostate, Muladhara Chakra. Prana finally rests in the seventh chakra, solidifying the creation."

Hart interrupted in excitement, "This has so much correlation to Jesus saying—God created and then rested on the seventh day."

"Sorry son, I have no idea of that." The lecture briefly halted.

"Satguru, please tell us about the pre-reverse and reverse order," I cued.

"The pre-reverse order is the process to approach this prana or kundilini lying in the Muladhara Chakra consciously and awakening it. By awakening it we prepare it to take on the reverse journey.

"The reverse order is the objective of meditation, to reverse this order of creation. But only practicing reverse order is like knowing that the ball resides inside the socks and trying to remove the ball from the outside. The pre-reverse order is a practice to see the ball from inside, approach it inside the socks, and then to take it out. Kriya Meditation is a master disciple system. The teacher must teach these kriyas to the willing soul in solitude. True masters have reversed the creation cycle and may awaken the kundilini of eager, capable disciples.

"Kriya meditation involves seven kriyas, combining meditation techniques. The foundational first kriya encompasses steps like, *Mahamudra*, *Talabya kriya*, *Navi kriya*, and *Yoni mudra*. Progressing requires mastering Talabya kriya and *Khecharimudra*. The second kriya, *Thokkar kriya*, guides tranquil breath to cross the dorsal knot, moving from the heart towards the coccygeal. The third and fourth kriyas are blessed, based on devotion to the Guru. The third unlocks the Naval knot, while the fourth breaks the Muladhara knot, awakening Prana for reverse ascent.

"The reverse journey, fifth, sixth, and seventh kriyas, are naturally guided by Guru and divine grace. Kundalini can only ascend via the Sushumna nadi, flanked by Ida and Pingala. These channels align with the spine, branching into seventy-two thousand smaller channels. Ida and Pingala mirror positive and negative forces, forming a complex circuit.

"Ida, Pingala, & Sushumna nadis originate from Muladhara chakra at the anus. All three proceed separately in the same direction, upwards. Ida from left of Muladhara and Pingla from right, end up at the Ajna Chakra, located between our eyebrows, while Sushmana, the spiritual nadi, terminates at the Sahasrara Chakra. Meditation activates the Sushmana nadi and directs prana to the Sahasrara Chakra."

Humbly, one of Satguru's students walked in and asked him to pause his lesson so that he could have some food. It had been almost two and half hours since Satguru began his talk. He paused and motioned for one of his followers to lead us to the cafeteria.

While looking out over the garden, we ate our lunch in a nook of the cafeteria. On the way back to Satguru's mansion, I couldn't stop thinking about this individual. There was something off about the stoned guy who ate dinner alone under the tree the night before, and who was now calmly sleeping under the dense shadow of the Banyan tree.

Satguru was ready to lecture when we arrived. He instructed us to place our fingers under our nostrils and disclose the dominant one again before starting. This time, my right nostril was dominant, Hart and Mr. Krishnan's left. Satguru grinned and said that my Pingla is more prominent now and Hart and Mr. Krishnan's Ida. He assured us that this is quite common. Ida and Pingla alternate between positive and negative energy every forty-fifty minutes.

"We discussed about the three veins Ida, Pingala, and Sushmana. Ida or Moon Nadi and Pingla or Sun Nadi are balancing veins. The spiritual Sushmana is the highway to bliss. The question is how to activate it. Sushmana only gets realised and stimulated, when the other two nadis, Ida and Pingala are purified and balanced. Till the time these two nadi's are not perfected, they act like chains around the Muladhara chakra. With one nadi being active at any point of time, the chakra is in constant motion. It's only when both these nadi's are balanced through meditation practice, does this chakra stabilise and the prana gets activated. Along with balancing the nadis, other kriyas need to be practiced, especially to control the mind.

"Mind needs to be devoid from thoughts to concentrate on this central path. Once the mind is totally concentrated on this path, the prana awakens and starts its journey, rising from the Muladhara chakra, moving upwards, crossing all the other chakras and eventually by gods grace reaches the Sahasrara, the door to enlightenment. This is the objective of Kriya Meditation."

A beaming smile appeared on Satguru's face as he gazed upon us one by one, starting with Mr. Krishnan on his left, then Hart. But as his eyes caught mine, the bright smile shrinked, as he saw that my mind was processing the lecture furiously. My thoughts were constantly deconstructing the presentation and attempting to solve the many unanswered questions in my head.

"You have some questions, son?"

I stayed quiet, unconsciously waiting for my mind to still. My friend Hart helped me out, he asked Satguru, "Will you kindly teach us this Kriya?"

Satguru smiled again and said, "Depends on your eagerness and desire, son."

"Desire". This word struck my mind like a bullet. This word is the catalyst for the brain. I politely and curiously asked Satguru, "Desire is that what you say is required to learn Kriya Meditation. If we generate this desire, learn Kriya Meditation and achieve the objective, we shall move out of this creation. Is the same desire, not the reason for this creation?"

"Precisely, you yourself are responsible for this creation and you yourself are responsible to get out of this creation."

"Am I the creator then?"

"Yes, you are the creator, the reason, and the source of this illusionary creation."

"So each one of us, every human, is the creator himself and has within him the power to create and destroy? If we're all so powerful and able, why does everybody suffer? Why can't I put an end to this creation?"

"Surely you can, through this Kriya Meditation."

"Alright, so if I reverse the order, go to the Sahasrara, and bring an end to this creation, would that guarantee that the desire won't ever come back to me and cause me to create all over again? Since you've taught us that the creative process begins at this Sahasrara level when desire enters, I'm curious how I might prevent any more creation once I am there. What guarantee do you have that desire won't rear its ugly head again? Where does this desire come from, is it a part of the creator in me or separate? If it is inherent to I, then it is always going to be there and can return at any time to initiate the creation; if it is external, then where does it come from?"

Satguru seemed to be in some discomfort. He shut his eyelids, moving his head backwards, resting on the head of the chair. After a few minutes, he raised his head, looking directly at me.

"Son, I am so happy, that you are on this path of exploration. The desire is not a part of the I, both are separate. Desire comes from the supreme creator."

I interrupted, "The supreme creator has desire? How can he have any desire? Is he our God with desire?"

"Desire is just the duality aspect of him." Everything in his creation is also just duality. Happiness-suffering, day-night."

I knew Satguru was diverting, but I was okay with it. He had come to the duality, which I already knew. I decided to get my other learnings also verified.

"Yes, happiness cannot exist in isolation, but what determines the magnitude of suffering or happiness. Why is one born a beggar and the other a prince?"

Satguru seemed in his comfort zone again. "Karma theory decides on the magnitude of suffering or happiness. It ensures that we reap what we sow."

I interrupted again. "Why am I responsible for my situations? I was created by him for his desire, then why am I responsible?"

Satguru's facial expressions kept on changing during our debate, "Yes, the creator is responsible for creation, but after creation, only you are responsible. If you do good karmas, you will reap good rewards and if you do bad karmas, you shall suffer, simple."

"Ok, then tell me this. Just after the creation was formed, what formed the basis of the creation, the 'I' did not have any good karma or bad karma, just yet. Did God give us this karma as the seed money?"

Satguru, got a little furious now. "These questions are from an undeveloped mind, which does not have the capacity to understand the answers. One must first enlighten the mind through Kriya Meditation, to be able to understand the answers to these ultimate questions. Kriya Meditation helps shift the focus from the deceptive external illusionary world to the spiritual reality inside. You yourself will provide answers to your mind, from the ultimate experience you shall have within."

I decided to keep an open mind and not let my ego dominate. I parked my questions on the side and concentrated my mind on the Kriya meditation.

"Satguru, I sincerely apologise if I have offended you. But I still have my doubts. I completely agree with you; that creation is nothing but the experiences we register in our mind through the senses. But whether these experiences are external or internal, how does that matter. In all our experiences, whether external or internal, we are just sending some signals to our mind, which interprets it, based on the accumulated data it has. So, experiencing the material world externally or experiencing the spiritual world internally are both a part of this creation and no different to each other.

"Till the time we are experiencing anything, our mind is at play. Experiences are just projections of what we already know. How can we experience something we have never known? In our spiritual experiences, that which we recognise, is something which was already there in our memory, which was already planted in our mind, what is already known.

"The mind lives on these experiences. It keeps craving and striving for newer experiences. This desire of the mind keeps it striving for knowledge and all the experience comes out of what is already known by it, the knowledge already stored in its memory. So be it materialistic or spiritual experiences, aren't both of these just illusionary projections of one's mind based on memory?

"Now that you have educated us, that the first three Kriya meditations will help us stimulate the mooladhara chakra, this has been processed and stored in my brain's database. The day my mind intensely wants such an experience, it would instantly hit the database and experience that the mooladhara chakra is stimulated. If I had not heard about this mooladhara chakra, there would be no memory of it in my brain, will I ever experience it then? It's getting harder for me to understand how Kriya meditation is talking about something apart from these illusions of mind. To me experiences whether it be internal or external are all manifestations of mind."

Satguru was exhausted by now, he had given up on me and wanted to conclude, "Kid, your mind seems to think too much, just stabilise it. Give it peace and you will understand Kriya meditation. Kriya meditation, needs you to have faith in the Guru."

After saying this, he got to his feet and left the room. We waited, uncertain of whether he'd come back or if he was finished with us. In the end, all it took was a tap on the shoulder from Mr. Krishnan, and I understood. We ate dinner and went to bed early. The next morning, while we were returning to our cottage after the meditation session, we saw Satguru's car leaving the Ashram's gate. Mr. Krishnan received word that Satguru had left a message for the guests. He needed to make an urgent trip to Kolkata, but he insisted that we stay put. He promised to come back in three days and meet us.

We hadn't made any plans yet. Everything about this ashram was pleasant; from the cottage we stayed in, to the delicious meals, and the extensive library we had access to. We decided to stay. During our three days at the Ashram, Hart and I quickly became well-liked there. My primary goal in talking to the disciples was to learn about their personal Kriya meditation experiences. I wondered if there is anything other than a *desire for desirable experiences.*

At first, I had a hard time getting the disciples to feel comfortable sharing their personal stories with me. But Hart came through for me in the end. He tagged along whenever I went to chat with strangers. That worked wonderfully, as people quickly warmed up to Hart and expressed genuine interest in becoming his friend. There were some who were freshers, some who had been practicing the first kriya for years and very few I hear, who had mastered the first three kriyas. We were told that there was only one person in the ashram who had gone beyond the fourth kriya.

Everyone spoke about their life-changing experiences as though they had some special insight to impart, as if they were proud of being the blessed ones. All the experiences revolved around defining the location, colour, and shape of the chakras, as well as the numerous lotus flowers therein and the mystical experiences.

Newcomers and experienced practitioners of first kriya meditation had very similar responses that centred on Satguru's teachings. Those who had attained a certain level of kriya mastery had varying responses. The stark difference was in the spiritual trance experience each has had within. Some said that everything disappears except for an inner light; some said that they could see the gods and goddesses of each chakra; and some said that their third eye had opened and they could see things unimaginable by common humans; some said that they could see Satguru within; some said they could heal others by the power of chakras within; one said that he had seen the garden of Eden within; yet another said that he had seen the realms of Heaven and Hell within.

Their experiences covered everything considered or perceived to be spiritual by the human brain, in this world. All the things we have heard about spirituality were covered. It was also quite relative. A person who has been born a Christian and was on this Kriya meditation path, talked about one light and the garden of Eden. A person born a Hindu, would talk about seeing various gods in the chakra's experience.

The experience was also influenced by peer pressure or the desire for visibility. On one occasion, a young disciple was revealing to us his feelings of misfortune and lack of experience. One of the senior members of the commune joined us and was boasting about his experience and about how the ashram ensures that even new practitioners have these experiences instantly. The young guy confirmed on being asked.

Once the senior left, I confronted him about his earlier deceit and asked him why he lied to us. With disappointment on his face, he said that all his juniors, peers, and seniors, boast of experience of some kind. He will be looked down upon as having a polluted soul if he makes no claim to having spiritual experiences. He claimed that he acted them out during one of the sessions because he didn't want to be left alone while everyone else was jumping up and down in a trance. That enactment gave him an experience and hence he believes that such experience will someday come naturally to him.

He also said that the ones who have such experiences can only go closer to the Guru and hence he desires and strives for such experiences.

After dinner on day four, I went outside and sat there by myself. The conversations, insights, and perspectives shared over the past two days have forced me to wonder. Why each experience was so unique.

The source of all these experiences is the mind and the experiences developed in the mind are dependent on its own database, which has been formed by past knowledge. No two databases can be identical; hence no two experiences can be the same. Once again, everything vanishes into the abyss of the mind, leaving us helpless to escape it.

As my thoughts reached their limits, my eyes gazed out and saw the person who cherished the banyan tree. With a broad grin on his face, he strolled up to the banyan tree, laid his head and spine against the trunk, and spread his legs out to relax. I desperately wanted to be that calm and content. I was drawn to him because of how at ease he seemed. I got to my feet and made my way slowly towards the banyan tree.

I moved closer to him, wanting to ask if I may join him,

but he looked to be lost in his trance, and his eyes were closed. I didn't want to wake him up, so I sat in a similarly relaxed position. As I was resting, I noticed other disciples glancing at us and exchanging puzzled glances. After waiting for perhaps ten minutes, I gave in and asked him, "May I get to know you?"

He replied, "I don't know myself," in a hushed voice. Gathering courage, I asked him about his whereabouts, "Where do you come from, are you part of this commune?"

He swiveled his head to face me and said, "I know not." His droopy dark eyes were fixed on me. It became awkward for me, and I got up to leave. He grabbed my hand and asked me, "Do you know about yourself; Who you are? Do you know where you come from or where do you want to go? Why aren't you afraid of yourself then?" I was speechless in the face of his questioning gaze.

He laid his hands on my shoulders and whispered, "They are fools and know not the easy way out," as he gestured towards the cafeteria. I heard an intoxicated guy telling the truth and felt compelled to engage him in conversation.

I remarked, "These men aren't fools; they are learned and experienced people, so punctual, so disciplined, and so dedicated."

He laughed, "Yes, they are, but what have they achieved with that?"

I knew where this was going, "They have mastered Kriya meditation and are experiencing the mystic spiritual world inside."

He gave away his resting position, leaned towards me and affirmed, "I have experienced it all." He noticed the curiosity on my face and continued,

"I have also mastered these kriyas and have experienced the various chakras and the prana flowing through these chakras inside. I have had ecstatic experiences inside, but nothing used to stay, they were temporary. This went on for almost five years. I got frustrated as these experiences were becoming common and nothing new was happening, while my desire to see something new kept intensifying. It's like how a baby reacts to his first exposure to the world; everything is new and fascinating. When he gets older, none of these things excite him, they just seem like the norm. Higher experiences like Samadhis are like experiencing ecstasies without dope. It's only one's intensified desire which leads him to have these spiritual experiences."

He stopped for a moment, got to his feet, and started to walk. I decided to go with him. We sat on the wooden bench of a small lake on the far east corner of the ashram. All I wanted to do was pick his brain.

"You say that meditation only leads to experiences, coming out of the intensified desires of mind, so is meditation of no use in finding God?"

He took a deep breath and with his eyelids opening and shutting slowly, replied, "What is meditation? It is nothing but a process of arresting or stilling the ever-vibrant mind.

Mind is nothing but play of thoughts between the past and the future. The thoughts one after the other, without a nano second's gap, keeps the mind alive. Meditation of any kind is just a process of slowing down the mind, by forcing it to concentrate on a particular thing, rather than roaming without any leash. All kinds of meditation in this world tell you to start with focusing, concentrating your mind on a particular thing. It is a matter of choice; it can be a word, an object, an image of god, the image of guru, light, energy ball, chakra, or any other thing.

"The image of the concentrating point is already installed in your brain and then one is asked to focus on it. With practice, the mind gets trained in focusing on this known image for hours together. Knowing that the mind will eventually get bored of the process and try fleeing off the leash, they ask you to move forward to a different higher image, in higher forms of meditation. The deeper one goes in meditation, the deeper levels of imagination creep up, but at the end of the day, it is just imagination, created by the mind. In every stage, the concept remains the same, leashing the mind to a preconceived image. What meditation does is just slows down the speed of the mind, it drugs it and makes it dull.

"True meditation is when there remains no divide between I am meditating and not-meditating."

"Satguru said that it requires willpower and desire to reach the Sahasrara or the crown chakra. Only then the mind

gives up and blends with God and that's the ultimate aim of progressing in meditation."

The gaze left the lake and looked at me, "First of all, willpower and desire are activities of the mind, how can they possibly still the mind? Secondly, every form of meditation, keeps God, or his abode, as the final destination. This to keep the mind desperately desiring the destination. The mind keeps imagining and desiring this destination. *This is destination addiction.* Is meditation solving its purpose to still the mind or just aiding it by giving it more desires and destinations to reach? *And if you desire liberation here, will you not desire liberation there.*"

"So very true," I nodded.

"God exists now, in this very moment, in everything around us, in you, in me, in the lake, in this tree, and in this grass. The day we are able to know ourselves, and stop imagining God at a destination, we will realise that there is nowhere to travel to, he is with you, he is you. There is nothing except him.

"If you already know your God, there is no possibility of knowing him. These authorities do not want you to be content with what you are and what you already have—God. They want you to condemn yourself and God. They want you to perform actions, follow rules, give up to authorities, to change yourself and achieve the God, who they claim to know.

"With emotions in his intoxicated eyes, he continued, "And I know this, God loves you the way you are. He has made you that way, why will he not love you that way. There is no need to change, no need to seek. God is with you right here, right now, there is no need to aspire for a distant location and find God there.

"Have you ever thought why do you search for God? You search for God, for your own existence, for protecting your identity. In your subconscious, you know that if you accept God right here, right now, the divide will be broken, and you will have to dissolve in him. *To seek God is to deny God.*"

Silence engulfed us. But I so wanted to see my God, in that moment. In all my enthusiasm, I asked him, "So, how do I experience him, how do I get to know him, how do I see him?"

He stood up, collected his jacket and was about to leave. "*He cannot be experienced, his image cannot be formed to see, he cannot be known by this mind. He is the vapour, you are the ice, he is the fruit, you are the seed. Ice can only burn, melt itself and be vapour, it cannot see it. Seed can only grow unencumbered and become fruit, it cannot see it. You cannot see God, you can melt yourself and be him. The experiencer, the questioner, the knower, the known, the mind needs to vanish. Only then he comes in.*"

On the bench, he abandoned me. But I did not have a sense of isolation. There was a hint of night jasmine in the air. Something beautiful sat on my arms; a *juganoo* (firefly), bright as the moon. For fear of scaring it away, I stayed very still when I caught a glimpse of it. What a revelation; a being whose natural intrinsic light banishing the darkness of night. It seemed my God was showboating, to impress me. I spread my legs and rested my head on the arms of that bench, allowing him to continue his show. The wind and the lake sung a lullaby and put me to rest. He hung the stars in the sky, so I may feel safe.

The next day was Satguru's birthday. The ashram was decorated with flowers and lamps, but Satguru wasn't there. The devotees had congregated in the hall, facing the enormous portrait of Satguru, and were profusely crying, missing him on this auspicious day. That afternoon, I found the crazed man under the banyan tree once again. In a friendly manner, he greeted me.

"I agree that all the physical actions and the experiences had during meditation are nothing but deep desires of mind for spiritual experiences and for visibility in the commune. But what of the tears in the eyes of the disciples, their love for their master, that can't be false?"

"The monks and the disciples have come this far for God, because they do not know or realise the God within.

Most of them were born in this commune while others have acquired it. All of them have been trained to focus their mind, concentrate on the guru, trained to be dependent upon the guru, trained to lean on the support system of the guru. They have been made to believe, that they alone are incapable of knowing and acquiring God, that it's only via guru's blessing, that one can achieve God. They attach themselves to the guru, whom they believe is the only possibility to reach God.

"They feel disabled, in desperate need of a support system—a commune. Within this commune, the competition to be closer to the Guru, to be his favourite, to be Guru's chosen one, to be above the others, to be respected and admired by others, to be of some worth in the commune, is immense. It's obvious that you start loving or are trained to love someone you attach your whole life to, someone you completely depend upon, someone without whose blessings you would be ruined. You need to show your love towards him, so that he can recognise and bless you. *They tell you that love should only be for one, but trust me, if true love blesses you, it would never be only for one, it would be universal.*

"Crying or any emotions are just reactions coming from thought process. Please understand how mind works. The mind works on stimulus, actions, and reactions. Stimulus is derived from words, images, or symbols. These words, images, and symbols are nothing but pre-stored knowledge. The mind is programmed to act and react in a particular pre-defined way once the stimulus is activated. Image of the

Guru and the emotion of missing him create a stimulus and a pre-defined action is activated. No person will do anything new, he will not dance, when everyone is crying. All responses of mind are predefined and methodical.

"Yes, there is one more crying, but that is without any image, without the process of thought and mind."

The crazed man pulled a bottle out of his coat and started drinking. He made a generous offer by reaching out to me. I could tell it was alcohol just from the aroma. Since childhood, I have been conditioned to be a teetotaler. As a result of my upbringing, I was programmed to immediately contradict,

"This is bad, this is wrong, that too in an Ashram!"

He smiled. "You fear this intoxication? This is harmless. You live your life intoxicated with money, power, pride, and ego that's far more harmful, trust me. And only because I do the wrong things or bad things, are you able to proudly do your so-called right things or good things and carry your ego. Without my bad things, how would you have defined the good things you do and feel proud of. This ego which you carry is subtle but the most harmful in the way to God.

"It's easy to love good things and the perfect God. True love is when you can love everything undivided. I just enjoy God's creation, both internally and externally without differentiating. Good and bad is man's creation. He divides, in order to own up good and expand his ego. To me everything is good and God, and there is no bad.

"Dig deep. Your religions deliberately want to condemn all things which give pleasure to humans in this world. They want us to lead a miserable life. What would be their need, if every human was content and happily living in this heavenly earth. *They have to make this heavenly earth hell for the humans, so they can sell the drug of Heaven.*

"Religions even condemn or reject God. God is right here, right now, all around us, on this heavenly earth. There isn't a place he does not exist. If everyone realises and experiences God on this heavenly earth, who shall purchase the drugs sold by these religions. For a heart filled with love, this earth is a heaven. For a heart filled with chaos, even heaven would feel like hell.

"You search for God because you have created a divide between him and you, between Heaven and Hell, between good and bad, between past and future. Your mind, that is you, can only stay alive by creating this divide and transiting between the two. You, your mind, will die, the moment you bring down these divides. Tell me, will you search for God, if you experience him right here, right now, not in the past, not in the future?"

"But that's not possible, is it?"

"Yes, he is already there. You have just dwarfed the God within you to a point that you do not recognise him anymore."

"So teach me, how do I experience him now?"

"I can teach you my love song, but that will not help you fall in love with my God. *Remember this, what I have experienced will only liberate me, but the same will inevitably slave you.*

"Do not run from a smaller mirage to a bigger one, just stop running. You or God are already there. You have always been the one you have been seeking. You just need to stop seeking, stop following authorities. Stop running and you will arrive."

Saying this he walked away, hummed a tune, as he took very small steps—"*Barf ka woh sharif tukda, jaam mein kya gira, badnaam hogaya, deta jabtak apni safai, woh khud sharab hogaya.*"

I have no idea what his name is, but he seemed to be touched by God, the most contented, cheerful guy I had ever encountered. He reminded me of a Zen proverb—When an ordinary man attains knowledge, he is a sage. When a sage attains wisdom, he is an ordinary man.

Before returning to my cabin, I sat for some time on the wooden bench by the tiny lake, where God had demonstrated his existence. I felt as though my Eden was all around me. I fell asleep on the wooden cold bench, engulfed by God. The following morning, after finishing breakfast, I sat down with my diary.

Religions, having divided us and God, Heaven, and Earth, now had to devise a path towards him, which they can sell. This path cannot be made simple, or it would lose its value. Whatever they sell had to be something tough, arduous. Knowing that human ego takes pride only in pursuing something unachievable, they manufactured this mysticism path. The harder you make the path, the more believable it becomes. Also, by making it complicated, they could always blame the pursuer for not doing it properly, and protect the path from being questioned.

Religions inject in the mind; thoughts of fiery Hell, glorious Heaven, Imaginative God, arduous path, these superficial and spiritual experiences. The mind then desires to travel on this path and makes continuous efforts towards it. Finally, the desire, the aspiration becomes so strong that the mind triggers the memory and experiences it. These hallucinations or trance or samadhi, in various religions are not some drama, they are surely real but they are just intense emotional aspirations or intense yearning for some experience inside. Most of the time these experiences are just intense social aspiration or so to say the demand of the ego to be known as spiritual to the rest of the world.

The faith in one's religion gets established strongly on experiencing these made-up images. One considers other religions and other experiences as fake. One does not realise that how can such spiritual experiences be different in different religions, how can God have as many images as the number of sects and religions? One's own ego blinds him.

Dream imitates this state of trance or hallucination aptly. See a sci-fi or a horror movie for two or three continuous nights. The dreams then will surely take you to a sci-fi or a horror world. But how can an involuntary thing like dream be assigned spiritual status? That would defeat the purpose of an organised religion.

When religions want to claim supremacy, they need to distinguish themselves from others. Mysticism became an important tool, because it has something which can be experienced and felt to be the truth, something away from just faith and belief. Seeing the success of incorporating mysticism in one's religion, every religion now has a branch which is combining mysticism with their original beliefs. They market that the experience or brain thought they have at the helm of the spiritual path, which is close to impossible, is the abode of their God.

It requires strong determination and guts to return to logic after having experienced mysticism. Whenever challenged about the reality of his claims, a mystic will constantly point to the fact that his experience itself cannot be disputed. Powerful self-determination is required to verify it.

There is no denying the benefits of meditation, but without wisdom, its use in finding the truth is dubious. Practicing meditation can aid in calming the mind, increasing attention and concentration, and bringing about other positive changes in our well-being.

Meditation helps in understanding our mind, how it operates, the process of thoughts, and the actions and reactions of mind. By slowing down the thoughts, one is able to analyse them closely. How and from where they emerge, how they travel, and the whole mechanism of the mind. Meditation surely helps in bringing awareness and wisdom.

It helps realise the duality, the duality of the external and internal worlds. It helps in mind control but not the cessation of thoughts or cessation of desire, which is food for the mind and thoughts. Most mystics wrongly conclude mind control to be victory over mind and give in to the power of mind.

The mind creates duality, divides between experiences inside and outside, between God and man. It only can stay alive by dividing and desiring to move from one divide to the other. It only stays alive in motion; it cannot live in the present. My God is in the undivided present and hence mind cannot conceive it.

It was the seventh day since Satguru had left the Ashram. He had promised to be back in three days, but we heard that his homecoming was in doubt now. I made the decision to head back to Mumbai. The takeover of my company had been officially approved, and I was a member of the new management team, so I needed to report to my office. To get to Mumbai, I'd have to first visit Banaras, pack up my belongings, and then make the journey home. My friend Hart had made a lot of friends here and was keen to pursue this Kriya meditation path. He wished me luck for my journey, both, journey towards finding God and the journey back home. He requested me to keep in touch and share the journey's unfolding revelations with him.

Chapter 12

Mind's Confession and God's Voice

The trip back home via Banaras was delightful and enlightening. I was in constant introspection. I learned to recognise my mind's recurring habits and the processes at work within it. I realised that there is no one else who can do this introspection on my behalf. It's silly to put the onus of self-examination on any authority, whatsoever.

My mind revealed itself the moment I tried to analyse and examine it. My mind, the creator of me and my world, finally wanted to surrender and accept defeat. It was tired of its unappreciated work and needed a way out. In the process it wanted to reveal its true self and the truth about this creation created by it. It seemed like the autobiography of a dying thief who wanted to admit his guilt and make amends.

My mind's biography, as narrated by it:

"I am the I, the consciousness, the mind, the ego, the thinker, you name it, and I am it. I am the monkey about which the Devil was raving. I was born out of desire, out of thoughts of an individualised mind. I am nothing but accumulation of thoughts. Continued thoughts culminated in the materialisation of a world into which I found myself woven. Like my father I desired to individualise. For which, it was necessary to partition and colonise, to differentiate, between what is mine and what is not. Develop a distinct persona, an ego bubble, to stand out from the crowd.

"I am nothing but this individual bubble of thoughts or ego, different from others. It's only my bubble, which defines me, gives me my identity. At birth, I was a tiny bubble, with the thoughts of my name, my family, and my surroundings. As taught to me, a bigger bubble is the only way I could progress my individuality and be known. Helped by my surrounding, I started dividing and collecting more thoughts into my ego bubble. The thoughts of my nationality, my culture, my religion, my beliefs, my people, and my possessions. As a result, I claimed a larger share of the world as mine and desired to keep expanding.

"I have been trained to get upset if my belief, my ego, is threatened, and to feel elated if my ego is praised. I continue to put in long hours to assure the continued expansion of my ego bubble and the satisfaction of its inhabitants. The things I've imagined but can't own or bring into my ego bubble fill me with remorse and longing. At the same time, I fear losing anything, which is there in my possession, inside my bubble. The new thoughts I encounter, I either dismiss them, or use them to strengthen my conditioning, or skew them so that they fit my conditioning. Through it all, I've been able to protect my conditioned individuality.

"I find myself in this chaotic world, where every individualised mind is trying to expand its bubble at the cost of shrinking the bubble of others. I have come to understand now that this chaos is because of me, because I have created this divide between my beliefs and other beliefs, between my friends and foes. It takes two to war. *The beliefs outside my bubble are ever breaking in, while beliefs inside my bubble are ever breaking out.* I keep struggling to maintain this divide and protect my ego bubble.

"I am the creator and the created. I create the desired and am the desirer, I am the thinker and the thought. I divide sin and good, suffering and bliss, earth and heaven, God and human. This is my small illusionary world. I have successfully inflated my ego bubble to the point of self-entrapment. The realisation of which makes me guilty and exhausted, wanting to shut down.

"I now realise that I can only exist in the divisions I have created, past and future. Thoughts are my breath and thoughts can only exist in the past or future. There can be no thoughts in the present. I cannot be static, thoughts exist only in momentum, momentum between past and future, so do I. *If I dissolve this divide between past and future, I can stop and rest in now, in oneness. But how can I dissolve my whole identity, for which I have worked for ages?*"

I am ashamed of my mind. I wasn't using my mind; the mind was using me until now. But now that my thought is coming to understand itself, it is naturally wanting to stop. *I am becoming aware that I am not this mind, not these thoughts, I am the one who is aware of them now.*

Mind is the creator of my identity and my creation. It keeps us engaged in this game. It then smartly assigns all this creation to the God created by it, swiftly shifts all the blame and praise to the created God. It prefers to remain anonymous and safe. *It knows that its cover would be blown if discovered.* Everything is trapped in my mind. My God and devils stay in my mind. My beliefs stay in my mind. My knowledge, possessions, family, choices, judgements, quarrels, envy, and struggles all stay in my mind.

This journey has pierced my ego, and unravelled my mind. It is no surprise that my constantly processing mind is feeling weary and drained, wanting to be discovered and dissolved.

Mission Update

Thoughts require a thinker; hence it creates the thinker—mind. Once created, the mind keeps piling up thoughts in desire of continuity.

As *Descartes* said, "I think, therefore I exist", or "I exist, therefore I think."

The mind is conditioned by its surroundings, by the thoughts floating around it, social thoughts, religious thoughts, political thoughts, etc. All our thoughts then come out of this conditioned mind. There cannot be a thought which is free from conditioning. The questions coming from our mind and the answers coming to our mind are all just conditioned thoughts.

If we start being aware, think about what we keep thinking, our thoughts. If we start searching for, start analysing and questioning the thinker who keeps thinking, the mind reveals its truth. *One needs to be aware of this process of thinking, that's meditation. Flow of thoughts is creation, stopping of thoughts is non-creation and complete evaporation of thoughts is liberation.*

As *Plato* once said, "The mind keeps a running commentary, judging and labelling everything. Don't argue or resist them, just ignore them. Deprived of attention and interest, this voice gets quieter and quieter and eventually just shuts up."

"If you accept that mind exists, you will try to control it and manage it. This is mind trying to control mind. If you self-enquire as to whether mind exists at all, you will find that it does not. Mind itself is simply a thought. This discovery brings freedom." – *Jac O'Keeffe.*

* * *

At my arrival in Banaras, I quickly gathered my belongings, settled any outstanding expenses, and prepared to catch the train to Bombay the following morning. Hart also had me deliver a package he had sent to a mutual buddy. The last thing I did was the delivery of the package near a place called Lahertara. I got free around six in the evening. The delivery location was beside a tiny lake called the Lahertara talab. Grass surrounded the lake, providing a comfortable place to rest. I found a quiet spot and sat there.

I did not want my worthless thoughts to disturb me, so I tried rejecting any thoughts coming in. My attention was riveted on the placid lake. Open sky ensured that the lake had no reflection. The water was so still and tranquil. I so wished to be like that. As soon as I wished so, the water suddenly came into action. A group of young boys from the neighbourhood were playing across the way and tossing stones as far as they could into the lake. One of the stones entered, exactly at the centre of the still water, my eyes were focused upon. As soon as the stone infused itself with the water, ripples started forming. The ripple circles grew larger and larger, each one brighter in the middle and dimmer on the edges. The water seemed now to be full of action, vibrant, energetic, and vivid.

The still water was gone; it did not exist anymore. After about thirty-forty seconds, the waves calmed down and I could once again make out the motionless water below. As if the still water, which had assumed the form of the dynamic ripples, had decided to relax, and relinquish its lively form.

My mind reminded me of its similar state. Mind, or waves, or wind, only exist in momentum. Wind is born with the movement in air; waves are born with the movement in water. Likewise, mind is born only with the motion in thoughts. Then what needs to be done to shut down mind, wind or waves?

Nothing it seems. I cannot instantly stop. Both the wind and the waves will eventually calm down into rested water and tranquil air. Well, I suppose this is my mental state now. If I stay with this wisdom; ultimately, my thoughts will fade away, and I'll be in a place of stillness and serenity.

The ripples were gone, and the water was still again. My mind immediately felt at ease and relief. Almost instantly after that, the water was agitated once more by the ripples. Once again, the boys began their game of hurling stones. This messed with my head. Even if eventually my mind dies and I achieve the true tranquil still form, what surety do I have that desire will not allure it again. Just as the boys' stone throwing set the stagnant water in motion anew, so too will desire arrive and restart this creation. The ability to maintain my natural, calm state would be transient at best.

The only way out is to stop the stones from falling into the lake. That is to stop Desire. In my search for wisdom, I have been looking into desire and ways to overcome it. The further I venture, the closer I come back to the origin, each time elevating desire's importance and hegemony to new heights. The end of desires is the only road to my God, but can someone please teach me how to get there?

To some extent, I finally understand the nature of desire and its power over my mind. Since desire is responsible for the existence of the mind, the mind cannot destroy it. A child can't tell its parents to not create it. The ripples could not have put a stop to the kid's hurling stones at it. So, what is to be done of this desire? I thought for a while.

In my desire to achieve the pure, true, omnipotent, peaceful, passive, and unperturbed state, am I not just desiring? Is this state not just the opposite of my current vibrant state? Am I just desiring the duality element of my current state? In the other state, what assures me that I shall not desire to come back to my present state? Is this not the cyclic game of desire and duality, which keeps repeating infinitely? I so wished for answers.

The message arrived from him some twenty minutes later. As the darkness was giving birth to the silver star. He made me write it down in different ink.

What is the need for you to desire? Don't desire, desire nothing. You are the water, do not divide yourself into wave and ocean. Enjoy yourself waving with the wave and delight yourself in resting effortlessly in the depths of the ocean. Ocean and the wave or me and you are the same, where is the need of any divide or any desire? Stop dividing the oneness, just flow with it, just live it, have fun.

Dive into your desires. You will find that the purpose of all your desires is to achieve a state where you desire no further. You desire money, so that you do not have to desire it further. You desire God, so that all your desires are fulfilled and you do not have to desire anymore. All your desires are for desirelessness. So why desire in the first place?

You can desire anything, except one. The desire of not to desire. I am beyond desire and you cannot desire me. You can just dissolve your desiring self and be me.

In that moment all my desires were fulfilled. I heard my God.

My mind has divided everything. It says that it can be either wave or ocean, either peace or agony, either pure or impure, either dynamic or serene, either mortal or God. I understand now, the mind can only exist in momentum, so whichever state it is in, it desires to move to the opposite duality state, created by it. This way it ensures its existence. And with it, the existence of time, thoughts, and agony.

My mind like a rat has set the wheel of thoughts in motion. It gets so absorbed and habituated to the motion of thoughts that it forgets that it itself is the mover of thoughts. My attention has finally moved to the axis of this wheel, which is ever at rest.

I have finally come to terms with who I am. I am water, as vast and unending as the ocean. I'm just going with the flow of the ocean, waving with the waves. And so does everything and everyone else in this cosmos. Though they appear to be separate waves, they form part of the same oceanic tide. All is One. In this Oneness, there are only two choices, either one can create boundaries or destroy them. I chose to destroy.

But my mind has woven this veil over centuries, dividing me and God, ocean and wave. Though it realises this now, it fears its death. How hard I try, this veil persists. I feel some resentment towards God for not making an effort to lift up this veil of dualism and arrive.

God's voice tells me in the background that he's trying his best to pull back the veil. If I could help and not resist. I realise that I keep resisting and protecting this veil, because my survival depends upon this veil. I do not have the courage yet. I, the wave, fear merging with the ocean, which would dissolve my identity.

Chapter 13

I Met God

All my exploring and seeking led me nowhere. All that it did was help me introspect and realise the false. The truth, God, was always there.

At the Mumbai airport, my father was there for me. Home sweet home, at last. Having my familiars around me, comforted me.

Intrigued, my father sought to ascertain whether the Devil continued to make appearances at midnight. He questioned whether I had found the answers to respond to his warnings. With a wry smile, I replied that the Devil had transitioned from a figure of fear to a peculiar friend. His visits, once menacing and prolonged, had transformed into fleeting encounters, like an old acquaintance dropping by for a quick catch-up.

As of late, an unusual silence had draped over my devilish companion. The once animated discussions had given way to a wordless exchange of expressions—a series of glances, subtle nods, and a silent understanding. There were no longer relentless inquiries or probing questions. Just a simple exchange of "How have you been?" before he faded back into the shadows.

That night, my devilish companion reemerged, returning to the stage of my consciousness. As the moon's gentle glow bathed the surroundings, there he stood, a figure wrapped in shadows but adorned with a mischievous smile that played at the corners of his dark lips. *I met his gaze, his eyes held the clichéd past knowledge of ages, while mine held the spark of my newly found love for god.* A silent understanding passed between us.

Amidst this stillness, a distant whisper, a mere murmur, brushed against my ears like a fragile breeze. "You lucky one, God and Devil are both in your mind". They lingered for a moment, etching themselves into my consciousness, before melting away into the night.

My friend began to dissolve into the shadows. His figure wavered, like an apparition caught between worlds, and his smile slowly merged with the darkness. And then, just like that, he was gone. The night swallowed him whole, leaving behind a sense of enigmatic wonder.

His visage became increasingly muddled as the nights wore on. I did miss him, but I also felt a certain peace and solace within. My friend appeared to be trying to tell me something through that dwindling face. As if to imply that he has completed his task and is free from further obligation. I was overjoyed for him. It appeared that he had broken free at last. *The devil in my mind was gone.*

Back at my workplace, a buzz of excitement enveloped me as colleagues eagerly inquired about my father and my sabbatical. Responding to questions about my dad was natural, yet a hesitation lingered when it came to discussing the God journey. I thought many would not be interested in such a subject.

Despite feeling like my usual self, the collective perception of those around me painted a different picture. They insisted that I had undergone a remarkable transformation. According to their observations, I had become unperturbed, composed, and mysteriously unaffected by the opinions or words of others. A newfound buoyancy seemed to emanate from within me.

That weekend, I enjoyed some quiet time in the garden with my morning coffee, all to myself. I contemplated the transformation in me. Alterations were plain to see. The shift occurred, I think, because of my revised perception to life and love for God.

I understood how the mind works, why people do and say the things they say, why they are so stubborn in their beliefs, why they are so easily swayed by authority figures, why they are so easily manipulated by superficial ideas, and why their egos are so sensitive. This made me uninvolved and casual about things and emotions floating around me. I realised that I have started slowing down my thoughts and have control over them.

Reading and writing makes me happy. I can sit for hours with a strong black coffee, music, book, or mac. My interpretation changed drastically. The other day I was reading a book. The Adam & Eve tale which made no sense earlier, suddenly turned out to be a stunning allegory that reveals the complex relationship and dangers of ego, desire, and suffering.

Once they tasted the fruit from the tree of Knowledge of good and evil, they were able to divide between good and evil, between God and themselves. They acquired the knowledge of false self, creating their identity, their individuality. This self-centric awareness led them to ego. Ashamed of their nudity, they covered themselves with fig leaves and created a barrier between themselves and God.

Humanity has been building upon this barrier since then, fortifying the divide between God and Man. Man was banished from garden of Eden because of the divide he created, because of his knowledge of good and evil. *He shall be back in the garden of Eden, once he dissolves this divide, this knowledge, this ego, and becomes nude again with nothing to hold on to.*

Ego is like darkness in my room, I cannot do anything to reduce or remove this darkness from my room. Wisdom is like light. The only way to get rid of darkness is to bring in light, bring in wisdom.

My reading and writing time have increased recently. My happy and content mind allowed me some more downtime. It ceased future fretting, ceased ego projection and protection, and ceased wasting energy on inconsequential matters. I was slowly but surely falling in love with my God. His love letters were in the book, and mine were written on the pad. The plot of my love life was beginning to take form.

It was the last day of December. I was with my family in Karjat, a hill station near Mumbai. My love finally showed up. Sweet early morning enticed me for a walk. After which I relaxed besides a waterfall. Nature was mesmerising me. Something miraculous was happening that moment. A gentle whiff of cool jasmine breeze kissed me. The birds rhymed with the jiggling trees and bushes. The waterfall crackled down, setting the beat. Everything around me smiled and was wanting me to join them. I got up, walked down, facing the waterfall eye to eye, wanting to embrace them all. I spread my arms, looked up, the soothing sprinkles closed my eyes. I took a deep breath. God was pouring down the wine of love, intoxicating me. I bathed in his wisdom. I was his darling and he was caressing me. I felt myself in his heart. He wanted to celebrate this moment. He came down with a sudden burst, enlarging and engulfing me. I was completely drenched with his love. He was overflowing my tiny cup. *I went into a dance, to the beat of freedom and sang to him a love song. He held my hands, drew me closer, and squeezed me in. I eventually melted into him.*

Since then, he has been alluring my focus with perseverance. My lover was changing my perception every moment. My affection for him grew stronger by the day. I began to live my life with God as the centre of my attention.

I guess I wasn't unfamiliar with this feeling of Love. In fact, I have experienced something similar before now.

He, my God, reminded me of this beautiful girl in my eighth grade, I had fallen for. It was not only me, almost every boy in my grade had fallen for this bombshell. With all this adoration showered upon her, she naturally acted untouchable. I knew that I wouldn't be able to get her, but no matter how hard I tried, I could not stop her from playing with my mind. She started to rule my mind and govern all my actions.

I dreamt of her every night, woke up to see her again, stood in front of the mirror, started blowing my hair with mom's hair dryer, waited for her at the entrance of the school, hoping to accompany her to the classroom, captured her every giggle, her every hair swing in the classroom, saw to it that my eye records an image of her every few minutes, constantly tried things just to garb her attention. My whole day and nights were ruled by her.

Like God, she never spoke with me, but occasionally she would pass a smile at me, good enough for me to stay on my endeavor. It was only in my ninth grade that she started to talk to me, my efforts started to pay off. Our Maths teacher had done this magic. I was good at math and she wasn't. Whenever our Maths teacher praised me in her class, I drew her attention, and her one look would melt me.

One day I mustered up the courage to ask her if she needed any assistance with her mathematics assignment. Her "yes", worked as steroids to my imagination. Early on, our conversations centred primarily on mathematics, but that was fine by me. As days passed, our interactions expanded, to a point that everyone in our school started to notice and talk about us.

Then came the happiest day of my life, the first day our school resumed after the summer vacations. We had entered the tenth grade now. In ninth grade, my friend Prateek used to sit beside me. Waiting an eternity to see her again, I reached school early. All the students seemed excited to find their new classrooms and especially, if there were any new joiners. The reason for my excitement was constant. I met a few of my friends and then chose a desk in our new classroom and settled in there. My eyes fixed upon the classroom gate, waiting to be mesmerised by her morning face. My friend Prateek entered the classroom, waved at me and then coolly sat with another friend of ours, Deepak. Did he ditch me for Deepak? My mind had no room to process this question for now, as it only wanted to remain prepared to capture the first glimpse of her glowing face.

There she was, the pinnacle of all desirable things. The sun would have faded off seeing the radiance on her face. She appeared to be a goddess walking alone in slow-motion towards the classroom. The time had dilated, and my mind was processing everything in super slow-motion. Her open hair were dancing, her eyelids occasionally shutting themselves to preserve the priceless black pearls in them, her smile melted all the hearts around, and the rhythm of her walk matched the rhythm of my heart. As she came closer my heartbeat was ready to explode and it did so. She swung her bag, placed it on my table and occupied the seat beside me. My heart collapsed. That moment made me believe in God, what magic has he done. My mind was blank and my belly in my throat.

The entire class staring at my desk seemed as surprised as I was. She said, "Hi," and I couldn't reply. Thankfully, that awkward moment was intervened by our new class teacher, greeting us. I do not remember anything else which happened that day. The whole day faded away in the smoke of her fragrance, which had put me on a high.

I cared for her like crazy, I guess that brought her closer to me. We became the best of friends. I loved her everything, the good, the bad, the in-between, all of her. Every second with her was filled with passion and enthusiasm. Love makes you do impossible things. I had suddenly become a disciplined and chivalrous guy, as she wanted me to be so. That period was the golden period in my life. We never proposed to each other, as we thought that this would eventually happen. There existed no one in that golden period except me and her, we were Adam and Eve, roaming in the paradise. But history had to repeat itself, and then came the serpent and the fruit of good and evil.

In India, tenth grade is when we have the first board exams. My parents, teachers, and elders around, all acted like the serpent and advised me that these board exams will decide if I get to eat the fruit of good or evil in my career ahead. These serpents were successful in deeply rooting this thought inside my brain. I truly started to believe that this tenth grade exam was the most important exam of life and had the ability to shape my entire life. I totally forgot about my present life, worrying about my future. I gave most of my time now to prepare for my board exams. Our love life took a break and we both got busy with this tenth-grade board exam. Our life changed after eating this fruit, love gave way to worrying, aspiring, and preparing for our future life.

Then came the day which ended this golden period in my life. It was not God who threw Adam out from the garden of Eden, it was my father's super boss. My father is a banker, he was transferred to a different state. We moved reluctantly and I took time adapting to this new place, new school, and new friends. Time has the power to move mountains. In our case it was both space and time which were altering the canvas of our relationship. Love for her still stays in my heart.

I guess these love stories in our life's prepare us for our eternal love story with God.

This time, I am sure, I do not want to let go of my love. God is showering his love uninterrupted, and I want to drink every drop of it. Love is like a fire which eludes your command. How hard you try to spark it, it wouldn't unless naturally. And once ignited, how so ever hard you try to blow it off, it wouldn't.

I spend time with my lover now. At weekends I travel to mountains, forests, and beaches. The charismatic nature of my lover, his presence in everything, his powerful acts, his mysterious nature, his creativity, and his overpowering personality mesmerises me every time.

My God is untouched by the molds others have shaped for him. He dances beyond the confines of rules, untouched by the chains of laws and patterns. His brushstrokes paint unique shades onto the canvas of existence; no two birds bear his hues alike. He blooms even amidst the rocky terrain, defying the set norms.

He weaves his narrative free from the threads of predictability. His essence breathes without the weight of conditioning. In his image, I find inspiration, a call to abandon the shackles of patterns and conditioning, to embrace the artistry of spontaneity.

Unbounded by any expectations, his love flows as unconditionally as the wind. He sits not in judgment of my choices, offering no condemnation for my deeds. He needs nothing from me, not even my prayers. He is teaching me to love unconditionally.

He shows up everywhere, across the canvas of existence. I can hear him when the nightingale sings, when the river crackles down, in every note of a jazz melody. In the delicate caress of a fragmented breeze, I feel his touch, the soft brush of his fingers across my skin. I can smell his hair when the morning mist unconsciously infuses the soil. And oh, the taste of him in a simple bite of mango cheesecake.

My connection with him extends beyond senses and flavours. I find myself playing with him on the seashore, he chases me in every wave. I chase him from pink rose to yellow jasmine in the garden of Eden. Dance with him as he comes down pouring from the thundering clouds. Sing with him driving solo in the mountains. Laugh with him without reason when I see him giggle in the cradle. Cry with him, when he returns to me after a long time.

I breathe him with every inhale and exhale. He pours into my being until there's no separation between us. Every heartbeat is a testament to our unbreakable bond, a steady drumbeat that echoes his presence within the chambers of my heart.

When his warm embrace dips below the horizon, painting the sky with hues unimaginable, I'm reminded of his boundless artistry. And then he twinkles to life like precious gems, each one a reminder that his presence illuminates even the darkest corners of the universe.

In the quiet moments of contemplation, his whispers of wisdom resonate in the chambers of my heart, like the faint rustling of leaves in a mystical forest. It's in these moments that the wonder of his presence envelops me, a sense of awe that transcends words and logic.

And when I close my eyes to rest, he pulls me in, close to his bosom, lulling me in a cocoon of peace. His comforting hands patting me and watching over me through the night. His presence wraps around me like a warm embrace, an unwavering companion in the grand tapestry of life.

I refrain from beseeching him. I just want to thank him for this wonderful life. I do not pray him, yet, my soul sometimes erupts in spontaneous melodies of devotion, a musical language he seems to cherish. I comprehend him intimately, and this understanding fuels my fearlessness.

His love has transformed my very essence, cultivating tranquility, and a composed spirit. Lessons learned from him echo in my actions—I no longer judge, hate, or form hasty opinions about others. Instead, I honour their space, their freedom, as he, my God always does.

It dawns upon me now that he has been loving me unconditionally all my life, writing me love letters all the while. Only now have I noticed him and accepted his love. What a moron to have resisted his approach all my life.

It's him, only him, who lifted the veil I unknowingly weaved over time, between him and me. As I look back, I marvel at the grace that unfolded, orchestrating our union.

It was the seventh month back home. My buddy Hart called and said he wanted to pay a visit to me in Mumbai. I couldn't contain my enthusiasm at finally getting to meet him. Together, we had a fantastic time. He was a changed person, and he gave all credit to the madman at the ashram. We talked for hours about God. Envious of my divine love story, he shared an intriguing tale he had heard from the madman, drawing parallels to our connection with God.

God had two sons Alpha and Beta. He gave them two boats and asked them to explore the sea and the islands he had just created. Alpha knew that father must have kept some hidden treasure, and wanted the best son to win it. He desired to explore the boundless sea in the quickest time. He rowed his boat with might and kept going deeper and deeper. He overcame wave after wave. Each wave grew his confidence and strength. He collected food and other possessions to ensure safety and continuity. He went deeper and deeper in his search. There came a huge thunderstorm, he passed one but a series of them followed, toppling his boat, and taking away all his possessions and food. He got furious, cursing the storm, and wanting to fight and defeat it. He did not want to give up, he took it upon himself to conquer the sea and find the hidden treasure. He went deeper and deeper, fighting his battles, some he won and celebrated others he lost and grieved. In his pursuit, he had gone so deep that he had forgotten all about his father and his home.

While Beta was a lazy guy, he had no desire to explore the boundless sea. He decided not to row the boat at all. He simply raised the sail and let the wind do the hard work and take the boat wherever it wishes. On his journey, he started enjoying the flora and fauna of the sea and the islands. He was in awe seeing the creativity in various weathers, various species, various plantations. The thunderstorms came by, some so strong as to topple his boat and take away his food and belongings. He never felt disappointed, as he started discovering the taste of various other fishes he never collected. He thanked his father for the variety and started enjoying his journey even more. Every day he woke up to experience new magic each day.

Finally, God decided to call back both Alpha and Beta. He made the wind flow vigorously in his direction. Alpha felt the strong wind and saw it as a challenge, as a hindrance in his journey, like any other storm he faced. He fought the wind with all his strength and perseverance. Eventually winning over it and continuing his journey in the boundless sea. While Beta lying lazily with his sail open, in no time was back with his father.

We agreed. Everything is taken care of. Life is a gift, cherish it, never condemn or fight against it. We are free, to either keep struggling and going deeper and deeper, or to open our sails and enjoy this creation.

Desire is nothing but the distance between our imagination and our current state. We become slaves to our own imagination. The key is to shift the focus from our imagination to our current gifted state. Only the desire for happiness and freedom, creates suffering and slavery. The desire to be something else, to be more happier, more successful, more respected, more liberated, keeps us away from being happy and free right now. If we need to go to Hell, we will need to keep aspiring, keep striving, keep getting better, like Alpha. If we wish to go to Heaven, we will simply have to stop all this nonsense. The path to Heaven is just love. Love knows no desiring, no striving, no rules, no practices, no path.

We keep escaping life by trying to find purpose in it. While the purpose of life is to enjoy every moment of it, to live fearlessly, independently, without any rules or authority and with total awareness.

The want for continuity, security, and assurance in life, is a hindrance to wisdom. To explore the unknown, unintentionally, brings in wisdom.

Hart finally returned to his country. He also found God and started his love story. We love sharing our love songs these days. I thank God for this friendship.

God is all around us, irrespective of us wanting him to be here and now. He rises bright every day, irrespective of us being happy or sad. He is ever present to start our love story if we accept him right here right now. I realise now, there was not a time, not a place, he was not with me.

I just love him here and now. Desires, hopes, and fears were associated with self and my God is slowly dissolving this self. *I have no destination to reach, all roads are good. I find my God travelling with me everywhere I go.*

I see him everywhere. One morning, I was observing his reflection in a garden nearby. It had rained last night and the leafs were still soaked up. My focus was forced on a tiny droplet on the leaf of a Plumeria shrub. It was vibrating as the leaf jingled with the wind. Soon it moved, dropped from the leaf, and merged with the droplet on the leaf below. A few other droplets merged with it and the big droplet dropped from the leaf and fell onto a very small stream running on the ground. The tiny stream merged with a bigger stream, where every small stream was merging. I could hear my God sprinkling and crackling in the flowing stream.

I so wish to dissolve with it and flow.

I realised. I am a tiny droplet, all I need to do is keep moving with the flow, not to resist the flow, not to allow any conditioning any authority to obstruct my flow. I need not protect my boundaries; I need to let go of them and just flow.

I am the water in the pond, still and foul, enslaved within the walls. I need to break these walls of authority and flow to be fresh water again.

I am the bottle in the ocean with water within. I need to break the bottle and dissolve my water in the ocean.

I am the circumference of the circle, and my God is at the centre. I need to wipe off the circle and then there shall be no circle and no centre.

The distance between him and me is just me. The moment I dissolve in him, the duality gets crushed. The seeker seeks, until he realises that he is the only obstacle.

I went in search of him and became him. The seeker becomes the sought. To love is to dissolve in the lover.

As I dissolve myself into God, I see God also dissolving into me. We are one.

How innocent was I, in order to find him, I hid him from himself.

He has been desperate to colour me, but I have been resisting all my life. I veiled and turned away my face, what else could I have done. With such desperation over the years, have I decorated this masked face, to be admired and envied by others. How could I let him unmask and colour me.

Today he came to me with colours. I resisted again, but he held my hand and forcibly snatched away my veil. He coloured me in his colours. We both looked the same now. He hugged me and we became one.

My God intends to make love to me right now, in this very moment. In my ignorance and fear, I keep postponing it. Thinking that I am not worthy of it right now. Only if I do this, follow this path, obey these rules, perform these actions, go to this destination, will I be worthy of his blessings and love. God laughs at me, but he respects my freedom. His abundance and grace leave me to my state and allows me my time.

And I understand now, he requires no conditions, no rules, no shackles, he just wants to love me. And if I break all the conditioning and allow him to make love to me right now, I shall be satisfied. A satisfaction so complete that all desire and duality will dissolve.

Chapter 14

Presence of My Own Absence

"A human being is a part of the whole called by us as the universe, a part limited in time and space. He experiences himself, his thoughts, and feelings as something separate from the rest, a kind of optical delusion of his consciousness. This delusion is a kind of prison for us, restricting us to our personal desires and to affection for a few people nearest to us. Our task must be to free ourselves from this prison by widening our circle of compassion to embrace all living creatures and the whole of nature in its beauty. The true value of a human being is determined primarily by the measure and the sense in which he has attained to liberation from the self."

– *Albert Einstein.*

I knew God, until they made me search for him. Me and my God were always together, we were one. The religions then divided us, kidnapped my God, and exiled him in a faraway abode. Then they blackmailed me, that if I needed my lover, I would have to be their slave and do as told. I realise this now, they could not separate that which is one, so they simply hypnotised me to believe their story. My God came to make love to me and seeing that I was hypnotised, he shook me, and I am finally regaining awareness. He is with me, right here right now. Then why should I search for him, why should I fear anything or follow any imagined path and follow the rules of that path. Let the ones who have kidnapped God and imprisoned him in a faraway imagined abode do all this nonsense.

He was ever flowing in me, but I was never thirsty. Rather than seeking, I wish to dig within and quench my thirst permanently. I know he is overflowing with joy within me. As I start to drink it, I realise that it is drinking me too.

My south pole wants to blend with my north pole and be one, ending the duality, the polarity. It's not only that I am getting attracted to my God, even he is eager and attracted to meet me. We both are coming close each moment and we know that eventually we will be together, this makes the separation and the journey fun to carry on.

I am the drop of water on the leaf. I have started to move towards my river now. I've been hesitant to take the first step towards the river's unknown depths, but now I am up for the adventure. I met other droplets on my way, and I thank everyone of them. They have accelerated my speed and helped me in my flow. Every one of them from my father, Hart, Devil to the Madman, saints and others, everyone has been my Guru, as they were leading me towards him. I am aware that if I continue my flow, I shall drop onto the ocean and be one with it.

He is helping me lift this veil. The way forward is being with my beloved and the way back is me and my illusions. I feel possessed by him. It seems that the one I was seeking, has always been seeking me. By trying to win him, I was losing. The day I decided to lose, I started to win him.

I am now seeking the presence of my own absence.

We have been calling for him, shouting, crying, and praying for him to come to us. But my God pleads.

Asking, "How should I come? I am already holding your hand. You are the only one who has trouble accepting me for who I am. You want me to be somewhere far away in a place imagined by you. You want me to be imprisoned in a temple, in a church, in a mosque, in heaven, anyplace will do, other than with you. You view me not as a friend but as a glorified tyrant. You demand me to hand down rules and a path to your imagined abode. You have made me your accountant, wanting me to keep record of all your deeds. You want me to bless good deeds and punish bad deeds, as a ruler. You want me to be a judge, who follows a rule book, and you also want me to be a forgiver. I am fed up of this job. What you think I am, is just a version of you, it's not me.

"I am incapable of living up to your standards. I pray to you, accept me as I am—your friend, always with you. Never judging you and never imposing rules on you. Please just accept me and allow me to love you.

"You have been made addicted to destinations. You search for me in the future, in the heavens or in the past,

scriptures. I am not in the past or in the future, they do not exist for me. I am not at the end of a path or starting of a path, I am travelling with you on the path, now. You are afraid that if you accept me Now, your future and past will all be gone, all your imagination will be gone, all your hope will be gone. All your hope for enlightenment in the future is bogus. One, because the future does not exist and second, because I am right here, right now. You have been looking for a key your entire life, when the door was always open.

"You keep desiring freedom but do everything to enslave yourself. It's a mystery, how have you managed to become so miserable and sad, when I am raining love all around you. How are you achieving the impossible task of living in darkness, when only I, the light exists?"

I have come to recognise my god's voice coming from within. If the voice is about the past or the future, I know it's coming from my time-bound mind. While if the voice is not referring to any past or future, it is of my God.

God is the silence beyond words. His abode is the space between two thoughts. A timeless and wordless state. As Jesus said, enter through the narrow gate. To enter this space, one needs wisdom, one needs awareness. The wisdom that one need not learn and become something, but keep unlearning and unbecoming everything he is not. *Keep unlearning every word.* The wisdom that one need not seek answers, but dissolve the questioner himself.

The awareness that, enlightened one already is, he just needs to stop trying for it. Or to say he shall be enlightened only when the "he" who is trying or desiring, is no longer there. The awareness that one cannot unhook his mind or his thoughts, he can just unhook or dissolve himself. In this state of awareness, the words, the thoughts will come and go, there will be no mind to absorb it, no thinker to think over it, and no memory to pile it up.

It's all about leaving. When I left my blinds, my beliefs, my crowds, I became a seeker. I left seeking and found myself. And now that I am trying to leave myself, I am getting closer to my God. The distance between me and my God is my left over individuality, ego, "I".

"I believe the main task of the spirit is to free man from his ego." – *Einstein.*

"Amongst the greatest things which are to be found among us, the being of nothingness is the greatest." – *Leonardo da Vinci.*

Know Thyself - He is You, You are Him

With complete awareness I kept finding myself, trying to know "who am I?". The deeper I went to search for myself, the more I realised that there is no "I". It is just the thought thinking the thinker, not realising that they are not different, they are the same.

There is no way to know God, because he is not in this illusionary game of Duality. While the "I" which wants to know him, is an illusion in this illusionary game of duality. Till the time "I" am there, my God can only be my imagination. The duality ends with the dissolving of "I". The duality illusion exists only when the "I" individualises. In wholeness, in oneness, there remains no "I", no duality.

"I" is just an allusion and non-existential. It is only he, my "God" who exits. This awareness helps in dissolving the "I" and once "I" is dissolved all that remains is "Him", my God.

"I" cannot know "God", but by dissolving, I can be him. As I let go of this "I", I realise that I was holding onto nothing.

"Take this 'I' from me so that all that remains is 'You'." – *Anonymous.*

I cannot see my God. Because I do not exist, it is only he who is seeing through my eyes. It has always been the eye searching for itself. In its search it can only search for something apart from it and hence it creates a fictional God. The eye needs to stop searching to realise that it is it.

"True peace exists only when the one seeking it is no longer there." – *Wu Hsin.*

"*Atma so hi Parmatma*" and "*Aham Brahmasmi*" meaning "You are Him."

"Music heard so deeply that it is not heard at all, but you become the music." – *TS Elliot.*

"Lovers do not finally meet somewhere. They are in each other, all along." – *Rumi.*

Oneness:

In duality, "I" creates God in his imagination and the same "I" desires his imagination. One can either keep desiring and imagining God as far as he can or be aware of his imaginations and stop it. This imagination stops us from knowing God, as he is, or to say it stops us from knowing ourselves, as we are.

One can only imagine things he knows, not of things he does not know. God is not known and hence cannot be imagined. Our instinct is to fill up the unknown with an imaginary known, Imaginary God. All our imaginations are of a God, made known to us by our society, by our culture and by our religion.

In oneness, there exists no imaginary "God" and no imaginary "I", no Imaginer and no Imagination.

My God is Wordless beyond Word

Word is the language of mind, the creator of thoughts and time. Every thought is a word or sequence of words. Words stimulate thoughts. God experienced through words or thoughts is just imaginary, a self-projection. If I exist, I cannot know him. Only when I am aware, when I stop fragmenting time and live in the wordless now, do I live him. Only when I am empty can my God live through me in all his creativity, his newness, his wonder.

He is beyond words; hence nothing of him can be written in words. If I write that he is the flower, he says I am the fragrance too. If I say he is the fragrance in the air, he says I am the air too. I say air, he goes within me, becomes me and says I am you. I say he is me, he goes out, blooms into a flower and says I am the flower too. I say he is the flower; he rises and expands engulfing the entire horizon. I can know him only by being him, being spontaneous, being free, being aware, and being creative.

Don't live to die but DIE TO LIVE!

We have been conditioned not to believe in this creative God, right now. Not to accept him right now, not to accept ourselves right now, not to accept where we are right now. To keep fearing the thoughts of the past and keep desiring thoughts of the future. Making our life miserable.

This desire for him in the future is just a way, not to accept his love right now. The moment we become aware of his/our presence right now, we will know him, love him, live him.

Drop onto the ocean, dissolve. You are the endless ocean, enjoy waving with the waves. If you are entrapped, be curious, make an effort, take the first step to flow, break the boundaries and continue to flow onto the sparkling ocean. Empty yourself and let God live through you.

"Do not grow old, no matter how long you live. Never cease to stand like curious children before the great mystery into which we were born." – *Einstein.*

"Most people die at 25 and aren't buried until they're 75." – *Benjamin Franklin.*

"Our purpose in life isn't to arrive at a destination where we find inspiration, just as the purpose of dancing isn't to end up at a particular spot on the floor. The purpose of dancing and of life is to enjoy every moment and every step, regardless of where we are when the music ends." – *Wayne Dyer.*

"And those who were seen dancing were thought to be insane by those who couldn't hear the music." – *Nietzsche.*

"The meaning of life is to find your gift. The purpose of life is to give it away." – *Pablo Picasso.*

Light at the end of the tunnel is not an illusion, but the tunnel is.

My God, the light is omnipresent. The society and religions, have built a tunnel around us and they keep us slaved in it. They keep building this tunnel, to secure their throne, in the fear that if one person escapes or breaks this tunnel, others will follow suit. The light which we see at the end of the tunnel is not fake, it is real, my God is real. But society and religion, will ensure that we keep travelling in this infinite manmade tunnel, keep desiring light, but never be one with it. The moment you are curious, the moment you stop travelling, and scratch the tunnel walls, the light makes all efforts to enter through that scratch and break the tunnel for you. So be curious, ask questions, start scratching.

My God, the light is the only existence. Darkness or tunnel is non-existent, it is only the absence of light. Blindfolded by religions and society, we are trapped in this darkness. The moment we realise that this darkness is fake and is only the absence of light. The moment we stop working on this darkness and simply open our blindfolds, the ever-waiting light will flow in and embrace us.

My God, the light, is seeking us, we cannot seek him, there is no path to him. No path, no road takes you anywhere. We the blind, have not to search for the light, but simply unwrap the blindfolds and open our eyes.

I thank the religions and the society for pushing me into deep dungeons of darkness. This forced me to realise that I am the light, I was always searching for.

My God, cannot be put down in words. All what I have written is meaningless, once the eyes are open. No authority, no book, can open your eyes. My only attempt here is to take you out under the open sky, where the ever-present light, the sun, can warm you and excite you.

My God has unfolded my blinds. His glorious rays are helping me open my ever shut eyes. The blurred face of my lover is so appealing, so magical. He is drawing me towards him, helping me to open my eyes fully.

He is dissolving me and teaching me the art of becoming artless. This love affair continues, and I keep writing with my half open eyes, for whatever it's worth.

Chapter 15

The God Exercise

A simple way to discover God and connect with him.

GOD	MAN

A. Answer the following questions, not from what has been taught to you, but from the depths of your soul. Place a ✓ or ✗ in the column 'GOD', for the given prompt.

IS GOD:

1. Love?	2. Unconditional?	3. Non-judgmental?
4. Free of any Beliefs?	5. Free of any Authority?	6. Free of any Desire?
7. Free of any Envy?	8. Free of any Nation?	9. Free of any Religion?
10. Free of any Rules & Rituals?	11. Free of any Customs & Traditions?	12. Free of any Caste & Creed?
13. Undivided between Good & Bad?	14. Undivided between Success & Failure?	15. Undivided between Happiness & Sadness?
16. Undivided between Societies & Communities?	17. Undivided between Heaven & Earth?	18. Undivided between whom he Loves & doesn't?
19. Fearless?	20. Boundary less?	21. Non possessive?
22. Egoless?	23. Satisfied & Content?	24. Creative?
25. Joyful?	26. A Dancer?	27. A Painter?
28. A Friend?	29. A Lover?	30. GOD.

B. Place a ✓ or ✗ for the same questions in column 'MAN', for the given prompt.

IS MAN:

C. Answer the same questions for the given prompt.

IS A NEW BORN:

D. Did you conclude: Man was born like God? If so, what in your view, has transformed Man and made him so different from God?

____

____

____

____

____

E. With you and God situated at opposite ends of the spectrum, is there potential for you to bridge the gap and get to know him?

F. With the complete awareness of your metamorphosed self and the willpower to meet God, if you discard the acquired knowledge, unlearn, and be childlike again, simply transforming all the crosses to ticks—would you not dissolve your individuality and merge with God?

The thing is, we all are well aware of this path. But putting it into practice is far more challenging than simply acknowledging it. Summoning the resolve to defy societal norms and patterns is nearly inconceivable. To annihilate your ego, to dismantle your very identity. You've been conditioned, meticulously cultivating your individuality over time. How could you possibly dissolve your sense of self now?

The only way possible is, living with complete Awareness, in Oneness, all the time. Start with seeing the presence of the divine in every soul, rather than their transformed outward selves. Once you see the glory of God in everyone, you shall recognize him within you, and eventually unite with him in Oneness.

Request you to keep this book handy and consult your ✓ & ✗ on the previous page regularly. Try to transform all your ✗ into God's ✓. And here's the secret—the moment you transform one ✗ to ✓, the rest will transform effortlessly.

Take the first step and God will take the next with you, being you.

You are God, live like one.

Acknowledgements

I owe this book to the one I loved, the best I could. The very essence of my being. To the one who was godlike to me, beyond divinity. Envious of this and to save his divine stature, God separated us forever.

This pain ignited the spark for my quest, so I wish to thank God.

I extend my deepest gratitude to the digital realm, the scriptures, and the vast library of books that illuminated the path during my quest. My heartfelt appreciation also extends to the untamed spirits, the audacious thinkers, the relentless rebels, and the brilliant minds who dared to challenge convention—Einstein, Socrates, Kahlil Gibran, Rumi, and countless others—who, with their unwavering curiosity and embrace of free will, served as beacons guiding my transformative journey.

I extend my acknowledgments to my cherished circle of friends and family, the dedicated team at Nu Voice Press, and Shweta, the talented sketch artist, whose contributions have breathed life into the pages of this book.